I0819940

THE MARK AND THE MATCH

RACHEL LANGLEY

THE MARK AND THE MATCH

Palmetto Publishing Group
Charleston, SC

The Mark and the Match

First Edition

Printed in the United States

Hardcover ISBN 978-0-57843-763-7
Paperback ISBN 978-1-64111-271-0

For my brother Zachary—
You told me to write you a story.

Without knowing you, loving you, and losing you,
I wouldn't have been able to write these pages.

CHAPTER 1

[LANEY]

Antonia. Another dimension. Lightning travel. Had it all been a dream, a nightmare? Were we finally waking up from it? My father had made sense of it by imagining he'd been in a coma after being struck by lightning. Antonia was the place he'd been trapped—enslaved—in his coma.

But, no. It was *real.*

We'd been struck. The lightning had taken us there. And now it had brought us home.

The sun was shining on my face. I could feel its heat on my skin and see its orange brightness through my clenched eyelids. The mockingbirds were whistling a morning tune—that was how I knew I was truly home. A content smile spread across my face.

"Why are you smiling?" Hollister whispered in my ear. He was home too.

I hadn't opened my eyes yet, too afraid it would all be a dream. But my hand still held tightly to Hollister's; I never wanted to let it go again. Blinking slowly, my eyes adjusted to the brilliant sunlight—everything seemed so much more beautiful than anything Antonia had to offer. I stared into Hollister's light-green eyes—eyes I had not seen in weeks. "We're home," I replied softly. He nodded without taking his eyes from mine.

It took all my willpower to look away, to look around me. We were in the same field we had walked to when we'd traveled to Antonia just two days earlier. It felt like a lifetime since that day.

My father was sitting in the grass beside us, weeping silently, washing away the momentary joy, knocking me back to reality, back to our loss. Hollister appeared alarmed, giving me a questioning look. "My mother . . . ," I answered quietly.

"Your mother? Where is she? Why isn't she with us?" he asked, suddenly aware of her absence. He didn't know.

I shook my head, holding back tears. "She died this morning. Or yesterday morning. I don't know what day it is."

His eyes glossed over. "How?" he mouthed the word, briefly glancing at my father.

We had so much to talk about. "I'll tell you everything later," I said, squeezing his hand and nodding my head toward my father. Then I knelt beside my father, putting my arm around his shoulders. "Dad, let's go home."

He dropped his face into his hands, and I could barely make out his muffled words as he cried, "I said I wouldn't leave that place without Lizzy."

"I know you did. You were very adamant about it." I tried to coax him to stand, but he wouldn't budge. Where was Leela? She would know what to do. Where was my twin sister? She should have been beside our father.

"Where's Leela?" I asked Hollister. He glanced around. Our scrutinizing gazes stopped on Curwen, who was squatting against a tree about twenty feet away, his phone—the transporter—in his hand, a defeated look upon his face. He felt our stares and looked up. His eyes were tortured, and he slowly shook his head at us.

Where was my sister? What did he mean by shaking his head?

I marched in his direction, Hollister by my side. "Curwen, where's Leela?" I demanded.

"She didn't come with us." He shook his head again, looking down at his hands, not meeting my eyes. "She must have let go . . . "

"Why would she have let go? Go back and get her!" I yelled.

"I can't. I've been exiled. My phone has been deprogrammed." He dropped his face into his hands as if he might cry like my father. But he didn't cry. He just rubbed his face and then started inspecting his phone again, desperate to make it work.

"What do you mean—exiled?" I asked.

"My punishment for helping you." His answers were succinct as always, never offering any extra details or explanations. He had told us the punishment for his treason would be death. Instead, he'd been exiled. For now, at least—would they send someone here to kill him?

"Can't you call somebody?" I suggested, my voice panicked.

"No." He appeared annoyed with my question. "Everything in the phone has been deprogrammed, not just the travel ability. Gigandet made sure of it."

I glared at him, my temper flaring. "Why would the king keep her there? Is that part of the punishment too? What did you do to make him so mad?"

"It's nothing *I* did," he said, standing. "It's what your sister did." He was angry with Leela.

"What do you mean?" Hollister asked calmly, trying to prevent me from becoming more upset.

"I think she sacrificed herself so all of you could be free. So *I* could be free. I should have known there was no other way Gigandet would let us go. I should never have brought her there." Curwen spoke the last part more to himself than to us, continuing to make sense of things in his own mind rather than helping us to understand.

Why would Gigandet want Leela?

"What does Gigandet want with Leela?" Hollister asked, reading my mind.

"She's the one with the mark . . . the mark that can break the curse."

"What mark?" I demanded. "What curse?"

"Her birthmark, Laney," Curwen explained, losing his patience. "The king has to marry her in order to break the curse about the sickness spreading among the people."

"You *never* told us about any curse!" I wanted to slap him but clenched my hands into tight fists instead. "Why would you have taken her there if you knew she had this mark?"

"I told her to stay behind with Corey and Annabelle!" he defended himself. "She wouldn't listen!"

"Because you didn't tell her *why*!" I argued. My sister was stuck in that place, and it was something she chose. Or did she? What if the king had threatened her? What if they had found the mark and she had no other option? How did Curwen know she had sacrificed herself? Even as I asked myself that question, I felt it was true—because that's who she was, that's what she would do. But I refused to accept it, to let her marry that man.

"We have to go back for her!" I cried, tears filling my eyes.

"We will," Hollister said, nodding at me in assurance. "Right, Curwen?" His voice sounded menacing, urging Curwen to give the correct answer.

"Yes," he agreed. "We'll figure it out. Gigandet won't hurt her. He needs her. And contrary to what it may seem, he's not an unkind man—to most people."

"He's not unkind to people—just to *bodies*," Hollister accused, glaring at Curwen.

Bodies. There it was, that word, the one Antonians used to refer to the slaves. Because the slaves weren't people. They were just *bodies*. Hollister had been a *body*. My father had been a *body*. My mother had been a *body*. And she had died. I choked back tears, swallowing the lump in my throat.

"Who is this guy, anyway?" Hollister asked me, gesturing at Curwen.

"The name's Curwen," Curwen said, his nearly black eyes meeting Hollister's determined stare as they both weighed each other. Hollister at six foot five stood a few inches taller, his golden hair whiter than usual after so many days working as a slave in the Antonian sun. Curwen did not appear intimidated, holding his own.

"Curwen's our . . . ," I hesitated, unsure what word to use, " . . . friend."

Hollister grunted an acknowledgement of my words, balking at the idea. "Some friend he is," he muttered before he turned away and nodded his head toward my father. "Come on. Let's get him home to Corey and Annabelle. Then we'll come up with a plan."

These two men—Hollister and Curwen—they were both planners and leaders. Would they be able to work together? I needed them on the same team. In that moment, I almost felt as though I knew what to expect from Curwen more than from Hollister. Hollister seemed different somehow—harder. I remembered Leela talking about how our parents and Hollister would be different from the trauma they had experienced these past several weeks, being enslaved in an alternate dimension. At the time, I hadn't wanted to listen to her, but she was right—how could they not be changed?

Hollister was weak from whatever the scientists had done to him the previous night, but I could tell he was trying hard not to let it show. Did he know what they had done to him? Could he remember? Would he be willing to share with me? Only if we were alone, maybe.

We approached my father, still seated in the same position. "Come on, Dad," I tried coaxing him again. He wouldn't move or acknowledge me.

Hollister gave it a shot, pulling on his arm, trying to convince him to stand. But he also received no response.

After a minute of our failed attempts, Curwen knelt on the ground before my father. "Dan," he said, quiet but firm. My father lifted his head, meeting Curwen's eyes. "Dan," Curwen repeated, "I am very sorry for what happened to your wife. I'm sorry that she died."

They continued to stare at each other for a long moment. Hollister and I exchanged confused glances. Then swiftly, without warning, my father punched Curwen in the face. Curwen fell backward, throwing his arms behind to catch himself. His lip bleeding, he rose quickly. "Get up, and do it again!" he challenged my father, his fists ready for a fight.

My father stood, his fists also clenched, his face angry, his cheeks flushed.

Worried, I glanced at Hollister, thinking he should step in and stop it. With his eyes narrowed, interested to see how it would play out, he shook his head gently and pulled me a few paces away to give them some space and observe from a distance.

"You're not sorry for anything!" my father shouted as he lunged toward his opponent. Curwen dodged the blow. My father stumbled to correct his balance and then turned around to swing again. Curwen ducked out of the way, anticipating his moves. They went on sparring like that for a couple minutes, Curwen never hitting back but always moving quickly enough to avoid any more contact with my father's fist.

My father's cheeks became redder, his face wet with tears, snot streaming down his face as he yelled more insults at Curwen—at Antonia—with every missed swing. My father looked exhausted. Curwen moved in, taking the opportunity to get into a clinch, pinning my father's arm down and pulling him close.

My father grappled one arm free and slammed it into Curwen's kidney. Curwen groaned; he nearly buckled, but he maintained his grip and managed to get both of my father's arms under control. My father struggled to get free, but Curwen did not let go—he was stronger than I'd realized. Eventually, my father gave up, exhausted, his forehead on Curwen's shoulder. Once Curwen was certain that my father had truly surrendered, he nodded for us to approach. He pulled away slowly as he transferred my father's arms to our shoulders—Hollister on one side, me on the other, so we could support him on the walk home.

Curwen wiped the blood from his lip with his shirt, breathing heavily. "Now we can go," he said, gesturing for us to lead the way. My father didn't say anything but just hung his head, his chin to his chest, defeated, too tired to cry anymore. With my free hand, I wiped his nose with his shirt as we headed toward the house.

Curwen trudged along behind us. From what I had just witnessed, I knew Curwen had let my father hit him. His senses were too keen, his reflexes too quick, for him not to have seen my father's fist coming toward him. To me, it'd come without warning, but he'd seen it coming and let it happen. How'd he known that's what my father had needed? Had he purposely provoked him? Was he punishing himself for being Antonian, for lying to us? What had he done by lying to us, by not fully explaining the risks for Leela? Had she really sacrificed herself for our freedom? *That is such a Leela thing to do.* If Curwen hadn't let her go, if she hadn't sacrificed herself—if that's what she did—would any of us be walking home now? Too many questions scrolled through my head like an unending teleprompter.

The house sat in the distance, that old farmhouse with its wraparound porch and slamming screen doors, the one my father had refinished for my mother in the early days of their marriage. How would the sight of it affect him? He didn't look up to see it, his eyes downcast. But my heart began to flutter at the thought of surprising my younger siblings with our arrival. How had Corey and Annabelle been since we'd been gone? Had my thirteen-year-old brother been able to care for our little sister without any problems? Had they needed to hide from the police or teenagers trying to break in? In Antonia, there hadn't been time to worry about them. But now, so close, a million concerns rushed at me.

How would they react to Leela's absence? She had promised them she would return. How could I tell them about the death of our mother? Our mission had not been a complete success. *We failed.* The women—my mother and Leela—who should've returned with us weren't with us. And our neighbors and friends were still "missing." How many of them had died like my mother?

We didn't get the chance to surprise my siblings, though. Corey's shouts interrupted my thoughts as both of them came running out the back door, the screen slamming behind them, hurtling toward us through the wide-open field. They must have been watching for us. Corey practically tackled our father. If Hollister had not pushed against his back for extra support, he might have fallen over. I dropped to my knees, and Annabelle threw herself into my arms. I embraced my four-year-old sister, stroking her blond hair, breathing her in.

When she pulled away, she shyly eyed my father and Hollister, waiting for one of them to invite her in. My father knelt and opened his arms to her while Corey hugged Hollister and shook hands with Curwen. By the end of the reunion, we were all in some degree of tears, some of us with glistening eyes, some of us blubbering and wiping our noses.

But neither of them had asked us about Leela or our mother.

Hollister held Annabelle. Looking her in the eyes, he said, "Leela told me I had to help you speak again. What did she mean?"

"Leela is with the king," Annabelle whispered.

She spoke. She was speaking. I hadn't heard her voice in more than a month.

And she knew what had happened to Leela. My eyes wide, I looked questioningly at Corey.

"You won't believe it," Corey said, shaking his head. "Annabelle has been drawing nonstop since y'all left. You have to see for yourself. Come on." He led us back to the house. None of us spoke, too curious to discover what it was that we wouldn't believe. I was still in shock from hearing Annabelle's voice. She had pinky promised that she would speak if Leela returned, but Leela hadn't returned. Why had she decided to speak?

When we entered the house, the entire wall in the foyer and hallway was covered in Annabelle's drawings. They were all over the walls, tacked on the banister, and sprawled across the floor. As I scanned each sheet of paper, I realized they depicted everything Leela and I had been through the past two days.

Curwen carrying Leela after the lightning travel.

Curwen and I at the state records office.

Hollister in the fields.

Sheldon and me at the carpentry warehouses.

Leela and Curwen in the gardens.

Dinner at Phaedra's house.

Mara and Leela being arrested by the guards.

Our mother in the hospital.

Leela speaking with the king and some other woman. *So maybe she did sacrifice herself.*

It went on and on.

How could she have drawn everything that had happened so quickly? When had she slept? When had she eaten? Had her tiny fingers not grown weary? She jumped out of Hollister's arms, running to pick up her sketchbook, and brought it to us. Holding it up, she asked with a smile, "See? Leela is with the king."

The drawing depicted Leela and Gigandet standing together in the meadow we had just left. "What happens next?" I asked her.

She shrugged. "Ain't happened yet."

Corey explained, "She doesn't seem to see *everything*. But it's pretty consistent, every hour or two. Look! Starting from before, when the lightning first struck, until now, I have put all of her drawings in order. It tells the whole story."

Curwen scanned the pages quickly. "Here it is." He pointed at a drawing, one that showed Leela and Mara in the palace prison. Mara was pointing at Leela's neck, at her birthmark. "Mara told her about the mark."

"*You* should have told us," I accused.

"I didn't tell *anyone* because I didn't want something like this to happen. It's been my mission for the past two years to find the one with the mark—for Durham and Gigandet. But once I met her . . . I didn't want this life for her." This time he really did seem like he might cry. It was the most open he had ever been.

"Well then, how are we going to get her back?" Hollister demanded.

"Maybe Sheldon will come here to take us back," I suggested with hope in my voice.

It was the wrong suggestion. Curwen turned and glared at me. "You think Sheldon is still *alive?* Were you not there?"

There. He referred to the palace jail. The place we had last seen Sheldon as he was dragged away through a door, as Curwen had begged to take his place, to barter his life for his best friend's. Like Leela had done for us.

He thought Sheldon was dead. Mara too, probably. But what had Leela just told me before we were struck? I struggled to remember her exact words. "No, Curwen," I said. "Leela told me, before you brought us home, that Sheldon and Mara would be released from prison and that they would be safe. She's there—she'll make sure of it."

"She can't make sure of anything," he said with anger. "She's just a pawn in their game. Like all of us. He will never let Sheldon live." *He*. I knew he meant Whirl. That cruel man who had shocked us into submission, backslapped Leela for uttering a word, and ordered Sheldon to be taken away. It was clear he hated Curwen. What was their relationship? But before I could ask Curwen about him, he walked out the front door, the screen bouncing shut behind him.

Our father had been silent this entire time, sitting on the stairs just listening, still catching his breath. When he finally spoke, he said, "I'm going upstairs to bed. Wake me up when a plan has been formulated." The four of us watched him as he took each heavy step, and we didn't make a sound until his bedroom door—his and our mother's bedroom door—closed behind him.

Hollister, finally allowing himself to appear weak, suggested we sit in the living room. Annabelle snuggled between him and me. Corey seemed too energized, too restless, to sit still.

"Corey," I began, "do you both know about Mom? I saw the drawing of her on the wall."

Annabelle and Corey stared at each other for a long moment before he nodded. "Yes. Annabelle saw what happened. She cried hysterically for an hour until she could draw it for me to understand, to let me know why she was upset."

"She wasn't talking yet?" I asked. I forgot that I could ask her directly now that she was speaking again.

He shook his head. "She spoke for the first time this morning when she saw that y'all were on your way home."

"I said, 'They're coming,'" Annabelle said softly, her eyes lighting up.

Hollister was quiet, but I knew he had a million questions and didn't understand what we were talking about. He didn't know what it had been like for us. We didn't know what it had been like for him.

Turning to him, I explained, "The day you were taken, when the lightning struck you, Annabelle saw it happen. From that moment on, she wouldn't speak. Not a word."

"But she began drawing things that we couldn't understand," Corey explained further, holding up the drawing of Hollister in chains, enslaved.

Hollister pulled my little sister closer to him. "I'm sorry you had to see that, Annabelle," he said. "I know it must have been very scary."

She nodded, her eyes wide, remembering. "But I'm talking now," she said softly. "I promised Leela."

"Leela also promised she would come back," Corey complained. "Curwen promised he would bring you both back."

"Sometimes promises have to be broken according to circumstances," Hollister said in Curwen's defense. Perhaps they would work well together. "When did y'all begin to understand the drawings?" he asked.

"When Curwen arrived and told us the truth," Corey said.

"How long ago was that?"

"About a week."

There was so much I needed to fill Hollister in on and so many questions I wanted to ask him about his own experiences. But I could see he needed to rest.

"Why don't we let Hollister take a nap?" I suggested. "Once Curwen comes back, we can decide how to get back to Leela."

"I'm going back this time. I'm going to help bring her home," Corey announced with confidence.

"No, you aren't," Hollister and I spoke simultaneously.

"Yes, I am." He was determined, but we wouldn't argue with him, knowing he didn't have a choice in the matter. It would be hard on Corey. He was closer to Leela than he was to me. All of us were closer to Leela than we were to one another; it was as if the axle upon which we all turned was missing.

"I don't understand why she would have chosen to stay there," I said.

"She did it for us, so we could be free," Hollister said.

I shook my head. "That's just what Curwen thinks. He doesn't know. What if she had no choice? I will not let her stay in Antonia. Or marry someone she doesn't love."

My twin sister was stuck in that place. My mother had died in that place. I wanted to yell at somebody, but not at any of the people who surrounded me. Where was Curwen when I needed him? I needed an Antonian to verbally punch, and Curwen was the only one around.

"Laney, it's okay." Annabelle patted my arm sweetly. "Leela's okay."

"How do you know?"

"Because I can see her now."

She squirmed off the couch and ran to her sketchbook.

CHAPTER 2

[LEELA]

They were gone. My sister. My father. Hollister. The lightning had come and snatched them away from me. Curwen had taken them home. *Home.* Would Antonia be my home now?

King Gigandet stood behind me, leaning close to examine the mark on my neck, the mark that made me different from my twin sister, the mark that was needed to break the Antonian curse. *If it's real. Which it isn't.* It couldn't be. Did I believe in this curse? The Antonian people did. The king didn't say anything for a long time, and I began to wonder if he needed more light. My arm ached from holding my hair up.

"Do you understand what this means, Leela?" he spoke softly so the guards couldn't hear.

I simply nodded. I couldn't speak yet. If I spoke, tears would start, and I didn't want to cry in front of any of them.

He sat beside me, leaving a little space between us. "It means we'll have to get married . . . " The way he said it, it sounded like he was explaining it to himself, convincing himself of a new reality, one that disappointed him. *He doesn't want to marry me.* But duty required it.

"I know," I said. "And it means that Elodie will hate me." I wasn't sure why that was my first thought. Why did I care how she felt toward me? *Because I admire her strength, her sacrifice.*

Elodie—she was the one he wanted to marry.

"What makes you think she doesn't already hate you?" he asked, bitterness on his tongue.

I looked at him, surprised by his question and tone, but gave no answer.

"She doesn't hate you," he admitted after a moment of silence. He hated me though, or at least my role in his story. He stared at the outline of purple mountains in the distance, not really seeing them. I knew he was picturing Elodie's face instead. He whispered, "Elodie could never hate anyone."

The way he spoke about her, with so much love and so much sadness, I was tempted to tell him to forget the whole plan. Forget the Antonian people. They weren't really *that* sick. I hadn't seen any sickness. There was only rumor of it. So why did we have to break this curse? This curse that *wasn't real.*

"What is this sickness spreading among the people?" I asked. "I haven't seen any signs of it. Everyone seems fine."

"It's there. People are dying. We're containing it, keeping it underground, but if you know what to look for, you'll see it," he said. "It's the same sickness from before. They never found a cure. I thought that perhaps it was from your dimension, that maybe your doctors had been able to find a remedy. But we haven't found anything there to help . . . except for you."

They didn't find me. *Curwen* did. But I wasn't all they had found. I wanted to broach the subject of the thousands of people they had found and enslaved. And killed. *My mother*. Even though my father and Hollister were home now, the rest of my town was still in Antonian captivity. And my mother was dead.

It wasn't the right moment. I couldn't risk making him angry. Or could I?

What could he do to me? He needed me. Did I truly have the upper hand in this situation?

No, probably not. He could always send someone to capture my family again. He knew my weakness. And I knew his—Elodie. How would this relationship work?

"What are the signs to look for?" I asked, curious about what I might have missed in my own observations. I hadn't seen as much of Antonia as Laney had. Most of my time had been spent traveling back and forth to the palace gardens, but Laney had moved among the people in the marketplace, in the state records office, to the fields, and to the warehouses.

"We can talk about that tomorrow, when your training begins," he said.

"Training?"

"Yes, of course. You not only have to learn how to be queen, but how to be Antonian." He said it with an air of annoyance, not directed at me, but at the fact that I wasn't who he'd expected. I almost wanted to laugh. What *had* he expected—that the slave, the *body* who created this curse would make it easy on them? It was a curse, not a blessing.

Gigandet ordered all the guards except one to return to their posts. "Allen," he addressed the remaining guard, "please send a request for the doctor to come to the palace at once. And send word for a room to be prepared."

Without hesitation or question, Allen obeyed. He began making the necessary phone calls as he walked some distance away from us. I was grateful he was there instead of Whirl. Whirl, the guard who said he was *the king's most trusted advisor*. When would I have to contend with Whirl again? Never, I hoped.

"Let's return to the palace," he said, rising from the ground, offering his hand to pull me up. Was I allowed to hold the hand of the king? I took it hesitantly and stood. "You need to get cleaned up and let the doctor look at that head wound."

I had almost forgotten about it—the dried blood crusted in my ear, my blond hair stained red, my head pounding. This wound was a reminder of my mother, of my last moments with her in that orchard, where she pushed me away, trying to spare me from punishment or death. Death spared me but took her. None of it seemed real, but the wound reminded me it was.

I followed a couple steps behind Gigandet, Allen a few paces behind me. It was the middle of the night—the stars and moon lit up the black sky. With every step, my body felt heavier, the adrenaline dissipating, the exhaustion finally setting in. The mission complete—for today, at least. How much longer would I be required to stay awake? My brain couldn't think or care about anything.

I was no longer in the dark stone prison cell. *But Mara was.*

"Gigandet, where did they take Sheldon?" I asked. "Is Mara still locked in the prison?"

"You mean, your accomplices?" he asked with disdain. "Yes, they are both still in the prison. I will decide what to do with them in the morning."

"But Whirl could be torturing them right now," I protested.

He raised his hand to silence me. "Whirl does nothing without my permission." I was sure Whirl did *plenty* of things without his permission. "*I* will decide what to do with them in the morning. Speak no more about those traitors."

Those traitors. I couldn't say they were my friends—I had known them only two days—but they had tried to help my family. Gigandet thought he would decide what happened to them. But he would see. I would have a say—in the morning.

We entered the palace through the rear courtyard, a way I hadn't been before. Guards lined the outer brick wall, standing at attention every ten feet or so. What did they think of me, entering the palace with the king in the middle of the night? We ascended a few stone steps to a terrace, which led to a wall of glass that contained three sets of double doors. Would I be here long enough for this place to become familiar to me? A guard at one of the doors opened it for us, and we entered the grand hall. Though I had seen it only a few hours earlier, I was in awe of its beauty and splendor once again. The walls, floors, and ceiling appeared like pure gold, with a shimmer of jewels of all shapes, sizes, and colors encrusted in them. A small part of me—a very small part—was excited to see what it would look like in the morning with the sunlight pouring through the floor-to-ceiling window.

This time, I noticed the throne as we passed by it. There was only one. When—if—I married Gigandet, would there then be two? At the front of the grand hall, there was a curved staircase covered with plush crimson carpet. Before we headed upstairs, I stopped them. "Wait," I said. "When can I see my mother's body?" It hurt to say those words, like a knife to the gut, inserted and then twisted.

"Your mother's body?" Gigandet asked. "You want to see her? That's an unusual request."

"Where I'm from, it's a very normal thing to do." I stared him down. "I *will* see her."

We stared at each other for a moment longer while he weighed my request, while he determined just how much power he would allow me to have in this situation, while he decided which battles he would fight. Again, I wondered: *How will this relationship work?*

"Allen," he said, "call and make sure they haven't cremated 3126. If they haven't, then tell them to await further instructions."

My breath caught in my throat. "She might already be cremated?" I whispered, blinking back tears.

"Maybe," he said, sounding apologetic. "But with so many deaths recently due to the sickness, she may be on the waiting list, especially since the disease wasn't her cause of death."

Allen had walked away to make the call. Seconds seemed like minutes as I waited for the verdict. When he returned, he simply said, "They will await further instructions."

The king and I simultaneously breathed a sigh of relief. "You can see her in the morning," he said. "For tonight, you need to see the doctor and rest."

I was satisfied with his answer and trusted his word. We began to climb the stairs, and each step was harder than the one before; my body was so fatigued. *Stay awake.* I took a deep breath and blinked my eyes rapidly to keep myself alert. When would this night end?

At the second-floor landing, we had to walk a short distance down the hall, my eyes focusing on the red carpet beneath my feet, until we stopped in front of a set of double wooden doors with an intricate pattern carved into them, something like my father would create, something that made them feel familiar and welcoming.

"These will be your living quarters," Gigandet said as Allen opened them.

Inside, the floor became a mosaic marble, almost grander than the gold floors below. Two comfy chairs and an inviting couch encircled a fireplace, a fire already burning inside of it. I wanted to fall down on the couch and sleep—that was the only thing I could think of. But I still had to see a doctor. Where was this doctor? How much longer could I remain conscious waiting for him?

To the right was another set of double doors that at that moment burst open. Gigandet was startled, and Allen jumped in front of him, ready to defend his sovereign. But then a young woman appeared—she had smooth, tan skin, and her thick black hair was in braids; her amber-brown eyes scrutinized us.

"Henley!" Gigandet nearly shouted, recognizing her, trying to cover his fright. "What are you doing here?"

"Preparing everything for your guest," she replied nonchalantly.

"But why are *you* here, doing that?" he asked, irritated that he had to ask for further explanation, that she hadn't offered it freely.

"Elodie sent me. To care for your guest."

Gigandet's muscles tensed up when Henley spoke her name.

Elodie. The king's true love. The one he wanted to marry. How did she know I would be staying here, in the palace? Did she know I was the one with the mark, the one who had to marry the king instead of her? I hadn't told them. But she was perceptive.

"That won't be necessary," Gigandet said. "We can have one of the other girls take care of her." He talked about me as if I weren't standing right beside him, but I had no energy to be offended. I didn't need anyone to take care of me in that moment—I just needed to sleep. They could argue without me. Without awaiting further instruction, I went to the couch and sunk into it, pulling one of the throw blankets over me, the warmth from the fire feeling like a sweet embrace.

• • •

A log in the fire fell, breaking, waking me, my eyes opening. Where was I? *The palace. Antonia.* There weren't any windows to let me know if it was morning yet. Other than the light from the fire and a dim lamp in the corner, it was dark. My head didn't ache until I moved it, turning to look at my surroundings—what I could see in the faint light.

"Are you awake?" a voice from the darkest corner startled me. I had heard the voice earlier. Gigandet had said her name. She had scared him too. But what was her name? I couldn't remember.

Sitting up cautiously, holding my head in my hands, I asked, "What time is it?" My throat was hoarse and dry; I was dehydrated.

"Six," she said, still not moving closer.

It was morning. I would see my mother's body soon—that much I could remember. The need to see her and the dread of seeing her warred in the pit of my stomach, wrestling each other until I felt sick.

"May I have some water?" I whispered. She didn't say anything but rose to pour a glass and handed it to me roughly. *She doesn't like me.* "Did the doctor come last night?"

"Yes. He closed up your wound with some stitches," she said. "You can't shower for a couple of days, so even though I tried to clean your hair as best I could, it's still bloodstained."

I groaned quietly as I ran my fingers over the stitches on the side of my skull. She had cleaned the blood out of my ear also. "Thank you," I said.

"Don't thank me. I'm only doing my duty since I've been assigned to you."

"By Elodie?" I remembered that too, from their conversation. "What's your name?"

"Yes, by Elodie. My name is Henley." Her answers were short, no elaboration.

"Why did Elodie assign you to me?"

"To watch you."

"Why?"

"She said you were important." I didn't feel important. "She just didn't know *how* important." Her voice was accusing and bitter. She must have seen the mark on my neck; she knew who I was and what role I had in replacing Elodie. I wished I could see her face in the dark.

"I'm genuinely sorry," I said. I didn't want this role either.

"Me too," she muttered. "When you're ready, Gigandet said I could take you to see 3126."

"*My mother*," I corrected her. "I'm ready." But was I?

"You're not ready," she replied bluntly. "You haven't even tried standing up, and you need to eat something. I'll get some breakfast for you." She disappeared before I had an opportunity to protest, closing the double doors behind her. I could hear her saying something to someone in the hallway—maybe a guard—but couldn't make out the words.

What had I committed myself to? How could any of this be real? My mind wanted so much to doubt this new reality, but the physical pain I had felt traveling here through the lightning and the current pain I felt from the wound caused by the guards slamming my head into a brick wall made it all too real. Dreams, nightmares, could never be *this* real.

Standing slowly, I walked to the wall and turned on the light. I didn't like the lack of windows in these living quarters, but after opening the other set of double doors which led into the bedroom, I discovered a couple of windows on each side of the bed. I looked out to see the sun was just waking up, peeking over the purple mountains in the distance. Purple. The color of the bruise on my side from being kicked by the guard in the orchard.

The heat made everything look like it was melting together, like an oil painting—one I would want to purchase—with hues of blue and purple, green and yellow, white and black. But something was missing. Red. The color of the blood in my hair. The color of the flowers in the windows of the safe houses, a sign of those who belonged to the underground resistance.

The palace was slightly elevated above the city so I could look down on it, view it from a different angle. Every building, every home, including the palace, was built with concrete blocks or stone and painted white to keep cool in the hot climate, and they all had solar panel shingles on their roofs. The homes in the living quarters were specks of white and black in the distance, past the meeting quarters. Which house was Curwen's? Or Sheldon's? Or Phaedra's?

Phaedra. She had a red flower in her window—a safe house, a safe place. An urge, an ache, formed in my stomach, a longing to go to her, to be wrapped in a mother's embrace. But she wasn't my mother—she belonged to Curwen, Sheldon, and Mara. *My* mother was dead, and she was waiting for me to come to her—*not her, but her body*. I shuddered, feeling nauseous.

A mirror over the dresser revealed the true state of my appearance. Henley had cleaned the blood and dirt off of me pretty well, but I still felt unclean. Stands of my white-blond hair appeared pink. The dark circles beneath my blue eyes were proof that I hadn't slept long enough.

Henley returned while I was washing my face in the bathroom. "Here are some new clothes for you to wear," she said, sprawling them across the bed. "Elodie picked them for you."

Again, I was confused by Elodie's role in this. Was she being kind, or was she being controlling? Was Henley my servant—or her spy? How would I know whom I could trust?

The clothes were unlike any I'd seen in Antonia. Everyone wore neutral colors—black, white, tan, gray, navy—except for the slaves, who wore bright colors—yellow, orange, red. But what was laid out for me, what Elodie had picked out for me, was a light blue, the color of my eyes. What did this color say about my place in Antonian society?

Not ordinary citizen, not slave. But I was *important*, according to Henley, according to Elodie.

"Does Elodie know I'm the one with the mark?" I asked.

"Of course she does. She and Gigandet have no secrets between them," she said. "Now dress quickly so you can eat. I set some pain medicine out for you. When you're done, you can go see 3126—I mean *your mother*."

As I finished eating, she took my dirty clothes, the only ones I had left from my home, my dimension, and she threw them in the fireplace before I could stop her. She washed her hands immediately, seemingly disgusted that she had to touch them in the first place. I stood from the table, still feeling sick about what came next. Henley opened the door, inviting the guard inside. He was tall with dark-brown skin and dark eyes; he was wearing white, like the other palace guards, rather than the customary black that guards outside the palace wore. He also wore a friendly, brilliant white smile, which was in striking contrast to the constant frown on Henley's face.

"This is Greer," Henley introduced him. "He's the guard who has been assigned to you."

"Hi, Greer," I said, forcing a small smile despite the throbbing pain in my head.

"Good morning. If you're ready, I'll escort you to the hospital morgue." He said it in a sad tone, as though he wished to express his condolences but didn't dare—not with Henley there.

"I'm as ready as I'll ever be," I said, following him out the door. When Henley didn't move, I turned and asked, "Aren't you coming?"

She shook her head. "No. That place is overrun with disease. You may be immune to it, but I am not." That's right. Antonians weren't immune to the sickness, the curse. I had the advantage, yet she said it in a way that made *her* sound superior. I nodded to Greer that he could lead the way.

He took me to the left, down the hall with the plush red carpet and around a corner, not the same way as the night before. Around another corner, at the end of the hall, Greer pulled back a thick curtain, revealing a large metal vault door. He entered a series of codes into a keypad and then turned the wheel until it opened. I peered inside. There was a long flight of concrete stairs; they went down, down, down into a deep darkness so the bottom was not visible.

Looking at Greer and pointing into the darkness, I said sarcastically, "Yeah, that's not creepy at all."

"You'll be all right." He grabbed the electric lantern off the wall just inside the vault, turning it on.

Where was he taking me? "Where are you taking me?" I asked.

"To the hospital morgue, by way of the underground tunnels."

"Underground tunnels?"

"Yes, there's a system of tunnels under the city," he explained. "They are not open to public use, and most people don't even know about them."

"Why do we have to go this way?" I asked, not wanting to enter the darkness.

"You'll be all right," he repeated, confident. "It's nothing but walls and dirt. No monsters, I promise. Just keep your hand on my shoulder so you don't trip. You still seem a little unsteady on your feet this morning."

"Yeah, that's what happens when your head is bashed into a brick wall," I joked, trying to psych myself up—physically, mentally, emotionally—for the task before me.

"I'm sorry about that," he said with sincerity. "You can trust that it won't go unpunished. And I'm sorry about your mother as well."

My mother. She was at the other end of the darkness. Well, *her body* was there. Not her, but her body. Her body, her flesh. More loss, more darkness.

Anger welling up in me again, I used it for motivation. "I'm ready. Let's go."

CHAPTER 3

[LANEY]

Leela was sleeping by a fireplace. That was the last thing Annabelle had drawn. She was still alive. "Is she dead?" I had asked, panicked.

"Noooo," Annabelle had replied, annoyed. "She's sleeping."

Annabelle went to bed after that. Corey explained they had been staying up most of the night—since it was daytime in Antonia—so Annabelle could draw the events as she saw them happening. Hollister wanted to stay awake, to ask a million questions, but his eyes could barely stay open—he was still on Antonian time—so I insisted he rest as well.

This allowed Corey and me to have some time alone together, rocking in the chairs on the front porch, watching for Curwen to return. Though impossible, it looked like Corey had grown five inches in the few days we were away, but maybe I had not been paying attention before. I had been preoccupied, swallowed up in my own despair, longing to find Hollister and our parents. But Hollister was with me now, asleep just inside, and I took a minute to observe my brother. He was taller than me now. This thirteen-year-old was becoming a young man, and now he had his father back to teach him and help him transition. But he no longer had his mother.

"Corey, I'm sorry about Mom," I said, examining his face, his maturing profile. The words felt inadequate—because they were. He didn't respond, but continued staring off into the distance, pretending to study the landscape he already knew so well he could draw it with his eyes closed. I prompted him, "How are you feeling?"

He cut his eyes at me before returning them to the horizon. "That's a dumb question. How are *you* feeling?"

I sighed deeply. "I don't know. It doesn't feel real. It feels like she's just still in Antonia. Not like she's gone forever."

"So, you didn't see her at all when you were there?"

I shook my head and whispered, "No."

His eyes glossed over, like he would cry. "But Leela saw her?"

"Only for a few minutes, and she said Mom wasn't herself, like she was disoriented or something. She didn't understand what was happening."

"How did she die? Why did she die?" Tears had begun slowly, one by one, to roll down his cheeks. "Annabelle's drawings only explain so much."

"You know Ms. Patty?" I asked. Before being enslaved in Antonia, Ms. Patty had owned the florist shop in town; she had been friends with my mother. He nodded. "Well, she worked in the same area with Mama, and she told Leela that Mama hadn't been doing well for a while—she couldn't adjust to the climate there. The hospital listed her cause of death as heat exhaustion."

"Do you really think that's what it was?"

I nodded. "I think so. . . . We can try to find out more when we go back."

"I want to go too."

"I know you do." *But I won't let you.*

We sat in silence for a long time after that. Silence was unusual for Corey. I expected him to ask so many questions about Antonia, to go on and on with his comments and curiosity. But instead, he was quiet and still, except for the occasional creaking rock of his chair. I closed my eyes to rest; it was nighttime in Antonia—I should be sleeping. How long had I been awake?

The last time I'd slept, Leela had been beside me in the bed, in Mara's house. She'd fallen asleep before me; I had lain awake for a few minutes listening to her breathing. And when I'd waked, she wasn't there beside me. But I'd not panicked. I'd not been worried at all, sure that she was just downstairs and that she knew how to take care of herself. Mara had been the one to worry, for her own reasons, of course—not because she actually cared about Leela. We had found Leela next door in the kitchen with Phaedra, deep in conversation. I never had a chance to ask Leela what they'd been talking about. Was it anything that could help us now?

"Hey." Hollister's voice made me jump. "Sorry, didn't mean to scare you."

I had dozed off, and my neck ached when I lifted it from the position it'd been in. The sun had made its way across the sky. "What time is it?" I asked.

"About four," he said, still standing in the doorway, not coming out on the porch, not coming near me. He had changed his clothes, finally removing the bright yellow garb, the color that the field slaves, *bodies*, were required to wear. He was wearing his own clothes.

"Where'd you get those clothes?" I couldn't remember him having left any at our house.

"Corey and I ran over to my place real quick." Corey was no longer in the chair beside me. "The power's been shut off."

"Yeah," I said, standing and stretching. "I expected that to happen any day now."

"I pulled the generator out of the shed. But we've gotta get some gas for it."

As I moved toward the door, Hollister pushed the screen open wider and stepped back, allowing me to pass, ensuring we wouldn't touch. It felt weird. Distant. Once inside the foyer, I said, "I remember seeing some full gas containers at Mr. Hammond's place. We can walk over." Mr. Hammond's farm had provided for us many times since everyone had disappeared. I knew he wouldn't mind; he was like a grandfather to us.

"I'll come with y'all!" Corey exclaimed, coming from the kitchen.

"No, why don't you stay here?" I asked, eager to have some alone time with Hollister to figure out what he was thinking.

Corey glared at me. "No. I'm so tired of being told to stay here."

"Yeah, Laney," Hollister chimed in. "Let him come! He's been holding down the fort long enough. Let him stretch his legs." Was Hollister trying to avoid being alone with me? Or was he just being himself, trying to make everyone feel included? I couldn't tell. Leela had said he would be different when he returned, and I didn't want to overanalyze him, but it was hard for me not to.

Corey grinned broadly while I stared him down.

"Who's going to watch Annabelle?" I countered.

"Her father," came my dad's voice from the stairs, startling us. How long had he been standing there, watching us? All of us knew the sound of our father's heavy steps on the stairs, but this time he had silently snuck up on us.

"Are you sure you're up for that?" Hollister asked. "We can take her with us."

"I'm quite capable of sitting with my daughter," he replied firmly. "Where is she?"

"In her room, napping," Corey said. "Want something to eat?"

"I'll find something. Y'all go on now. The sooner you leave, the sooner you'll return."

I was hesitant, unsure of my father's mental and emotional stability. Would he be okay with Annabelle? Would she be okay with him? I glanced at Hollister to see what he thought; he nodded his head ever so slightly, encouraging me that it would be all right.

"Let's go, y'all!" Corey hollered from the back door, slinging his hunting rifle over his shoulder. I was grateful we would be taking it with us—not leaving it with my father.

"You got ammo in that thing?" Hollister asked as he headed out the door with Corey, the two of them falling into step beside each other, same as the last day they saw each other. I grabbed a basket from the back porch as I hurried to catch up with them, ticked off, wondering what was up with Hollister and angry that I had to share him with my brother.

"Have there been any issues with the cops since we've been gone?" I asked Corey once I reached them, inserting myself between them.

"No," he said. "It's been pretty quiet. Just their usual routines. The police scanner that Curwen left helped us keep a watch on things."

"Why are y'all having to look out for cops?" Hollister asked.

"They're still monitoring the town," I explained. I kept forgetting he didn't know. "After all of you were struck, they closed the town off and ordered anyone who was still here to evacuate so they could conduct their investigation. Obviously, we didn't leave and have been hiding from them."

"Was there anyone else who had to evacuate?" he asked. "Anyone else who wasn't struck?"

"Just Angie Stover and the baby," I said, hesitantly, knowing that Hollister was good friends with Angie's husband. "Did you ever see Rick?"

He nodded, his jaw tightened. "Yes. He's part of my barrack." He was silent for a long moment, then asked, "So the baby is okay?"

"Yes," Corey jumped in. "Laney saw them the day it happened. They didn't see her though. She hid. And then she made all of us hide in the cave until it was clear to come home. Well, she didn't really make me, cause I wanted to stay. But Leela didn't."

"So Leela did what Laney wanted? No surprise, right?" Hollister joked sarcastically, he and Corey sharing a laugh at my expense. I had stayed to find him. He wouldn't be here otherwise.

"Where do you think Curwen went?" Corey asked me. "And who is Sheldon? That other guy in Annabelle's drawings?"

"Sheldon is Curwen's best friend—they're like brothers. He helped us with the mission," I replied. *And he's my favorite Antonian who I hope isn't dead.* "Curwen probably went somewhere to think. . . . You know how he is."

"Are you sure he'll come back?" Hollister asked. Would he?

"He always does," Corey answered for me.

"You mean, in the entire *week* you've known him he's proven himself faithful?" Hollister asked, again with sarcasm. It wasn't like him. "He did lie to y'all about Leela having the mark."

"Technically, he just didn't tell us. I'm sure he had a good reason," Corey defended him.

"Still a lie of omission," Hollister argued.

"Look!" I raised my voice, anger spilling over. "If it weren't for his help, we wouldn't have found any of you, and you wouldn't be here right now! Stop being so critical." They both stared at me wide-eyed, surprised by my outburst. I was usually the critical one—not Hollister.

We had arrived at Mr. Hammond's farm, so I walked away from them, headed for the greenhouse, hoping to find some produce worth picking, hoping it had been all right without our constant care. How much longer could we last here? Now that our father was back, he, Corey, and Annabelle could evacuate the town together while Hollister and I went back for Leela. Would they agree to that? What could their story be if—when—the authorities discovered they were no longer missing?

As I opened the greenhouse door, I found Curwen already inside. *Faithful.* His lip was swollen from earlier, from my father punching him.

"Hey, thanks for defending me back there," he said, continuing to inspect the pepper in his hand, not looking at me. "I just caught some fish for our dinner and thought I would stop by here for some vegetables."

"Sorry you had to hear that," I replied, embarrassed. I couldn't remember a single moment I'd ever been embarrassed by Hollister before. Changing the subject, I asked, "Is there anything good here?" I set my basket down beside him.

"Some of it's still good. Some of it's been infected with those creepy-looking alien insects." He flicked one of the little orange hatchlings off an unripe tomato and shuddered in disgust. I almost wanted to laugh at him.

"Leaf-footed bugs," I explained. "I hate them too."

"We don't have them in Antonia."

"Antonia wins!" I joked.

He smiled for a brief moment, and then it faded. "Do you really think Leela will make sure Sheldon and Mara are okay?"

"I think she'll do everything in her power to make sure of it. Just like you did everything in your power to help us."

"But did I? I should have done more," he said, still never looking at me.

I had thought I was angry with him—I wanted to be, but somehow, I couldn't muster it. He was only one man. And he was hard enough on himself; he didn't need us to make him feel worse. *That's something Leela would say;* I heard my mother's voice again.

"Hey, Laney, we got the gas tanks. You ready . . . " Hollister's voice trailed off when he turned the corner and saw Curwen standing there with me. This time, Curwen looked up; I knew he would show no weakness in front of Hollister. I was surprised he had shown it in front of me.

"Hi, we never officially met," Curwen said, sticking out his hand in greeting. Hollister set the gas tanks down, stepped forward, and squeezed Curwen's hand firmly. Hollister's eyes held suspicion, and his handshake conveyed warning. "I've heard a lot about you."

"I've heard a lot about you too," Hollister said, finally releasing his grip. What did he mean? He had heard very little about Curwen from us. Had he heard things in Antonia, things we didn't know about, bad things about Curwen? Or was he just saying that to sound threatening?

"Laney, I'm starving. What have you found?" Corey whined as he came into sight. Once he saw Curwen, a huge, relieved grin spread across his face. Curwen tossed an orange to him, which he caught with a disappointed look. I knew he was tired of fruits and vegetables. "Can we *please* raid Mr. Hammond's pantry?" he begged. "Ours is empty."

"No," I said firmly. "We can't risk setting off the alarm and having the cops show up."

"Let's get home," Hollister said. "Looks like a storm is moving in." The wind was picking up, and a blanket of clouds was slowing making its way across the sky.

Curwen added, "Yeah, we need to get these fish grilling."

"Fish!" Corey's eyes lit up. "I haven't been able to catch anything since y'all've been gone!"

We headed home, and even though I expected Hollister and Curwen to have a lot to talk about, they remained silent—unsure, and probably distrustful, of each other. They should have been discussing Antonia and the plan to get Leela back—they were both strategizers—but they said nothing, except for quick replies to Corey's occasional question or comment.

When we reached the house, Hollister went to work setting up the generator while Curwen and Corey focused on dinner. I found my father and Annabelle sitting on the couch together. They had opened all the windows to let the storm breeze blow through; the curtains were dancing through the room. Annabelle was drawing.

"Leela's awake," my father explained. "She's eating breakfast."

"She's up early." I sat beside Annabelle to look at the paper in front of her. These drawings were the closest connection I had to my twin. It felt surreal. It was one of those moments where none of this felt real, where it all seemed like a dream, a nightmare. Everything from the travel light to my little sister's new psychic abilities—it just didn't feel real. Annabelle tossed her current sheet aside and began a new one. Was this what it would be like for her, awake all night, her crayons rapidly flying across the page?

"Annabelle," I began, "since you're talking again, couldn't you just tell us what you see rather than drawing it?" Even though she moved quickly, I was still too impatient to wait for the finished product, eager to know what was happening to my twin.

"No." She shook her head. "I draw it."

All three of the guys entered the room, announcing that the generator was hooked up and that supper was on the table. But I didn't want to move from my spot beside Annabelle, transfixed by her creation because there was another person in the drawing—not just Leela this time.

"Who's this guy?" I asked Curwen, pointing at the picture. "Do you recognize him?"

His eyes went wide for a second, surprised by Annabelle's abilities. "That's Greer. You know, Annabelle, you draw really well for a four-year-old," Curwen complimented her.

"Almost five," she said with a coy smile. Her birthday was soon—the first one she'd have without her mother. Our mother had been planning such a huge celebration for her baby's fifth birthday. I feared it would pass just like any other day.

"Who's Greer?" Hollister asked, his demanding tone jarring me from my thoughts.

"He's a trusted member of Gigandet's guard."

"Just like you, huh?" Hollister accused.

"I'm not a member of the guard." Curwen remained steady, unfazed by Hollister's tone.

"But you work for him. You're *trusted* by him."

"Not anymore."

"Hollister," I interceded. "Let's go outside, now." I grabbed his arm, pulling him out the front door. "We need to talk." The rain had begun to fall at a slow drizzle, but I left the porch anyway.

"Where are we going?" he asked when I kept walking down the driveway, farther away from the house, away from people who could hear us. "Laney, let's go back. We're going to get soaked."

"No, we need to talk."

"Talk about what?" He stopped in his tracks, not budging another step.

"Why are you being like this?" I demanded.

"Like what?"

"Distant. Rude. Sarcastic. Angry." When he didn't say anything, I added, "I knew you'd be different, changed somehow, but I need you to explain where your head's at."

He sighed, looking at the ground. "Laney, I've had many days and nights to think about what I would say to you if we ever saw each other again. But now, I'm not sure how to say any of it."

"Just say it the best way you know how."

He paused for a long moment, then sighed. "I'm afraid you'll distract me from what's important."

His words felt like a quick jab to the ribs. I hesitated, absorbing the hurt, before demanding with controlled anger, "Am I not important?"

"Yes, of course you are," he said firmly. "That's not what I meant. See? I told you I don't know how to explain what I want to say."

He was frustrated with himself, I could tell. He didn't want to hurt me, but he wanted to be honest. So even though every part of me was hurt by what he had said, I didn't want to react on my feelings. *Be slow to take offense*, I heard my mother's voice warn me, as she had many times before. Even in death, she knew that his words were going to be hard for me to hear. I took a deep breath and asked, "Would you please try again to explain?"

He copied my example, taking a deep breath before starting again. "First of all, you do not need to doubt that I love you and that I still want to marry you. Those two things will never change. Okay?" I nodded, wanting him to continue. "My whole life has always been about us . . . when I thought that was gone, when I thought I would never see you again, I found something else, something greater than you and me, to fight for." He paused, waiting for my reaction, but I remained stoic, trying hard not to reveal my feelings on my face. But he had known me long enough to know how his words were making me feel. So, he said, "That doesn't mean that we aren't important. It only means that all of the people, the *bodies*, who are enslaved—they are important too."

I paused before responding, letting his words sink in. But then, not slow to take offense, I yelled, "Of course they're important!" How dare he imply that I didn't care about the slaves!

"I know you would say their lives matter, that they are important. But what I'm saying is they are important enough that I *need* to go back and help them," he said, staring me directly in the eyes. "And hear me when I say this: they are important enough *that I'm willing to die for them.*"

"No." I shook my head, anger and tears in my eyes. "No. You will not risk your life. If Leela talks to Gigandet, maybe she can help them. We are not going back there so you can fight an impossible battle! Don't you know that I saw you in the fields, being shocked with that collar? And that I saw them drag you back into the barracks unconscious?" *After being taken to the scientists.*

"Laney. Don't *you* know that I did all those things *on purpose*?"

"What do you mean?" I asked, almost not wanting to hear the answer.

"To gain information," he explained. "I was able to see more of Antonia on my way to the scientists than I had seen all the weeks prior to that. I was able to see what they do there, and how it works and who's in charge. I was able to look for a way of escape for all of us *bodies*."

"Why did it have to be you?" I remembered him writhing on the ground in pain. "There are plenty of other *bodies* for that task."

"I volunteered," he explained. "The men—not *bodies*—of barrack twenty-seven, my barrack, my men—we've been planning an attack for weeks. And now, because of Leela's decision, I won't be there to help them. It's happening soon, and I won't be there. I *need* to get back there now." He said all this through clenched teeth.

"Are you angry at Leela—that she saved us and brought us home?" *He doesn't want to be here . . . with me.*

Sighing, he said, "I'm angry that I can't be there to help my men. I didn't get the chance to tell any of them about my trip to the scientists." Would he tell me about it if I asked? I shuddered to know. "They don't have the information they need. I'm angry that some—maybe all of them, including Rick—may die, and I won't be there to fight beside them." He paused and then grabbed both of my shoulders, forcing me to give direct eye contact. "But I'm not disappointed to see you again. Or Corey. Or Annabelle. Or your father. Y'all are my home. And that's what I'm afraid of."

"What do you mean?" I demanded.

"It would be easy to stay here. With you. Be comfortable. Be married. Be home. Forget about Antonia." He was right. It would be easy. As long as Leela was okay. "But I don't want to forget. I want to fight."

I was quiet for a long moment, studying the fierceness in his eyes. It told me he wouldn't give up. So I determined, "Then I'll fight with you."

CHAPTER 4

[LEELA]

The flight of stairs seemed like it went a mile deep as we descended farther into the depths of the earth, into the ground. The ground—the place where my mother's body should be buried. But they would cremate her. Would I get to keep her ashes? Did I want to keep them? I wanted to give them to my father.

Greer walked at a slower pace for me, not complaining or appearing impatient, even though I could tell it took a conscious effort for him to change his stride. My ribs were aching and bruised from the guard's swift kick to my side. I hung on to Greer's words that the guard would not go unpunished. How would he be punished? I could think of a million ways.

"It's not much farther," Greer said. How could he tell? The lantern lit up the walls, but there were no signs to indicate where we were, how far we'd gone.

"I'm sorry you've been assigned to me," I said, thinking there must have been plenty of other things he would rather be doing—assignments other than taking a girl to see her dead mother's body.

"Don't apologize, Leela," he said. "I'm honored to be assigned to this position."

"Honored?"

"Of all the guards he could have chosen, Gigandet chose me."

Did he know I had the mark? "Do you know who I am?" I asked.

He smiled, his teeth gleaming in the dark. "Of course. Gigandet assigned me as head of your security. He said I had to protect you with my life. I had to know why."

"You wouldn't have done it even without knowing, just because he ordered it?"

"Of course," he replied without hesitation. "But when you know the value of what you're protecting, you're much more motivated to protect it well."

"Would I have less value without the mark? Would I be any less human?"

He was silent. I could tell he was thinking hard about my questions. But before he could reply, there were footsteps and another light coming toward us. He stepped in front of me and lifted the lantern higher, straining to see. "Who's there?" he called out, deep and strong.

"Dr. Brandon," came a softer male voice, a voice I had heard before. He was close enough that we could see him now. He was medium height and build with light-brown, tightly curled hair. His face held a kind but surprised expression.

"Oh!" he exclaimed when he saw me. "I was just coming to see you." He was the doctor who had visited me last night. I vaguely remembered his voice giving instructions to Henley regarding my care. "Why are you here? How are you feeling?"

"We have business to attend to," Greer answered for me.

Business. Seeing my dead mother. Was our *business* a secret? The doctor had to know who I was—there was no way he'd cleaned and stitched my wound without seeing the mark. I decided to answer his other question. "I'm feeling okay."

"Are you weak? Tired? In pain?" he asked.

Not wanting to be examined right then, in the dark, in the cold, I gave a succinct answer. "It hurts to breathe with these bruised ribs. But other than that, I'm fine."

"Your ribs? I didn't know to look at them last night."

"It's okay," I said. "They're not broken."

"How do you know?"

"Because I've had a broken rib before. I know how it feels."

"How did you break a rib before?" He appeared shocked.

"Softball injury."

"Softball?"

"It's a game—"

"Look," Greer cut me off, "we really must be going. King's orders. If you need to examine Leela, you can come to the palace later. Call ahead." He grabbed my arm gently, now aware that I was in discomfort, and led me away.

Dr. Brandon's lantern light became smaller and smaller as we left him behind, and then we turned a corner, and it disappeared completely. "Was I not supposed to talk about softball?" I asked quietly.

"The doctor knows you have the mark. He doesn't know that you aren't from Antonia. And, at least at this point, we need to keep it that way," Greer explained.

"Why is it a secret—not being from Antonia?"

"Do you know that for centuries Antonian parents have longed for their baby girls to be born with the mark? So they could marry a king, become royalty. There will be plenty who will hate you for taking that from them, and if they know you aren't Antonian, I can't imagine what they might do." Probably more riots in the meeting quarters. Of course there would be an uprising for a slave—a *body*—marrying their king. "For now, it is best kept secret." He stopped walking. "We're here."

Where was here? He shone the light to our right. There was a metal door.

"Wait," I said. "What is my story then? Why am I visiting the morgue?" I didn't want to say the wrong thing again.

"You won't need a story. There won't be anyone here. They've been ordered to clear the area for the next hour." When he finished speaking, he pulled something out of his pocket—a medical face mask—and put it on. He wasn't immune to the disease. He was taking a risk bringing me here, a risk Henley had not been willing to take. After entering the access code, he pulled the door open.

The flickering fluorescent lights were almost blinding after walking in the dark for so long. Greer gave a moment for our eyes to adjust before we entered the hallway, the basement of the hospital, the place where morgues always seem to be located. If possible, it felt colder in the hospital than in the tunnels; I was grateful for the pants and long sleeves Elodie had provided. Perhaps, though it would be strange, she would be my ally.

Greer led me down the hall to a desk, our footsteps echoing on the concrete floor. Grabbing a clipboard, he scanned through a couple of pages. Was it filled with the names or numbers of those who had died recently? Was the sickness, the disease, really taking that many lives?

"3126," Greer said. The number assigned to my mother. "She's in cooler number three." Her body was there—not her. "She's scheduled to be cremated this afternoon."

"What will they do with her ashes?" I asked.

"They . . . " He hesitated. "They just dispose of them."

"What if I would like to have them?"

"I'm not sure. That's not our practice. But we can talk to Gigandet about it." He led me through another door, into an autopsy room, where the coolers were located. My eyes zeroed in on the one with the large, black number three engraved above it. "I'll give you some time."

"No," I objected. "You should stay." Someone needed to be here, to witness this, to see the reality of what they had done to this *poor, weak female slave*, as Gigandet had called her. Gigandet should have been there—not Greer. This would have been his mother-in-law, *if we end up married*. I shuddered at the thought. "Will you open it?" I asked him, my hands beginning to tremble and my stomach feeling sick again.

He turned the metal latch. It made a screeching sound, and the hinges of the door squeaked when he opened it. The frigid air that gushed out made us both shiver. He grabbed the handle on the rack and slowly pulled out the tray. Her body was in a zipped bag.

With shaky fingers, I began to unzip the bag, just enough to reveal my mother's face and neck. Other than being cold, she simply looked like she was sleeping. Her blond hair—the same color as mine—lay in soft curls around her ears. It was an illusion, a trick to the mind, thinking that at any moment she could open her eyes—the same color as mine—and smile, awake.

But it was just her body. Not her. She wasn't there.

There was pressure behind my eyes, like water pushing against a dam, tears that wanted to flow but wouldn't. I almost couldn't feel anything but empty and numb. Her mouth—the same shape as mine—would never speak again. We would never talk again; I'd never hear her voice. My mother wasn't there. I had seen her for the last time the day before, the day I had failed to rescue her. I had been the last one from my family to see her alive—and now to see her dead. This body, it wasn't her.

Grabbing a pair of scissors from a nearby tray, I cut a lock of her hair with the hope to one day give it to my father. It was a better option than trying to obtain her ashes. Without my noticing, Greer had found a small plastic bag, one used for autopsy specimens, for me to put it in.

"We can get a better bag or box later," he said.

"Thank you," I whispered, surprised by his kindness. I kissed my mother's cold cheek and then zipped the bag closed. "We can go now." Greer slid the body tray back inside, securing the latch on the door. I almost wanted to stop him, to stay there forever, for a few more minutes. But it wouldn't change anything. She wasn't there.

As I clutched the little bag in my pocket, I thought about Corey and Annabelle. How had they responded when my mother and I hadn't returned, when they'd heard that their mama had died? Every cell in my body, my living body—this body that could feel and breathe and contained a soul—every cell in this body, longed to hold Annabelle, to embrace Corey. With them, I could cry.

As we entered the foyer again, I heard a child crying from behind a set of double doors at the end of the hallway. Greer had said the floor had been cleared out for our visit. But the noise of a child crying came again. "What's down there?" I asked Greer. My feet started moving toward the sound. But Greer gripped my arm tightly and pulled me in the opposite direction, back to the tunnels.

"It's a quarantine location. Until the patients can be moved somewhere else," he explained. Somewhere else. I had a feeling *somewhere else* was the morgue, and then the cremator.

Most of the way back to the palace through the tunnels, we didn't speak. But I finally asked, "Are we going to see Gigandet now?"

"Yes. I have a meeting with him about your security team," he said. "And I think you should be there."

"Security team? It will be more than just you?"

He nodded. "Yes."

"Who else will it be?" *Please, not Whirl, that evil, manipulative man.*

"That's what we'll discuss. It has to be people we can trust, people who can keep the truth about your identity a secret. We need to contain it to as few people as possible."

Sheldon. Mara. "What about Sheldon and Mara?" I jumped at the opportunity to help them. What had Gigandet done with them? He said he would decide their fate this morning. Had he already done that? Was I too late?

"The two people imprisoned for trying to help you yesterday?" he asked.

They were still imprisoned—not dead. Yet.

"Yes! They already know my true identity, and they would keep it confidential."

"They're accused of treason," he said bluntly. "How could I trust them?"

"I trust them. They wouldn't do anything to harm me," I argued.

"But would they harm the Crown? Are they traitors who want to overthrow the king?"

Were they? Is that what the underground resistance aimed to do? I had never asked. But I shook my head vehemently, dedicated to fighting for them, for their freedom. "No. No, they wouldn't do that. They only wanted to help me save my family."

"By breaking our laws," he countered.

I sighed. How could he be convinced?

We had finally arrived back to the palace, to warmth and light. He closed the vault door and pulled the curtain to cover it, and then he turned to look at me, doubtful of my suggestion. "We'll talk about it with Gigandet." I rolled my eyes, thinking that if I married Gigandet that was a phrase I would have to hear for the rest of my life—and I was already tired of it.

He led me past my living quarters, back down the curved staircase from the night before, to the grand hall—the place I had looked forward to seeing in the daytime, with the sunlight streaming through the floor-to-ceiling windows. It was more beautiful than I could have imagined, and if I had to remain in Antonia, married to Gigandet, that place almost made it worth it—that's how good it was. I wished I could have sat on the gold, jewel-encrusted floors, staring out over the city and the countryside forever, the purple mountains in the distance once again drawing me in. But Greer cleared his throat, indicating that we needed to continue. Gigandet was waiting. We turned down a narrow hallway, and I knew where we were headed: back to the king's library, the place where Gigandet had accepted my deal—my family's freedom in exchange for helping him find the one with the mark. *Me.*

Greer knocked. Allen opened the door. Gigandet was inside, standing over a large table I didn't remember seeing the previous evening. Books were sprawled across it, and without invitation, I couldn't restrain myself from rushing up to it. I recognized these books—they were from my dimension. They were all old, classics, first editions.

"These are Curwen's books! What are they doing here?" I demanded, feeling protective of them, of him. Even if he had been planning to betray me.

"Good morning, Leela," Gigandet said, drawing attention to my rudeness at not greeting him or waiting to be greeted by him. I couldn't tell which was the proper etiquette.

"It's not a very good morning," I replied, giving him a hard stare. Then I repeated, "What are these books doing here?"

"They were found at Curwen's when we searched the place."

"So, why didn't you leave them there for him? I know he's not supposed to have them, but they must have taken a long time to collect. It would be horrible for him to come home and find them gone."

He looked at me, confused. "Curwen's not coming home."

"What do you mean?"

"He's been exiled for his treason," he said bluntly. "I believed Curwen was my friend."

"I believed he was mine too," I said softly. Had he been my friend? Was he still my friend? How had he felt when he brought my family home and then realized he could never return to his own?

"He fooled us both, I guess," he said, a sad look upon his face. This man probably didn't have very many people he could call friend. "I'm sorry it hasn't been a good morning for you, and I'm very sorry about your mother." *He should be sorry*. I could hear in his voice that he was being sincere, but I had no ability to forgive him in that moment. So I said nothing. He added, "I lost my mother a few years ago."

"Oh. Did she die from being worked to death as a slave in the Antonian heat?" I asked. It came out of my mouth before I could stop it. All three men stared at me, caught off guard by my audacity and rudeness. I was caught off guard too. It was impulsive. Like Laney. Not like me. "I'm sorry," I apologized. "I'm sorry you lost your mother, but let's not pretend our situations are the same." He and his Antonia were the reasons my mother was dead.

He nodded and changed the subject. "Greer, come. Let's discuss security measures. You may sit too, Leela." He directed us to the chairs near the fireplace—no fire burned in it this morning. "Greer, who can we trust among the guard with this task?"

"Please don't choose Whirl," I answered instead, dread in the pit of my stomach.

"Why do you say that?" Gigandet asked.

"He's cruel, and I don't trust him."

The king smiled slightly. "Good. We don't trust him either."

I gave them both a questioning look. "But he said he was your most trusted advisor . . . "

"Did he?" Gigandet asked, surprised. He and Greer smiled at each other. "Good. Plan's working."

When I still didn't understand, Gigandet nodded his head at Greer, giving him permission to explain things further. "We've been watching Whirl for a while now—we know he's trying to make a play for the throne. We let him believe he has more power than he does, until we can figure out his plans and get proof of his treason."

"Sure seem to be a lot of people committing treason these days," I quipped sarcastically. Again, impulsive, my tongue wanting to lash out. My words appeared to make Gigandet sad; perhaps he was more sensitive than I had realized. "So, how do you know what Whirl is up to?"

"Like I told you last night," Gigandet said defensively, "there is nothing that happens here that I don't know about."

Staring hard at him, I wondered if that was true. Did he know about the underground resistance? Did he know that Durham was the leader of it? Or that Curwen and Sheldon and Mara worked for Durham? Did he know they had safe houses, marked by the red flowers in their windows? Were they safe, or was he watching them too, waiting for proof of treason? Everything within me wanted to warn them if he was—obviously my loyalty did not lie with my future husband. Again, I shuddered at the idea of the marriage.

"Anyway," Greer said, interrupting my thoughts, "Whirl will have nothing to do with you. We're keeping him busy with other tasks at the moment."

"Who in Antonia knows that you're not from here and that you have the mark?" Gigandet asked me.

"Other than the people in this room?" I asked. "And Elodie, Henley and Dr. Brandon?" *Sheldon and Mara.* Did Sheldon know about the mark? I was sure if he had seen Mara, she would have told him by now. Or had Curwen already told him before? Keeping up with who knew what would be a difficult task.

"Dr. Brandon doesn't know you aren't Antonian," Greer reminded me.

Gigandet sighed. "Who else can we trust?" he asked, directing his question to Greer and Allen, making it clear that I wasn't to answer this time.

"Leela actually had a . . . suggestion," Greer began, "that we utilize the other two people who already know the truth. They've been used for extra security at events in the past, and it will be good to have a female guard as well. And they obviously care about Leela to some extent if they were willing to risk their lives to help her yesterday." *To some extent.* To what extent did they care about me?

Gigandet's eyes narrowed, his face in a scowl. "You mean the two prisoners?" he demanded. Greer nodded, unfazed by the king's demeanor, confident under scrutiny. "What are their names?"

I almost answered, but Greer gave a slight hand motion for me to remain silent—he would convince Gigandet before I would. "Sheldon and Mara," he told him.

"They're being charged with treason—they should be put to death," Gigandet responded. For as sensitive as he sometimes seemed, he could also sound so cold. There were no gray areas for him. "What if they try to commit some other crimes or help Leela escape?"

"Wait a minute," I spoke up. "I'm not going anywhere. I've agreed to stay here so my family could go home. There is no escape plan." As the words came out of my mouth, a heavy weight settled in the pit of my stomach.

Gigandet looked at me, doubtful, weighing my words and whether he could trust me.

"Here's what I suggest," Greer began. "Let's give them an opportunity to prove themselves. You let Curwen go rather than having him killed. The people don't know what's happened here, so they won't know that you are showing clemency to Sheldon and Mara rather than making an example of them."

But *some* of the people knew something had happened. They had watched Sheldon and Curwen, my twin sister and my father—a *body*, a slave—be marched through the streets, under arrest. Some of them had seen Mara and me arrested in the gardens—at least the *bodies*, the slaves, must have been talking about it. What were they saying?

But I didn't open my mouth to mention any of that. The king was considering it.

Greer added, "Their servitude could be their punishment. For a trial period. If they don't work out, no big deal."

Finally, Gigandet spoke. "We'll try it. On one condition. They have to wear shock collars."

My eyes grew wide, remembering what it felt like to be shocked with the cattle prod in the gardens, remembering the sounds as Laney, Curwen, and Sheldon were shocked into silence in their jail cells. I wanted to scream *no*, to say that the collars were unnecessary, but again Greer's hand and eyes warned me to stay quiet.

"That's fair, sir," Greer agreed.

"If anything happens, you will be held responsible," Gigandet said, making sure he understood the full weight of what he was asking.

"I understand, sir."

"What do you think, Allen?" Gigandet asked.

Allen hadn't said a word—I had forgotten he was there. "I think it's worth a try. I have my doubts about which other guards we could trust—too many of them are loyal to Whirl these days. If these two can keep things confidential and not cause trouble, they could be a good solution. I'll help Greer monitor them from time to time."

Gigandet nodded. "We'll try it. Greer, you may need to have them seen by a medic—no telling what Whirl may have done to them by now. Make sure they are in good physical condition for the assignment."

"Yes, sir." Greer stood. I did as well.

Gigandet ordered, "Please take Leela back to her room. She needs to rest."

Before we could leave, I walked over to the table of books. "May I please keep this one?" I asked, holding up the copy of *Jane Eyre* I had been reading two mornings ago, the one Sheldon had pushed deeper into the couch cushions to hide, the one Curwen had put away while joking that Laney and I would be the death of him. I breathed a sigh of relief that he hadn't been condemned to death, but to exile. But was exile the same as death to him?

Gigandet nodded his approval. "Keep it in your room, somewhere it can't be seen."

I took the book, placing the lock of my mother's hair between its pages. "May I ask a question before I go?"

He nodded, curious.

"Why were all the people from my town struck? Why were they brought here?"

"Whirl did that," he said, disgusted. "A reckless move. We had intel that someone with the mark might have been in your area. I sent Curwen to investigate, but before he got there, Whirl struck all of them."

"Not *all* of them." Not me or Laney or Corey or Annabelle.

"Yes, thankfully, Whirl did not find you first. When he inspected all the bodies and didn't find the mark, he was so furious—it was almost comical." He and Allen shared a smile, remembering Whirl's reaction. Their smiles made me sick; all I could imagine was the humiliation my townspeople must have felt as strangers searched their bodies for the birthmark.

"Then why didn't you send all of them back?" I demanded. "My mother could still be alive."

"That wasn't our concern. We needed to find *you.*"

Their need to find me was the reason everyone was taken—the reason my mother was dead.

CHAPTER 5

[LANEY]

After several minutes of attempting to persuade me against the idea—the idea that I would fight with him—Hollister finally relented.

"Okay," he said as he began leading me back to the house, out of the rain. "But do not tell Curwen—or anyone—about the slaves' plan to revolt."

"Why not?" I asked. "Maybe he could help us."

"No. I don't trust him. I don't understand how you do. Leela is stuck in Antonia because he wasn't honest."

"You don't know him." I found myself defending Curwen against my better judgment. A week ago, I had held a knife to his throat, but now I sounded like Leela, giving him the benefit of the doubt.

"You don't know him either," Hollister said as he opened the door for me to enter the house.

After we finished eating, Curwen announced that he wanted to talk to us. So, we all ended up in the living room, much the same way we had been a week earlier, except now my father and Hollister were there. And Leela was not. My father sat in his chair, the one Leela and Annabelle had curled up in the last time we were here. Corey sprawled across the floor. Hollister and I took the couch. Annabelle sat at my feet, at the coffee table, with paper and crayons ready for any visions.

Curwen had to resort, again, to bringing a chair from the kitchen to join us.

"I think before I tell you my plan for getting back to Antonia, I should tell you a little more background on Antonia," Curwen said. "Not leave anything out this time."

"Ya think?" Hollister asked sarcastically. Although I had gotten him to open up and explain some of his feelings, I still wasn't sure why he had such disdain toward Curwen.

Curwen ignored him. "Twenty-five years ago, there was a rebellion in Antonia—nearly a revolution. It was a time of great social and political upheaval. People were disappearing all the time—that's what happened to my parents and Sheldon's parents and Mara's parents. There were three main factions—much like there are now—those who wanted to reform the government, those who wanted to usurp the throne, and those who remained loyal to the crown. Things were unstable, but they became worse when, in an attempt to maintain control, the government banned travel light."

"Wait," Corey interrupted. "You mean, the people from Antonia could travel whenever and wherever they wanted?"

"There was a process to apply for a permit and training classes, but it was open to the public to travel for leisure. We actually learn a lot about your dimension's history and geography—or we did—and it made people want to come here. But now only those with special government clearance are permitted to travel—and only for government purposes."

Hollister asked, "And you have one of those special government clearances?"

"I *did*. I obviously don't anymore."

"Why did you have one?" Hollister pressed. "You work for the king?"

"I *pretended* to work for Gigandet . . . in order to obtain a permit to travel."

"Well, who do you really work for?" Hollister stared him down as he continued to interrogate. Curwen didn't answer immediately; I could tell he was getting tired of Hollister's questions and attitude. Or was Curwen trying to keep his real work a secret? I wouldn't play that game. I wouldn't keep secrets from Hollister.

"He works for a man name Durham," I said. "He's leader of an underground resistance."

"Are they the group that wants reform or revolution?" Hollister wanted to know.

"Reform." Curwen hesitated, debating whether he wanted to explain further. "We don't want a complete overthrow of the government. More like a democratic monarchy. We don't know what would happen if we got rid of the monarchy—without a king to marry the one with the mark, what would happen to the curse? Would it go away? Or would the sickness continue to spread until all the Antonians were dead? Without that knowledge, overthrowing the government is too risky. And we don't want violence or bloodshed."

"So who is the group that wants bloodshed and revolution?" Hollister asked.

"A faction of guards. The king is aware of it, but he is still trying to see how deep it goes and how strong they are. I'm concerned he is wasting too much time, that they may strike first."

"Did you advise him of this?"

"I did." Curwen nodded. "That's why I was sent here the first time, to investigate why all the people from your town were taken. It's against regulation to strike more than two people from a certain geographic area. Gigandet knew the leader of the faction of guards ordered it, and he thought it might be because they had found the one with the mark. Obviously, the one with the mark is valuable to each group for different reasons."

The one with the mark. Leela. What did the faction of guards want with her? "Why do the guards want Leela?" I asked, worried. "What will they do if they find her?"

Curwen was silent. He didn't want to answer.

Finally, Hollister said, "They'll kill her."

"Is that true?" Corey cried, his eyes wide and scared.

"Probably," Curwen admitted. "They don't want Gigandet to be able to break the curse."

My father asked rhetorically, "Can you tell me again why you thought it was a good idea to take her there?" He had been quiet until that moment.

"I'm confident Gigandet will do everything in his power to protect her. That's why he assigned Greer—his best man—to her. That's why he made Whirl leave last night when we were about to come home," Curwen explained.

"Whirl?" Hollister and I both asked simultaneously. Did he know who Whirl was? *That cruel man.*

"What does Whirl have to do with this?" I demanded.

"Whirl is the leader of the faction of guards. *They* are the real traitors. Not Sheldon or Mara." Curwen said this with bitterness. Whirl was the one who'd had Sheldon dragged away, the one who may have killed Sheldon. *If Sheldon is dead.* I remembered the way Curwen and Whirl had glared at each other, so much disgust and anger from both sides. I remembered the way Whirl had hit Leela—not once, but twice—and the way he had shocked us into silence with the collars. I could only imagine the things he was capable of.

"Whirl?" Hollister asked again. "I've seen him. He's a sick man . . . sick in the head, I mean. Deranged. Enjoys the pain of others."

Surprised, I asked, "Where did you see him?" I was scared to hear the answer. Had Whirl enjoyed causing pain to Hollister?

Hollister shook his head, nonchalantly, indicating it was no big deal. "Just when I was with the scientists." My eyes grew wide. *The scientists.* What did the scientists do? "He didn't do anything to me," he explained quickly to ease my concern. "I just saw how he treated others."

"You're right," Curwen agreed. "He is a very sick man." *A cruel man.* "He has the scientists under his control as well, trying to find a cure for the disease before the king can break the curse."

Hollister said, "So if he can cure the people of the disease, he'll be the hero . . . "

"And they will give him their loyalty," Curwen finished his sentence.

"Are they really *that* stupid?" Corey asked.

"Son," my father cautioned him, "when you're watching your loved ones die, and then someone comes along who can help them, it's natural to believe they could be good and trustworthy and deserving of gratitude and loyalty. It's how many a dictator has risen to power. He may be a sick man, but he knows what he's doing."

Annabelle yawned as she picked a different crayon to continue her drawing. Periodically, I would ask her if Leela was all right rather than watching constantly over her shoulder as she worked. I figured she would become visibly upset if something went wrong with our sister.

"We're all tired and need to sleep," I said. "You had a story to tell us. We've gotten sidetracked."

"Wait," Hollister said. "I have one more question before you continue with the story. If the king wants to marry Leela and the revolutionaries want to kill her, what do the reformists—your underground resistance—want to do with her?"

"I believe it was Durham's intention to use her as leverage . . . to persuade Gigandet to create a representative governing body for the people."

"Why didn't you tell Durham about Leela having the mark?" I asked, curious.

He shook his head and shrugged his shoulders, seeming genuinely unsure of why he hadn't been honest with his boss, the man who had raised him. I remembered the night he told us the truth—he'd been gone all day and showed up soaking wet from the rain. His eyes had looked tortured, and now it made sense to me. He had been struggling with the decision to help us, his loyalty and his conscience waging war within him.

"I wonder if Durham knows the truth now," I said.

"I think Gigandet will be doing his best to keep Leela's identity a secret," Curwen assured me. "But back to the story. Twenty-five years ago, there was a rebellion in Antonia. The government banned traveling to civilians because it believed the traveling had exposed them to too many radical ideas, that the traveling was the root of the unrest among the people. The ban only made people angrier, and then when the king—Gigandet's father—died, all the political factions saw it as their opportunity to strike for the throne, to snatch it away from a six-year-old Gigandet. At this time, the leader of the underground resistance was a young man named Gibson."

"Wait," Hollister interrupted again. "Gibson?" Curwen nodded, trying to hide his annoyance. "I've heard about him from some of the older men in my barrack. He was a slave who attempted to free all the slaves." It was obvious from the look on Hollister's face that he admired this Gibson. Perhaps the stories he'd heard about Gibson had inspired Hollister's own fight to free the slaves.

"Well . . . " Curwen hesitated. "Gibson was the leader of the resistance, and he went undercover as a slave, to try and incite a rebellion among them, to cause more issues for the crown and make it easier to manipulate the queen into agreeing to the reforms."

"He didn't want to free the slaves?" Hollister asked, disappointed.

"I believe in the end, after living with the slaves, after seeing how they were treated and what they had lost . . . yes, I think his goal changed. He lost sight of the reason he started it to begin with; he did want to free the slaves. At least, that's what I've been told."

"What happened to him?" Corey asked, transfixed by Curwen's tale.

"His rebellion failed, and he went a little crazy in the head, so affected by the things he had experienced while living with the slaves. In order to keep him from being captured and executed, his cousin—Durham—sent him away, to this dimension."

We were all silent for a long moment, processing everything he'd just revealed.

"Why are you telling us this story?" Hollister finally asked.

"Because we need to find Gibson in order to get back to Antonia. He will have a transporter. He's never traveled back to Antonia or contacted Durham, but somehow—I'm not sure how—Durham has a network of contacts that have kept tabs on Gibson for him. Gibson travels around a lot, but he always goes back to this place in North Carolina. It's supposed to be some kind of community of ex-Antonians —those who were exiled or left illegally, or those who chose not to return when the ban was enacted."

"What if he's not there?" Hollister demanded. "Will we have to wait around until he gets back?" I knew what he was thinking. He didn't have time to waste—he needed to get back to his men in barrack twenty-seven; they needed him.

"I'm hoping someone there could tell us where to find him. Or maybe one of the other ex-Antonians has a working transporter we could use. Either way, it's our best shot," Curwen said with confidence.

"Sounds like a plan," my father said while yawning and stretching. "When do you leave?"

"First thing in the morning," Curwen and Hollister said at the same time. If both of them weren't so serious, it might have been comical. At least they had the same urgency to get back to Antonia, to my sister.

Curwen continued, "I rented a cabin in the woods about ten miles from here. I left my vehicle there. We can use it for travel. I thought perhaps Dan, Corey, and Annabelle could stay in the cabin. I've reserved it for a couple more weeks, and you'll have electricity and food there . . . won't have to worry about keeping the generator going or drawing attention from the patrol vehicles riding through town. What do you think, Dan?"

"That could work," my father agreed, not at all hesitant about leaving the home he had just returned to. Perhaps, without my mother, it didn't feel like home. Or maybe it felt too much like home and made it hurt worse, all the reminders of her around every corner. My father had always been a man of few words; would he tell me how he really felt if I asked?

"I'm not staying! I'm going with y'all to find Gibson!" Corey asserted. All three men and I instantly began protesting—absolutely, under no circumstances would he set foot in Antonia! In the midst of the chaos of voices, we almost missed it. Corey noticed it first, gesturing to his little sister, getting our attention. Silence fell. Annabelle had stopped drawing, her head still bowed, and she had soft, quiet tears streaming down her cheeks, falling gently onto the paper. "Annabelle," Corey spoke soothingly, moving closer to wrap his arm around her.

I leaned forward from my position on the couch to look at her face. "Annabelle, what is it?" I asked, panicked again. Every time she drew something, my stomach dropped in dread of what it might be. What had happened to Leela?

She took her little index finger and pointed at a figure in her drawing. "Mama," she whispered. It was hard to understand the drawing at first; it was obvious it had been difficult for her to do—her hand must have been shaking, even though I hadn't noticed. All of us, except Curwen, moved in closer to examine the paper.

"That's Mama?" I asked, pointing where her finger still lay. She nodded. "Where is she?"

"Someplace cold," she whispered. Leela and the man from earlier—Greer—stood beside each other. "Leela's seeing Mama."

"She's viewing her body in the morgue," Curwen explained. He didn't even need to see the picture to know what was happening. "I'm surprised Gigandet allowed that. Maybe Leela has more persuasion over him than I thought she would. That could be helpful."

"Would you shut up?" Hollister snapped at him. It was the first time I'd seen Curwen not be sensitive to the situation around him. He usually knew what people needed—like with my father that morning, knowing he'd needed to hit something, someone—but just then, he was too busy thinking strategically to pay attention to the mood in the room.

We were quiet, a moment of silence for the one we'd lost. I knew we were all imagining ourselves in the morgue with Leela. She and I had never had any sort of psychic twin connection, other than sometimes finishing each other's sentences, but in that moment, I wished we did so I could feel what she was feeling. I wondered if

Annabelle could feel it or if she could only see it. If only Leela knew we were watching her, sort of, then she would know she wasn't alone in her farewell to our mother. We were all saying goodbye in our hearts.

My father was weeping gently; Annabelle crawled into his lap. Would he be able to take care of my siblings when we left? Would they be a good distraction for him, a responsibility to keep him busy, or would he neglect them in his grief? The way I had neglected them in mine when Hollister had been missing and I feared the worst. But the way my father held and comforted his youngest child in that moment dispelled all my concerns. They would take care of one another. It was good to know that. After the brief conversation with Hollister, hearing about his desire to fight—and me insisting that I fight with him—I wasn't sure we would make it back from Antonia a second time. My father, Corey, and Annabelle would *have* to take care of one another. In my heart, I said goodbye to them as well.

Finally, I broke the silence, "Come on. Everyone needs to get some good sleep. We have a long way to walk tomorrow." I stood, stretching, and then reached to pick up Annabelle from our father's lap. "Come on, you're sleeping with me. No more drawing tonight," I told her. "Hollister, you can have her bed. Curwen, you've got the couch." Corey was already halfway up the stairs. He was upset about our mother and angry with us for denying him again. My father followed behind him, resting his hands on his son's shoulders, giving them an affectionate squeeze.

When we reached the landing at the top of the stairs, before Hollister disappeared into Annabelle's room, he turned to me and asked, "You believe everything Curwen told us?"

"Yes. He has no reason to lie."

"No reason we know of," he countered. "You good with his plan?"

"Yes. Are you?"

"Yeah. I just hope Gibson is there."

"Me too." I knew he was thinking about the men in barrack twenty-seven again, desperate to get back to them.

"Well, good night," he said, hesitating for a moment before closing the door behind him. I waited a couple seconds to see if he might come back, just to give me a hug, but he didn't. As Annabelle became heavier in my arms, I moved on.

Lying in the bed beside her, I thought about Leela and her empty bed next to mine. Who would have ever thought that the birthmark on her neck meant anything special, that it had huge significance to thousands of people in another dimension, that people would be working hard to find her—to use her, to marry her, to kill her? Hollister had his reasons for fighting, and I had mine. Her name was Leela.

CHAPTER 6

[LEELA]

It was dark and cold. The torches weren't lit. My arms stretched out at my sides, I ran my fingertips along the stone walls, trying to find my way in pitch blackness. Their voices cried out to me—Sheldon and Mara. They were somewhere in the darkness. I had to get to them. Though I couldn't see, I knew I was in the prison tunnel, the place I had been just the day before, beaten and bloody. But now it sounded like Sheldon and Mara were being beaten and bloodied. I had to get to them. Each step becoming more frantic as their screams grew louder and the air became colder. What was Whirl doing to them? No telling what Whirl may have done to them by now*—that's what Gigandet had said.*

There should have been a turn to the right, leading to the prison cell Mara and I had shared yesterday. Instinctively, I knew that's where they were, but the wall never seemed to end, to open up to a connecting tunnel. One foot in front of the other, I attempted to slow my breathing, my panic. There was silence now; their voices were quiet for a long moment. All I heard was my own heavy breathing.

Then Sheldon screamed, the sound reverberating through the tunnel with a gush of wind pushing me backward. I pressed against it, moving as fast as I could toward his voice, my arms out in front of me to keep from running into something.

I tripped and fell, landing on my hands and knees. But what had I fallen over? I felt the ground around me, beneath me. My breath not slowing, knowing what it was. A body. A cold body. I felt it in the dark, my hands moving across the cool skin and the clothes, up to the face. The features, I knew who they belonged to. Suddenly, out of the dark, Whirl's face appeared with a torch—I screamed, and my heart stopped from fear—and he said menacingly as he pointed, "Look at her!" Not her, but her body. My mother.

"Leela, wake up," I heard a voice say, a hand on my shoulder. I shot straight up, breathing heavily; my head ached from the sudden movement. The hand on my shoulder was the man from earlier, Dr. Brandon. "Are you okay?" he asked.

Henley and Elodie—the one Gigandet wanted to marry—stood just behind the doctor, watching me. Why was Elodie here? How long had she been here? In contrast to Henley's disdain, Elodie's dark-gray eyes appeared concerned. Her frame was small and delicate, her long brown hair curled in waves around her face. She was beautiful. And it felt uncomfortable, knowing I was taking her place—if I couldn't find a way out of it—while she was still hovering around, picking out my clothes and visiting me.

"Leela, are you okay?" Dr. Brandon repeated. I nodded, self-conscious with the silent women in the corner staring at me.

"What's going on?" I asked, somewhat defensively. "What time is it? Why are y'all here?"

The doctor removed his hand, seemingly put off by my demeanor. He said, "You certainly speak strangely. . . . What area of Antonia are you from?" That's right. He had been told that I was Antonian, but I suspected he wasn't fooled.

"What does that matter?" Elodie asked coolly. "She has simply picked up her manner of speech from the bodies who cared for her." Bodies—slaves, she meant.

"It's on our list of things to correct," Henley added, a smirk in her eyes. Is that what they had been doing while I slept—creating a list of things to correct about me, a list of ways to make me more Antonian? *I don't want to be Antonian.*

"What time is it?" I asked again.

"Late evening. You've been asleep for several hours," Elodie replied, her voice like music. I had almost forgotten how angelic she looked and sounded, almost wishing she weren't as perfect as I remembered. She had come closer now, standing beside the bed. "How are you feeling, Leela?"

Even though anger and bitterness swelled within me, her big, kind, gray eyes caused me to pause before reacting. I couldn't be angry with her. She'd lost something too. I'd taken it from her. "I'm okay," I finally replied.

"You seemed like you weren't sleeping well," Dr. Brandon observed.

"No." I shook my head, remembering Whirl's evil face and my mother's cold body. "I was having a bad dream." *A nightmare.*

"I see," he said as he jotted something down on a notepad. "Want to tell us about it?"

I looked at him incredulously and shook my head. "No, thank you." What was he thinking? He may have been intelligent as a physician, but he was inept at reading social situations. Why would I ever want to tell him, a stranger, about my nightmare, especially with two other people listening? I wanted them all to stop staring at me, to give me time to wake up.

"Okay." He appeared offended by my response. "Then let me do a quick exam of your head wound, and I'll leave you be. I've already spent too much time here today anyway." I sat up on the edge of the bed and tilted my head so he could see better. "Stitches look good. Keep them dry for another day. Are you sure your ribs are fine? Want me to check?"

"No," I said, clutching the edges of my shirt, holding it down so he wouldn't dare try to lift it to see my ribs. "They're fine. I told you they aren't broken—just bruised."

"Right," he said with a suspicious, knowing look. "Softball injury. A game."

"That's right." I glared at him. "A game I learned from the *bodies* who cared for me," I said, repeating Elodie's words, unsure what my backstory was supposed to be.

He continued to scrutinize my face with his suspicious eyes for a moment longer before turning to Henley. Addressing her, he said, "Just page me if I'm needed for anything else. Leela should be fine, but let me know if Sheldon or Mara need further assistance."

My ears perked up. *Sheldon and Mara.* He had seen them, examined them, treated them. What was wrong with them that they might need further assistance? *No telling what Whirl may have done to them by now*—Gigandet's words echoed in my head again. Dr. Brandon couldn't leave fast enough for me to find out. As soon as the door shut behind him, I asked, "Sheldon and Mara—where are they? *How* are they?"

"They'll live," Henley quipped, clearly not concerned.

"What Henley means is that while they do have some physical injuries, they will heal, and they have been approved to serve as part of your guard team," Elodie added with a much kinder tone and a smile. Henley rolled her eyes and muttered something under her breath as she left the bedroom. I rose to follow with Elodie close behind me. "We thought you might be hungry," she explained when she saw how I looked at the table adorned with plates of food. "Please sit, and let's have dinner together."

It was so strange—her being there. Were she and I supposed to be friends? How could she possibly want to be my friend, and how could I bear to be hers, knowing she belonged with Gigandet—not me? But I sat at the table because I was hungry. "When will I see Sheldon and Mara?" I asked before stuffing some bread in my mouth.

"That's a question for Greer," Henley answered, always maintaining a tone of disdain.

"Okay," I said as I gulped down some cucumber juice, the same juice Whirl had brought to Mara and me in the prison cell. "Where's Greer?"

"We'll call him shortly," Elodie said. "First I wanted to have some time with you."

"For what?"

"To explain things. To help you adjust."

"You mean to tell me all the ways I need to change and all the things that need to be corrected about me?" I asked defensively.

"Yes," Henley said.

"No," Elodie countered firmly, giving Henley a warning glance, telling her to be quiet with her eyes. "I want to help make this transition as seamless as possible for you," she added with a slight, sad smile. "I can appreciate the sacrifice you have made, not just for your family, but also for the Antonian people. And I want to make it easier for you, if possible."

The Antonian people. I rolled my eyes. "I appreciate your kindness, and I know this isn't easy for you either, but you'll have to forgive me when I say—I didn't make this sacrifice for the Antonian people." I didn't do any of this for them. I did it for my family, for *my* people.

She nodded gently. "That's understandable for now. But you will do it for them when you see babies dying and mothers crying—you'll do anything for them."

"Is that what you've seen?" I asked. The cries of the child in the hospital basement rang in my ears. My heart fluttered at the image of a mother with her dying child, the opposite of what I'd experienced that morning with my own mother. A child with her dying—dead—mother.

"Last week, yes. I went to one of the quarantine stations with Gigandet—he didn't want me to go, but I insisted. One of the children passed away while we were there. . . . I tried to comfort his mother, but what could I do? It's getting worse every day . . . every day you don't marry Gigandet." It was strange, the combination of sadness and determination in her eyes. Sad that it had to be this way, that I had to marry Gigandet to break the curse and defeat the sickness, but determined to make it happen to save her people. It felt like she cared more for the Antonian people than the king did.

"Do you believe that?" I asked with complete sincerity. "Do you really believe in this curse? Do you really think there isn't any other way?"

"How can it not be true?" she countered. "You exist."

She had a point. We sat in silence for a few moments. I stared down at my plate of food since there weren't any windows to look out. How nice it would have been to have a view of the purple mountains, those beautiful hills surrounding Antonia that always seemed to be inviting me, drawing me to them.

Finally, I asked, "But don't you want to marry Gigandet?" I realized it wasn't something either of them had ever said; I had simply assumed there was something between them, a deep love only they could understand.

She smiled softly, her eyes far away. "Gigandet and I grew up together. My father was leader of the guard then, so we lived in a small home beside the palace—where I still live. When Gigandet's father died, my father became a trusted advisor to the queen. So Gigandet and I spent much of our time together. We had a care and affection for one another, and it eventually grew to love. My father always cautioned me not to fall for Gigandet, always tried to introduce me to other suitable men. Because he knew this might happen." She paused before continuing. "We actually planned to get married a couple years ago, but then people started getting sick. You see, for centuries, every king has had to wait, to see if his reign would be the one upon which the curse would fall. Gigandet thought he was in the clear, so he proposed . . . but when we heard reports of the first deaths, we knew we had to cancel the wedding and begin looking for the one with the mark. *You.*"

Me. But I didn't want this. Again, I imagined transferring the mark from my flesh to hers. Henley had been quiet, but I wanted her bold and blunt opinion. "What do you think?" I asked.

"Do I think the curse is real? Yes. Do I think you're the only one who can break it? No."

"Henley," Elodie chastised her. But Henley just crossed her arms and shrugged her shoulders, unapologetic. Her opinion was her opinion. How well did these two know each other? Thinking of the previous night when they had brought me to this room, I vaguely remembered that Elodie had sent Henley to take care of me. As if I couldn't take care of myself. I also remembered that Gigandet would have preferred someone other than Henley to see to my needs.

As though she could read my thoughts—because she was so perceptive—Elodie said, "Henley also grew up with us. Her mother worked for my father. She's been my companion my entire life." So basically Elodie sent her best friend to spy on me. She quickly added, "But she's not here to keep tabs on you." How did she do that? She could read my mind in ways Laney never could. "I sent her because she's the only one I trust to keep things confidential and to work in your best interest. All the other servant girls and bodies are gossips." *Bodies*. She used that term again. I must have made a face, scowled or winced in disgust, because she quickly corrected herself. "Slaves, I mean."

"You'll have to get used to using that word though," Henley said, "if you're going to pass for Antonian. I don't know why it's so offensive to you people."

I cut my eyes in her direction. "There's your answer. You just said it. Because we're *people*. Not just *bodies* to be worked to death." *Like my mother.*

"I'm sorry your mother died," Elodie said. I know she meant it to be sincere, but it sounded hollow and out of place, and I couldn't bring my mouth to say anything in response. She needed to get out of my head, out of my room.

Just then, I was grateful for a knock on the door—anything to break up the strange and awkward tension. Greer entered. Instead of the bright white from this morning, he now wore the black uniform that all the other guards wore. Like Whirl. The thought of him made me shiver; I couldn't shake the image of his face from my nightmare. What had he done to Sheldon and Mara?

Sheldon and Mara. They appeared in the doorway behind Greer. They were here. Were my eyes deceiving me? They were also clothed in the black uniform. Gigandet had followed through and allowed them to be members of my security team.

When my eyes met Sheldon's, I couldn't help but smile, and my eyes glazed over with tears—which I quickly blinked away. I rushed to him and hugged him, not caring that it was deemed inappropriate by Antonian standards. He returned the hug but pulled away quickly, smiling sheepishly, his light-green eyes lacking their usual confidence.

One of those eyes was surrounded by an enormous purple bruise, and his cheek had a large cut, stitched up by Dr. Brandon, I assumed. Holding his chin, I turned his face back and forth to examine the damage. He gently brushed my arm away, uneasy with the scrutiny, and stepped to the side, allowing Mara to enter.

My breath caught in my throat at the sight of her. Her long, beautiful black hair that had cascaded in waves around her face—it was gone. They—he—*Whirl*—had shaved her head. And not without causing injury; there were gashes on her dark skin where the razor had sunk too deep. Mara saw the shock and pity in my eyes, and she didn't like it. Her face was fierce, like it had been since I'd met her only a few days earlier, and I knew a hug would not be welcome, so I grabbed her hand and gave it a squeeze. She gripped my hand tightly, but I could tell she was much weaker than she appeared.

Much the same way I couldn't stop myself from hugging Sheldon, my free hand couldn't resist reaching up to cradle her shaved head, to feel the raised stitches, the same as the ones in my own head. She didn't pull away but instead explained, "He thought that—because I'm a woman—my vanity would cause me to talk." She rolled her eyes and snorted with indignation.

"That's because he doesn't know you," Sheldon said encouragingly, putting his arm around her shoulder.

I barely knew her either. I could hardly call her a friend. Had she truly *not* surrendered any information to Whirl? The day before, in the palace gardens, when the guards had me pinned to the ground, when the female guard had threatened Curwen, she had immediately given them my name. Had Whirl not tried that tactic with her, to threaten the one she loved? That would have been better than cutting her hair. Whirl was cruel, but he seemed clueless to the motivations of others.

She soon grew uncomfortable with me being so close and touching her and drawing attention to her, especially with Elodie and Henley watching. They were always watching. But I couldn't help wanting to be near Sheldon and Mara. They were the closest thing to home that I had.

Looking to Greer, I demanded, "And what is being done about Whirl? That man must be stopped!" I could still feel the sting on my cheek from his backhand. "Why does Gigandet allow him to do these things?"

Greer's eyes flickered quickly to Elodie and then back to me, making it clear that he wouldn't, and I shouldn't, talk about Gigandet with her there.

Being perceptive as she was, Elodie said, "I'll take my leave now. Leela, we'll talk more later." She turned back at the door and added, "Please don't judge Gigandet so harshly. Give him a chance."

It took every bit of self-control I had to maintain a blank but firm expression on my face. What kind of chance had he given my mother? What kind of chance had he given Sheldon and Mara, knowing *there was no telling what Whirl may have done to them*? That's what he had said. He had left them in Whirl's care. A small voice in my head argued back—but he wasn't sending them to be killed, which should have been their punishment. He *was* giving them a chance. My face softened, and she seemed to be waiting for a response, so I gave her a slight smile and head nod. Then she left, and Greer shut and locked the door behind her.

Putting my arms around the shoulders of both Sheldon and Mara, I led them to the couch, and then I brought them plates of food from the table while they protested that I didn't need to serve them. But if I was still exhausted from the last two days, I could only imagine how they felt and what their night had been like. I wondered what injuries they might have that I couldn't see but didn't ask. The collars of their shirts came up high, which I thought was unusual, different from the other guards, until I realized why—they had to hide the shock collars around their necks, the ones Gigandet insisted they wear.

That's when I also wondered—did Sheldon know what was on my neck, that I was the one with the mark? Had Mara told him? Or Greer? Or Curwen? I was sure he must have been informed, and for some reason I couldn't explain, I hated that he knew. We sat in silence as they ate while Henley became more annoyed each second. Finally, she asked, "Greer, can't you take them across the hall to the guard quarters? They shouldn't be here like this."

Looking at Greer, I pleaded, "Please don't take them anywhere."

"They don't belong here," Henley argued.

"Neither do I," I said softly. At least, I didn't want to belong there.

"That mark on your neck would prove otherwise," she quipped. "Unfortunately."

"Yes. *Unfortunately*," I agreed. "I don't want to marry Gigandet any more than you want me to." I wasn't one of those Antonian girls who wished she had the mark so she could marry royalty. Couldn't she see that?

"Then don't marry him."

Greer, Mara, and Sheldon all looked at one another, confused, and then waited for my response. Henley and I stared at each other for a minute. What did she mean? She said she believed the curse was real. But she didn't think I was the only one who could break it. What did she know that the rest of us didn't?

"What do you think we should do?" I finally asked.

She paused before saying, "We need to talk to the Ancient Ones."

"Henley, stop," Greer ordered. "We're not doing this."

Ignoring him, Mara asked her, "What do you know about the Ancient Ones?"

"We all know they don't exist anymore," Greer answered instead.

Continuing to ignore him, Henley said, "I know that my great-grandfather was one of them. What do you know?"

I almost dreaded this alliance forming between Henley and Mara.

Mara smirked with a mischievous look in her eye. "I know how to find them."

CHAPTER 7

[LANEY]

"Laney, I'm not sure I can do this," my father said as he sat down on the back-porch steps. All morning, my father would have moments of strength and clarity quickly followed by moments of defeat and indecision. Hollister was putting the generator away in the shed, Curwen was repacking his gear, and Corey and Annabelle were inside, deciding what they wanted to bring with them. There was no one to talk to him but me, and I felt ill equipped for the task. I breathed deeply and channeled Leela, knowing she would have the right words and compassion.

Ask questions, I heard her say. Sitting beside him, I asked gently, "What do you mean?"

"We just got here. I thought I would never see this place again."

"Are you afraid you really will never see it again if you leave this time?"

He shrugged his shoulders, "I don't know. I know it's just a house. I want to stay, but I also want to run as far away from it as possible." It was a house full of the memories of his dead wife and the life they had built together. Part of him wanted to stay there forever, to never forget, and part of him didn't want to remember because the pain would swallow him, drown him. He sighed and stood, giving my shoulder a squeeze with his large, strong, calloused hands. Staring off into the distance, he said, "I love you, Laney." They were words I had heard a million times from that deep, gruff voice—words I never tired of hearing.

"I love you too." I smiled and grabbed his hand as I stood.

"Please trust that I can take care of your brother and sister," he added. "I will always grieve the loss of your mother, but I will also always take care of you kids. So, don't worry about that while you go get Leela back. You bring her home, you hear?"

"Yes, sir." I nodded. He pulled me in for one of his long bear hugs.

Just then, Annabelle came running out, the screen door slamming behind her, with a piece of paper in her hands. "Look!" she exclaimed, holding the sheet up for us to see. The drawing contained several figures.

"Curwen!" I shouted. "Come look!"

He came rushing around the side of the house, a look of concern on his face. "What? What's wrong?" he asked. It was obvious he didn't want to look, too afraid of what he might find. But I gave him a smile and shook my head, reassuring him all was well. The drawing showed Leela with Mara and Sheldon, sitting on a couch together, roughly sketched, but I knew it was them. They were alive.

Hollister had come up behind me. "What's going on?" he asked.

Curwen exhaled a huge sigh of relief. "They're alive. For now, at least." He leaned down to look my little sister directly in the eyes and said, "Thank you, Annabelle." She turned and hid her face in my side, suddenly shy of the attention, or perhaps overwhelmed by the intensity and sincerity of his gratitude. What a gift she had been given! Where had it come from, this ability, and how long would it last? Would her entire life be plagued with the need to draw these visions? Would she ever be able to focus on anything else? I picked her up and held her tightly.

"Come on, y'all," Hollister urged. "If we're goin', let's get goin'." He wanted to get to Leela, but more importantly, it felt like he wanted to get back to barrack twenty-seven. I was still bothered by the way he had implied that I didn't think the slaves were important—they *were* important—but I also couldn't bring myself to be more concerned for them than I was for my own sister. She was in imminent danger too.

Corey came out the back door, looking like he was ready to go on a nature survivalist show, his hiking backpack and hunting rifle slung over his shoulders. Even though he hadn't said anything directly about it since last night, I could tell he still wasn't convinced that he wasn't going to Antonia with us. He would mutter things quietly under his breath in a passive-aggressive way. None of us corrected him because we didn't feel like arguing, but we had all solidified our agreement with one another that he was not, under any circumstances, allowed to go to Antonia.

Thinking of Corey or Annabelle in Antonia made me shudder. And it made me wonder, *What do they do with the children?* So, I asked Curwen, "What do they do with the children when they're struck?"

"It's prohibited for children to be struck," he said in his mechanical voice, the voice he always used when I asked questions about Antonia. It sounded like it was something he had recited a million times.

"But they took the children from our town . . . "

Everyone was silent, staring hard at him, waiting for a response. Had my father or Hollister seen the children while they were enslaved? Did they know what had happened to them?

"*Whirl* took the children," Curwen clarified. "It's one of the reasons Gigandet sent me to investigate. But I don't know what he's done with them. Did you see them with the scientists?"

Hollister was caught off guard by the question but shook his head. "No, I didn't. But it was a large facility, and I only saw a small part of it. Yet another reason we need to hurry up and get back there." His jaw was clenched in anger.

"Let me get my stuff. Then we can head out," I said. In my bedroom, *our* bedroom—Leela's and mine—I stood in the quiet, looking around to see if I was forgetting anything. My eyes stop on the framed photo on the nightstand between our beds. It was the last family picture we had taken, at our college graduation, and our mother had framed it for us as a small gift.

"Laney, come on!" Corey hollered from downstairs.

I quickly grabbed the picture, wrapped it in a shirt, and stuffed it into my backpack.

As we were preparing to leave, my father said, "Corey, you're not taking the gun to the cabin. You don't need it. It's not hunting season. Go lock it up."

My brother argued, "I'm not taking it to the cabin. I'm taking it to Antonia."

No, he wasn't.

"You are most definitely not doing that," Curwen said quickly, firmly. "That is one of our strictest laws—guns are not allowed to be brought into Antonia." His face was fierce, and it was obvious this was something he felt very strongly about.

"But . . . " Corey wanted to protest further. One look from my father silenced him, and he entered the house with his head hung low. I watched through the screen door as he locked it away in the safe under the stairs.

Hiking was something we were accustomed to, but ten miles on a mission—*no time for leisure, must get to Leela*—was going to be a challenge. The terrain became steeper as we headed northeast toward the mountains, Curwen leading the way. Annabelle walked as long as she could, and then my father and Hollister switched off carrying her, her limp body growing warmer and her cheeks pinker as the sun rose higher. Despite telling her that she didn't need to draw last night, that she needed to sleep instead, I found her awake at three in the morning, sitting in Leela's bed with a crayon in her hand. All she had drawn was another picture of Leela sleeping. Why was Leela sleeping so much? *Annabelle* needed to sleep, so I was glad this journey forced her to put down the pencil and paper, to fall asleep resting her head on her father's shoulder.

Hollister didn't say much, and when he did speak, it was in response to one of Corey's many questions. I knew his mind was preoccupied with the men of barrack twenty-seven. Did he really think he could help them in some way? Had they already staged their attack, or would it be a quickly and quietly crushed rebellion? Would Rick Stover make it out alive, and if he did, would he end up with the scientists? I knew all these questions, plus a million more I couldn't fathom, were weighing on Hollister's mind, so I maintained my distance. Which was so hard. Because I just wanted to hold his hand. Though he had said he still loved me, still wanted to marry me, I couldn't *feel* it. I had to constantly remind myself of his words, remind myself of what I knew to be true; I had to be like Leela, to focus on my head—not my heart.

Hours passed, but we didn't stop along the way, walking at a steady pace, eating as we went. By midafternoon, Curwen announced that we didn't have much farther to go, and though we had become conditioned for this kind of travel, I couldn't wait to ride in a car again, to roll down the window and feel the breeze blow through my hair. We had been in the woods for a while; the tree coverage was a nice respite from the sun. Finally, as we crested the top of a hill, I saw a cabin emerge beyond the trees. It sat alone and isolated, a perfect spot of seclusion for my father and siblings to rest.

We ascended the creaky wooden steps to the covered front porch, and Curwen opened the door for us. It was stuffy inside, and my father immediately turned on the air conditioner, blasting the cool air; I had a feeling Curwen would go behind him and turn it up—he was used to Antonian heat.

"Hollister and Laney," Curwen began, "let's all take showers before we head out. There are two bathrooms."

"Y'all can go first," I said. "I'm going to see what I can make them for dinner."

"You only need to make dinner for Dad and Annabelle," Corey specified. "I'll take a shower before we head out too." He still assumed he was going. I couldn't tell if he was serious or not, but it was time for him to face the facts.

"Corey, you're not going with us," Curwen said firmly. "I wouldn't take you to Antonia a week ago, and I'm definitely not taking you now when things are even more dangerous." Corey looked from me to

Hollister to our father, pleading with his eyes, but we all shook our heads at him. In the time it took to blink, he had thrown open the front door and had taken off running.

Our father yelled after him, "Son, where are you going!"

"To the creek!" he hollered. "Don't worry about telling me bye! Just go." We had crossed a small creek just five minutes earlier. Corey always gravitated to moving water when he was upset; it soothed him and gave him time to think. He'd be back.

Our father was thinking the same thing. "He'll be back once he's cooled off. Y'all go on and get your showers done. We didn't hustle to get here so we could waste time worrying. I'll take care of Corey."

The guys went to take showers, Annabelle slept on the couch, and my father rested in the armchair, turning on the television; the sound of it was new and familiar at the same time. Left alone in the kitchen, I raided the well-stocked pantry and fridge, creating a couple of meals to last them for a few days. It made me think of my mother. When someone dies, friends and family bring food, usually an unnecessary amount. But we didn't have any friends and family to mourn with us, to bring us meals, to sit with us and weep—they were all enslaved in Antonia, or they were scattered across the country and believed we were all missing and possibly dead. But no—only my mother was dead.

As I was washing the dishes, Hollister came up behind me, startling me. "Sorry," he apologized softly as he reached around and took the sponge from my hand, holding my hand in his for a moment. "Let me finish here. You go get cleaned up so we can get on the road." That's all he wanted, all he cared about—*to get on the road*. Frustrated, I pulled my hand from his and left him there.

Once we were ready to head out, *to get on the road*, Corey had still not returned. I wanted to tell him goodbye, even though he had shouted for us not to worry about it, to *just go*. Annabelle had woken up; she didn't have any urge to draw though—she simply explained that Leela was sleeping. I sat on the couch, snuggling her close to me. Curwen was briefing my dad on everything he needed to know about the cabin.

“I went ahead and rented it for a couple extra weeks . . . just in case,” he said. In case what? In case the mission took longer than we expected? In case we never returned at all? I shuddered thinking about it, squeezing Annabelle tighter; she didn’t complain.

Hollister came in from putting our bags in the vehicle. “Y’all ready?” he asked.

“Almost. Dan,” Curwen addressed my father, “here is a satphone. I have one as well. The number is programmed in here. You’ll be able to reach us as long as we’re here.”

“I’ll call you before we leave,” I added. “And check in when we get where we’re going.”

“All right.” He took the phone from Curwen. “Y’all get going then.” He noticed my hesitation. “Corey will be fine,” he reassured me. “I’ll have him call you as soon as he’s back.” I nodded, standing, knowing there wasn’t any more time to waste. We had to go. Leela needed us. The men of barrack twenty-seven needed us. All the *bodies* needed us. But what could we do for them? The thought was overwhelming.

My father pulled me in for another one of his bear hugs before I slid into the back seat of Curwen’s rented SUV. Would Hollister sit beside me? He shook hands with my father and gave him a quick hug before jumping into the front passenger seat. I internally rolled my eyes. Curwen also shook my father’s hand before getting behind the wheel. Annabelle stood on the porch, her tiny hand waving to us, getting smaller as we took off down the gravel driveway onto a dirt road. It was strange to feel the tires beneath us; the last time I had ridden in a car, I had been blindfolded and wearing the prettiest blue sundress. Leela had been driving, and we’d been driving to my surprise anniversary party, the one where Hollister was going to propose, the one where we discovered all the townspeople had disappeared. It seemed a distant memory. Distant . . . that’s what Hollister was.

Curwen was kind enough to turn on the radio so we didn’t travel in complete silence. I pushed all the thoughts away, cracked the window, and focused on the scenery passing by. We reached a paved road and continued east into the mountains, toward North Carolina. "How do you know what to look for?" I asked Curwen. "Wouldn't this community of ex-Antonians be kind of secretive?"

"All I know is I'm supposed to go to a place called The Cracked Pot. It's where Durham told me to go if I ever got into trouble while I was here."

"The Cracked Pot? What is it?" Hollister asked.

"When I looked it up, it's a diner and country store. It didn't have a website, so yes, it probably is kind of secretive."

The Cracked Pot. I wondered what—who—we would find there. The sun dipped lower in the sky behind us as dusk approached. Would the store still be open by the time we reached it? The winding roads through the hill country and the lush green foliage had me mesmerized for most of the ride, thinking about family vacations and college weekend trips. I couldn't shake the feeling that life would never be like that again. Had that really been my life? It almost didn't seem real, like none of it had ever happened, like life hadn't really begun until the day the lightning struck. I had been living someone else's life before then. This was my life now. Listed as missing, presumed dead. But not dead. Alive. *Alive.* For now.

A couple hours later, the GPS announced, "Destination, five hundred feet ahead, on the left."

I leaned forward, peering between the front seats, wanting to get the first glimpse of The Cracked Pot. It wasn't what you would imagine when you thought of a country store and diner. It was a modern, concrete, cubical building, painted a matte black with white shutters and window frames. Pulling into the dirt and gravel parking lot, my stomach felt sick in anticipation. There was only one other vehicle parked there, probably an employee. It was eight, so perhaps the dinner rush had passed. Did diners in the middle of nowhere experience such a thing as dinner rush?

"Finally. I'm starving," came a voice from behind me. Corey's voice. The three of us were frozen for a moment before turning around. Corey was peeking over the seats, a blanket over his head, a big grin on his face. But the glare from all of us must have been intense because he slowly sunk back down into his hiding place.

"You didn't see him back there?" Curwen asked Hollister, accusing him because he had been the one to load our bags into the trunk.

"No! He wasn't there."

Still hidden under the blanket, Corey said in a muffled voice, "I snuck in after that. Don't blame Holli."

"You didn't hear him moving back there?" Hollister asked me. Now it was my fault.

"No. Because I didn't move," Corey answered instead. He popped back up. "I told you I was coming."

"We're taking you back *right now*," I said firmly.

"Can you at least let me eat first?" he asked, continuing to act nonchalantly about the situation.

"No. You should starve as punishment." I glared at him. "Do you know how worried Dad must be? You're going to call him right now and tell him what you've done. Curwen, give me the satphone." Before we could dial the number, though, it started ringing; I handed it to Corey to answer. As soon as he said hello, we could all hear my father yelling on the other end. The three of us exited the vehicle, leaving my brother to receive an earful.

There were four wooden rocking chairs out front beneath a red awning. Beside the door there was a giant cracked black pot with beautiful red flowers blooming. They seemed familiar. The light from inside cast a warm, yellow glow, and as I peered in the windows, I gasped in realization. There, in the windowsills, were more red flowers, the same ones from the pot, the same ones from Antonia, the ones that marked a safe house of the underground resistance. Is that what they were supposed to represent here—a safe place for all Antonians? It made me anxiously excited to go inside, to see who we might meet.

"Curwen, look," I whispered, pointing at the flowers.

He gave a single nod of his head. "I saw them."

"What do you think they mean?" I asked.

"Hopefully, that we'll be welcome here."

Corey opened the trunk and hopped out. "Here," he said, handing the phone to me with attitude.

"Hello," I answered cautiously, unsure if I would be yelled at also.

"Well, what do you want to do about him?" my father asked. "I have no way to come get him without a car."

"Don't worry. We'll make sure he gets back to you before we go to Antonia." I glared at my brother. "We've arrived at our destination, though, so I've gotta go. I'll keep you posted. Love you," I told him.

"Love you too." Then he hung up.

Curwen, Hollister, and Corey led the way as we entered the diner. A bell chimed as the door opened and shut, announcing our arrival. It was small, quaint, and cozy inside with black-and-white checkerboard floors and half a dozen round oak tables with matching chairs. A set of red double French doors on the right led to the store. A chalkboard wall behind the counter revealed today's menu, and a display case in front of it showed off all the desserts. I realized how hungry I was too. But there was no one is sight. Corey, impatient for food, rang the bell on the counter.

A young woman who couldn't have been much older than Corey came from the back, the kitchen door swinging behind her. Her long, wavy, black hair perfectly framed her face, and her big, bright smile accentuated the freckles on her cheeks. Wiping her hands on her apron, she asked, "What can I get ya?"

"Eight grilled cheeses and four soups, please." Hollister stepped in to order before Corey could have his pick of the menu. I could tell my brother was salivating over the dessert display; I wanted one of the cupcakes too. But we were all angry with Corey. His actions would cost us more time, and he didn't seem to understand that.

We sat at one of the tables and she brought our food not long after. Was she here alone? Just then someone entered from the store. I gasped. I'd seen her before. "Phaedra?" I asked.

"Yes?" the girl from behind the counter said. Was that her name too? I ignored her and continued staring at the other woman, the one who was identical—except for her cropped hair—to the Phaedra I had met in Antonia. She turned to look at me, surprised and suspicious.

"No." Curwen shook his head, a huge smile spread across his face, the first really joyful smile I had witnessed from him. "Phaedra's twin. Haleh."

CHAPTER 8

[LEELA]

They kept us up until curfew—9:00 p.m.—discussing their plans to find the Ancient Ones. Mara and Henley quickly developed a camaraderie that sparked a tinge of jealousy in me—why couldn't Mara have connected with me like that? I didn't say much during their planning; Sheldon only chimed in when he felt he had a good point to make, and Greer constantly argued against them, doubting that the Ancient Ones still existed. And even if they did exist, he didn't think they would have any new or relevant information about the curse, nothing that could change the fact that I needed to marry Gigandet. He could have stopped it—the planning; he held all the power. As the leader of my guard, he was the only one who could permit or prevent us from going anywhere. But it seemed like there was a part of him that didn't want me to have to marry Gigandet either. He had known and served Gigandet—and Elodie—for several years, and I was sure he couldn't imagine them not being together; I sensed there was a small part of him hoping the Ancient Ones could help us.

I sat beside Sheldon, both of us trying to keep our eyes open; we were interested, but exhausted. I wanted to ask him a million questions, but not with the rest of them listening. So I focused on what they were saying. They explained that the Ancient Ones were a secret group of individuals who recorded the history of Antonia. It wasn't always a secret, but when the government wanted to rewrite history—to erase some things, to justify others—it began to imprison the Ancient Ones, denying them the right to speak the truth. So they went into hiding—hiding in plain sight, as ordinary citizens. Henley's great-grandfather had been one of them, according to her mother; it was believed they had all been wiped out during the rebellion twenty-five years earlier. Were any of them still alive, and could they help change my future? I didn't want to hope for it, too afraid to want it and end up disappointed.

There was some argument about whether I should be allowed to join them on this search for the Ancient Ones. Henley wanted to go with Mara, just the two of them, but Greer would not allow it—he wouldn't allow Mara or Sheldon out of his sight while they were on probation. He needed to learn if he could trust them first. He needed to know that they wouldn't do anything to betray him or Gigandet. I needed to know that too. Were they still plotting and scheming for the underground resistance, for Durham? Did they have an agenda other than the one Greer had assigned to them, the one I had pleaded for them to have in order to save their lives?

"Then I guess we'll all go together," Sheldon concluded. He yawned. "Can we go to sleep now?"

"Yes," Greer responded. "Mara, you'll stay in here tonight. Allen will be posted at the door. Sheldon and I will be across the hall."

"And I'll be at home with Elodie," Henley added. "But I'll be back before daybreak."

"Can't wait," I quipped sarcastically.

She rolled her eyes.

"Don't say anything to Elodie," Greer warned her.

"I would never. I wouldn't want to get her hopes up."

When they left, and Mara and I were left alone. I breathed a sigh of relief and then immediately started asking her questions. "What happened after I left you?"

"You mean when I woke up alone in a cold, dark dungeon?" she corrected me with attitude.

"No," I countered. "I mean when I gave myself up to Gigandet so nobody would be executed."

"Fair enough," she conceded. "But I'm not going to talk about what happened next. You can see from my bald head some of what happened." Part of me was grateful that she didn't want to share those details, that she would keep her secrets to herself, that I wouldn't have to share in that pain also, but most of me wondered: Would I imagine it worse than it had been, or had it been worse than I could imagine? What had Whirl or his guards done to her and Sheldon? "Don't worry," she added, "I didn't say a word. I didn't tell them anything."

"I wasn't worried." *Liar.* I had been wondering what she might have told them, what they might have tortured out of her, whether she had revealed any information that could hurt us.

"Why don't you go to bed?" she ordered more than asked. "We have a lot of walking to do tomorrow."

Daybreak came and passed. Sheldon, Mara, and I missed it. Henley may have been there, but Greer didn't allow her to wake us. When we finally rose, Henley rushed us through breakfast, and Greer made sure that he, Sheldon, and Mara changed into civilian clothing so they would be inconspicuous in the Antonian crowds. Their shirts still had high collars, though, to hide the shock collars around their necks. It made me sick to my stomach to imagine Greer shocking them, and I prayed he would have no reason to—I didn't think it was something he wanted to do either.

"Will Gigandet know that we've left the palace?" I asked him.

"He has urgent business to attend to this morning," he said, not elaborating. I noticed Sheldon and Mara look at each other, their ears perking up, curious about this *urgent business*.

I decided to indulge them. I asked, "What kind of urgent business?"

"Nothing to worry about. Just affairs of the state." His tone made it clear that he wouldn't give more details, that the conversation ended there.

We exited the palace from a hidden side entrance, the idea being that we would appear to be ordinary citizens on a visit to the gardens. But we didn't enter the gardens; Greer didn't want to run into any of the guards who had shocked, kicked, and arrested me two days earlier. I didn't want to run into them either. Hadn't he said their actions wouldn't go unpunished—had he meant all of them or just the leader, the one who'd bruised my rib and slammed my head into the brick wall? He must have only meant that one, if the others were still on duty. I shuddered at the thought of any of them recognizing me. Henley had given me a hat to wear and braided my hair, pinning it in a position to hide the birthmark on my neck. I had felt Sheldon eyeing it as Henley did my hair, obviously curious about the mark he'd heard about since childhood; it made me self-conscious.

The air smelled sweet, like the jasmine my mother grew one summer—it didn't survive through the winter. It died because it couldn't handle the cold; she died because she couldn't handle the heat. Her body—was it ashes now? I breathed deeply, taking in the scent of the flowers, pushing the thoughts away, forcing myself to focus on the things around me. The white stone walls, the white concrete beneath our feet, everything white so the sun would reflect off it and keep the city cooler. The clear blue sky—I'd yet to notice clouds or experience rain in Antonia. The purple mountains in the distance—what made them purple?

"What makes the mountains purple?" I asked them.

"Some kind of shrubbery that grows there," Henley answered.

"I heard it's a flower," Mara added. "And that it's poisonous."

"Have any of you ever been to the mountains?" I asked.

"No." Henley shook her head emphatically. "It's strictly forbidden."

"Why?" I wanted to know. My other companions were suspiciously silent.

"You cannot survive there," Henley explained. "For our safety, we remain in the boundaries of the city." She sounded like Curwen used to sound when we asked him questions about Antonia, like she had memorized a list of rules to recite, like she didn't really understand the reasons behind the rules. I noticed Mara and Sheldon pass a sideways glance between them—they knew something more than Henley. I hated not being able to ask them.

We passed through the small forest with its lighted walkway into the meeting quarters—the place where people could gather for recreation and celebration. We had made it to the beautiful, tree-lined avenue with the large rectangular fountains; three days earlier, there had been a protest happening there, a protest Curwen had dragged me away from, a protest that had ended violently with citizens being attacked with high-voltage cattle prods. This morning, it was calm, peaceful, only a few couples lounging about.

We came to a locked gate, one that led to the working quarters. I could already hear the sound of the crowd, the hustle and bustle of life as business owners opened their shops and vendors sold things in the street. Greer scanned his card through the slot and entered a code. Before opening the gate, he instructed, "When we get into the crowd, close ranks around Leela. Our most important purpose, at all times, is to protect her." I almost rolled my eyes, thinking that would never be Henley's most important purpose. She walked through the gate first, then Mara.

I had never been to the working quarters. Laney had described them to me—the dirty walkway, the noise, the vendors shouting, the people brushing past and kicking up dust—a sensory overload after the tranquility of either the meeting or living quarters. It was almost as though the working quarters was the only place the Antonians were able to make a sound, to feel a sense of freedom, to be loud, to be passionate. It was overwhelming—but it was life.

I fell into step beside Sheldon, letting Henley and Mara lead us, with Greer taking up the rear. With the roar of the crowd around us, Sheldon and I were able to have a conversation without the others hearing. But I didn't know what to say. A million questions I wanted to ask, yet when the opportunity came, I couldn't get the words to come out right. I was determined to try though. "Are you really okay?" I asked. "How badly did Whirl hurt you?"

He sighed. "I'm fine. Nothing worse than what I received from training with my boss and Curwen." His boss? He must have meant Durham. But he didn't want Greer to hear Durham's name; he was still loyal to protect their resistance group. Was he still plotting for the resistance now, even in the midst of this new mission?

"I wonder if your boss knows what's happened," I mumbled. Where was Durham? Was he trying to find a way to help his children, or was he more focused on the cause of the resistance? Or had he cleverly found a way to combine the two? I glanced back at Greer; he wasn't paying attention to us, busy keeping a watchful eye around us. Sheldon was doing the same.

"I'm sure he must," he finally answered. "We need to go to the bakery." To Phaedra, to the woman whose arms I wanted to be wrapped in, to feel a mother's embrace.

"Do you think she'll be there?" My excitement at the thought was almost too much to contain.

"Probably, but shh," he warned.

I didn't like being chastised by him, feeling as though he found fault in me. I quickly apologized, "Sorry. I'm just excited to possibly see her. I've been wanting one of her mother hugs. . . . I know I need to be quiet, though, for her protection. I'm sorry."

He dropped his head. "No, Leela. I'm sorry. I'm sorry your mother died. I'm sorry I never met her. I'm sorry we didn't save her. And I'm sorry I didn't say this sooner. When I saw that word—deceased—on the computer screen, it was like time stopped and all sound faded away, and I didn't even want to believe it or look at your sister or father and tell them."

Tears filled my eyes as I blinked them away. "I didn't know that," I said softly, looking at the ground. He had discovered and delivered the bad news. What a terrible position to be in. We were silent for a long moment. Then, changing the subject, I asked, "Where's the bakery from here?"

"Just around the corner."

"Greer," I said loudly, "can we stop at the bakery? I didn't eat enough at breakfast because *somebody* was rushing us. And I need to get out of the sun for a moment." I fanned myself with my hand, trying to appear overheated—in reality, I had adapted to the Antonian climate quickly. Why couldn't it have been that way for my mother? Her cause of death: heat exhaustion.

Henley shot a look of disdain at me and said, "We don't have time to stop."

But Mara knew who owned the bakery, and she wanted to see her. "We can spare a few minutes," she argued.

"Seeing that Leela asked Greer—not you two—maybe we should let him answer," Sheldon countered, making sure to add a lighthearted smile, glancing back at Greer.

Henley rolled her eyes, annoyed.

"Sure, we can stop," Greer agreed. I could tell he still wasn't sure he wanted to be doing this anyway.

We turned the corner, and I saw the The Flour Shop Bakery and Cafe at the end of the alleyway. It became less crowded, less loud as we moved toward it. When we entered, the cool air gave me chills. The stone walls were painted a rosy peach, and the floor was a multicolored slate tile. There were a dozen or more tables spread throughout and only four customers. They glanced at us when we entered but quickly returned to their conversations. How would they act if they knew who I was, that I was the one with the mark? I still doubted that a birthmark I'd had my entire life could really mean so much to these people, that it had any power to break a curse.

As I looked behind the glass counter at all the pastries, cookies, pies, and donuts, I couldn't help thinking of my brother, of the way Corey had stolen—and eaten—the entire box of them when Curwen had brought it to us from Antonia, the first time he had demonstrated the lightning travel to us. Corey would have liked to have been in the bakery with us just then; I could imagine him drooling over all the baked goods, choosing to sample them all.

Behind the counter was a young man, waiting for us to approach and place an order. But I didn't want to see him. Three of us didn't want to see him. We wanted to see her. *Phaedra*. And he knew that. He knew she—their mother figure—wanted to see them too. As soon as he recognized Sheldon and Mara, he disappeared.

"What kind of customer service is that?" Henley complained.

Seconds later, Phaedra came bursting into the room, her arms outstretched, reaching for her children without hesitation. I noticed Greer searching for something in his pocket—perhaps a weapon, perhaps the remote to shock them—and I placed my hand on his arm, shaking my head and silently asking him not to do anything. Phaedra pulled Sheldon and Mara close to her, hugging their necks while weeping, tears of joy pouring down her light-brown skin, a beautiful smile spread across her full lips. I knew from the placement of her hands that there was no way she couldn't feel the shock collars on their necks, but she didn't say anything; she was just relieved to know they were alive, to see them, to touch their bodies, their living bodies.

"She's their mother," I whispered to Greer in explanation. He removed his hand from his pocket, but his eyes were angry—I could tell he felt like he had been tricked into coming here. Which he had. But couldn't he see that it was for good, for a family to be reunited? She stepped back from Sheldon and Mara and examined the bruises and cuts on their faces; removing Mara's hat, she rubbed her hand over her daughter's shaved head.

Pointing at Mara's scalp, she asked Greer, "Are you responsible for this?"

He seemed insulted that she would assume he was to blame for Mara's head. "No, it wasn't me."

"Good." Then she looked at me. That was all it took. I couldn't help it. I started crying uncontrollably. "Oh, Leela," she said soothingly as she pulled me into her strong embrace, my shoulders heaving with my sobs. I knew we were making a scene, I knew we were making the customers stare, and I knew Greer would not be happy about it. I felt another hand give my shoulder a squeeze and looked up to see

Sheldon giving me a comforting smile, his eyes glistening. *Stop crying now. Pull yourself together.* Henley's glare was telling me the same thing. I wiped my face and took some deep breaths.

"Here," Phaedra said as she led me to a table. "You all sit, and we'll bring you some food. It's almost lunchtime—I've got some hot soups on the stove and some freshly baked bread." Everyone took a seat, and she flashed a smile before disappearing into the kitchen, her employee following her. Phaedra was the kind of person who could genuinely, wholeheartedly, joyfully love the worst of us. She had a way of making any person feel instantly welcomed. But Henley and Greer did not appear pleased as they sat across from the three of us who'd been embraced by her.

"If there's going to be sneaky behavior like this, we can go back to the palace right now. And you two," Greer pointed at Sheldon and Mara, "can go back to the dungeon. Gigandet is holding me accountable, and I will *not* be manipulated."

"You're right," Sheldon said immediately, apologetic. "We did not intend to manipulate you—it wasn't part of the plan. But we were so close to the bakery, that the idea of not stopping . . . well, we just had to."

"You're wasting our time," Henley stated.

We sat in silence, eating our food. Phaedra joined us for a few minutes, but she didn't ask any questions, knowing we couldn't answer them honestly with Greer and Henley listening. I didn't want her to be considered an accomplice to our "crimes" either. Greer remained on alert, but she was slowly winning him over; Henley would not allow herself to be won. As we were finishing our meal, Phaedra excused herself to get back to the kitchen, and my eyes fell on the door; Durham had entered. I tried my best to act normal, not to draw the attention of Greer or Henley in his direction; their backs were to him.

He and Sheldon caught each other's eye. Sheldon gave his head a barely noticeable shake, pulling his shirt collar down for a split second to give Durham a glimpse of the shock collar beneath it, letting his boss—his father—know he wasn't a free man. Durham nodded slightly and turned and walked past us to a table in the corner where he could observe our situation. How much did he know about what had happened to all of us? How much had he communicated to Phaedra? Without Sheldon to hack into the Antonian system and find intel for them, how was their resistance group functioning?

There was another man with him who was talking loudly as they sat down. "The reports are saying that several guards were killed or wounded before the bodies were subdued," he said. *The bodies*. The slaves. Had they attacked the guards? My eyes went wide in shock and curiosity; Greer's eyes narrowed in suspicion. In his civilian clothing, they didn't know he was a guard. He turned his head to examine Durham and his companion.

"Greer, what are they talking about?" I asked. "What happened?"

"Nothing you need to be concerned about," he said. "And *they* shouldn't be either." He glared at them.

"Is that the urgent business Gigandet had to attend to?" I pressed for more information.

"He said don't worry about it," Henley answered instead.

"I just—" I began to protest, but Sheldon gave my knee a squeeze, indicating I should be quiet. He and Mara hadn't said a word either; I just wanted a moment alone with them to speak freely. What was happening? Was the slave revolt a plan set in place by the resistance, or was it something completely separate? Were the *bodies* finally fighting for themselves? Was there a way I could help them when—if—I became queen?

Almost as if he could read my thoughts, Greer said, "Let's get out of here . . . so we can figure out a way for you not to be queen."

CHAPTER 9

[LANEY]

Phaedra's twin. *That's right.* Phaedra had told me about her twin sister. What had she said? That she had traveled through the light and never returned, that she had fallen in love with a man and had chosen to stay here. I remembered Phaedra's sadness when she had spoken about her, and I wished she were here to see her sister now. Haleh stood before us with all kinds of questions and distrust in her eyes.

"Phaedra, go to the back," she ordered the young woman, who I assumed was her daughter. Phaedra, the Phaedra I knew, had said she always imagined the children her sister might have had. Little did she know that she had a niece and a namesake. Haleh's daughter obeyed her immediately. Turning to us, she demanded, "Who are you?"

Seemingly compelled, without being able to control himself, Curwen rose from his seat and moved toward her. "My whole life Phaedra has told me stories about you. My name is Curwen, and your sister has been like a mother to me." He held his hand out to shake hers. She didn't reach for his.

She narrowed her eyes at him, trying to decide if he was trustworthy. "Is this a trick?"

"No, not at all," Curwen replied.

"He's telling the truth," I added.

She threw a glance in my direction and with attitude asked, "And who are you?"

"I'm Laney. And this is Hollister. And Corey," I introduced us. We all stood.

"Sit down, sit down," she insisted. We did. "I can see you're Antonian," she said, gesturing at Curwen. "And you three are not. Which makes me think you have some sort of story to tell."

"How can you tell?" Corey asked, genuinely curious.

"Because I know my own people. Please, have a seat . . . Curwen."

He returned to the table. "I'll tell you anything you want to know," he offered. I had never seen him so forthcoming; he usually lived in a world of mystery and caution. But Haleh must have reminded him so much of Phaedra, his mother figure, that he felt completely, automatically comfortable with her.

"Oh, just wait a minute," she said, not wanting to be rushed. "I saw this guy," she pointed at Corey, "eyeing the desserts earlier. I think we all need a little something sweet before we start this conversation. What'll it be? No charge." Corey jumped up to help her carry things—a couple of pies, a few cupcakes, plates, and forks—to our table, and Haleh invited the young Phaedra to come back and join us. As she took a seat beside her mother, across from Curwen, I could tell the girl was hesitantly curious, unlike Corey who was boldly—and sometimes embarrassingly—curious.

When everyone was settled, Haleh asked Curwen, "So you know my sister? She's okay then?"

He nodded. "Yes, she's great."

"She told me about you," I added. "She said you fell in love and decided to stay here."

"Yes. My husband, Patrick. He'll be here soon. You'll meet him." She seemed to be letting us know that someone else was coming, warning us that we better not try anything, still unsure if she could trust us.

"When was the last time you saw your sister?" Corey asked with a mouth full of strawberry pie. "We're trying to get back to Antonia to see my sister now." Although Curwen had said he would tell Haleh anything she wanted to know, he seemed uneasy with not being able to control the things Corey might say. But Corey's easygoing nature helped Haleh relax a bit. I think she sensed Curwen's uncertainty, and she decided to ignore Corey's second sentence, though I could tell it piqued her interest; she would make her way back to it later. She seemed wise in knowing she needed to share some of herself, to be vulnerable, for us to feel safe to do the same.

"I suppose it's been about twenty-six years since I saw her," she began. "Things were very open in Antonia back then. Anyone could apply for a travel permit. Phaedra and I got ours as soon as we finished school. We were at a party on a college campus not far from here when I told her I wanted to stay, to enroll in college and be with Patrick. She became very upset, and we had a fight. Then she left, and I never saw her again. Not long after that, the Antonian government restricted travel, and I've always assumed that's why she has never come back. I've never left the area in case she ever wanted to come back and find me." Her voice dripped with a sad bitterness.

"Wait," Curwen started, "you think Phaedra just abandoned you because she was upset about you wanting to stay here?" He hesitated, glancing at all of us, as though we shouldn't be listening, before asking, "You don't know what happened to her?" *What happened to her?* I tried to remember my conversation with her—she'd said that being here hadn't been a good experience for her. What had happened?

"No. What happened?" Haleh asked with panic.

"I'm not sure this is my story to tell," he said, seeming to regret that he'd ever mentioned it. I could tell—all of us could tell—that Curwen wanted this to be a private conversation, but none of us moved because we all wanted to know.

"You've already started, and she's not here to tell it. I've waited twenty-six years for an explanation, so please don't make me wait any longer," she demanded in a polite, firm manner; she had a mother voice that you dared not disobey. Curwen was clearly struggling; here was this woman, who looked and sounded like the only mother he had ever known, requesting him to share something private, something that belonged to the only mother he had ever known.

As was customary for Curwen to do before he revealed something or launched into a story, he sighed deeply. "When Phaedra left the party, she was upset about you wanting to stay here . . . because she didn't want to be separated from you. But she didn't feel the same pull as you to remain. She was walking back to the place where you were both staying when two men approached her . . . and brutally attacked her." He paused, and I heard Haleh's intake of breath.

We all sat motionless, simultaneously dreading to hear more details, yet wanting him to continue. But respectfully, he didn't give any details. He explained, "They left her unconscious. When she woke up, she found her bag nearby, and thankfully, the transporter was in it. She was able to travel home before she passed out again, and Durham found her and took her to get the medical help she needed." Imagining Phaedra being hurt like that almost had me crying; tears were streaming down Haleh's face. "That incident made her never want to come back here. But she has always missed you, Haleh." Haleh's daughter put her arm around her mother to comfort her. "And she will dance around her kitchen to know you have a daughter with her name," Curwen added with a closed-mouth smile to comfort her.

"She and Durham—did they ever marry?" she asked.

Curwen shook his head. "Neither of them ever married." No. Durham had broken her heart, I wanted to correct him. And Durham didn't deserve her. She was too good for him.

"So, she never had children," Haleh observed to herself; it wasn't a question.

But Curwen answered it anyway. "Just us orphans—me, Sheldon, and Mara. There were many orphans after the rebellion ended. Durham took us in, but we spent most of our days at Phaedra's house or bakery when we didn't have school."

"Bakery?" Haleh asked.

"Yes, she owns one of the only—and the best—bakeries in Antonia. I'm sorry, but haven't you enquired of her all these years to the other Antonians you've encountered? I'm sure they could have told you something." I think he was just curious, but his tone sounded accusatory, and I was worried our host would be offended, especially when it was obvious that she was already feeling a great deal of pain about the previous revelations. I gave his forearm a hard pinch under the table in warning, a reminder that he needed to be more sensitive. His eyes flinched, his jaw clenched, and he pulled his arm away in a subtle but quick movement.

Before she could respond, the door opened, the bell chiming, and a man with orange-red hair, and freckles just like young Phaedra, entered. Patrick. Haleh immediately stood and went to him, whispering quietly to him while he eyed us suspiciously. What was she telling him? Did he know the truth about her past, about where she was from? I assumed he must if his daughter did. His daughter knew not to move from her spot, knew her parents needed a few moments, but she watched intently, trying, as children do, to get a read on the situation, on how her father would respond to what her mother had to tell him. He made sure to turn his back to us when he replied to Haleh so we couldn't read his lips.

Eventually—it was only a minute later but seemed like forever—they walked over to us. Haleh introduced him as her husband, Patrick, and then she told him our names. He shook hands with all of us and said, "Welcome to our home." He squeezed his daughter's shoulders and gave her a kiss on the head; she seemed a bit embarrassed by the display of affection in front of strangers.

"Phaedra, would you get some food for your father please?" Haleh asked. She obeyed without protest or grumbling. Patrick sat in the chair beside his wife and attempted small talk until his daughter returned with a sandwich and soup for him.

Then he became serious. "I appreciate that y'all have brought news of my wife's sister, and you are welcome here. But why have you really come? We don't get new faces around here very often, especially new Antonians." He looked at Curwen when he said that. What were we going to tell them? The truth? But how much of it? *Everything*? That would have been my preference, but I had no idea what Curwen wanted to do. Or Hollister.

"Have you ever been to Antonia?" Corey asked Patrick before anyone else could speak. "I'm trying to get these guys to let me go back with them." He rolled his eyes in our direction.

Patrick smiled at him and shook his head. "No, I've never been. And it might be best that you don't go. I certainly wouldn't allow Phaedra to go." He gave his daughter a smirk and a wink—it was obvious they had talked, perhaps argued, about the subject before, possibly many times. "But what brings y'all here?" he asked again.

"We need to get back to Antonia," Hollister stated firmly. He was impatient to get there. We all were.

Curwen didn't like that Hollister answered, so he quickly jumped in. "Durham always told me if I needed help, I should come here to The Cracked Pot. I didn't know who I would find here, but I'm so glad it was you, Haleh."

"But we're looking for someone named Gibson," Hollister asserted.

Curwen's jaw was clenched in annoyance.

"Gibson?" Haleh asked in surprise.

Patrick continued, "How's he going to help you?"

"We need a transporter," Hollister said.

"Because mine's been disabled," Curwen added.

"Because you've been exiled?" Haleh asked. Curwen nodded, looking ashamed. "Why?"

"Gigandet feels I've betrayed him."

"Have you?" she pressed. She had that mother look, the one you can't lie to.

"I work for Durham. I went undercover to work for Gigandet in order to gain access to a transporter. But things were just so much more complicated than that. Factions conspiring against one another and against the king. And this family," he gestured at me and Corey, "who were caught in the middle. . . . I was just trying to do what I thought was right."

"What he means is that Laney's sister is the one with the mark, and she's stuck in Antonia, and we need to get back to her," Hollister said. I kicked him under the table. He wanted to get back to his men in barrack twenty-seven. Curwen didn't say a word but gave Haleh and her family time to process what Hollister had so carelessly revealed.

After a moment, Haleh reached across the table to put her hand on mine. "I'm sorry, Laney. I know what it means to be separated from your sister. What's her name?"

"Leela," Corey answered. "Her *twin* sister. Everyone from our town was struck there and enslaved. . . . Leela sacrificed herself so Hollister and my dad could come home. But everyone else is still there."

"And your mom?" Patrick asked. Those three words knocked the breath out of me. This is what it would be like for the rest of my life—having to explain to strangers that my mother was dead, followed by that awkward moment when they are caught off guard and don't know what to say.

"She died there two days ago," I said. "Heat exhaustion."

Haleh breathed deeply, feeling the weight of it. After a brief pause, she said, "I'm sorry my people did that to her."

I nodded, accepting her apology. "Me too."

"And I'm sorry they enslaved you, Hollister," she added with sincerity. He simply nodded, unsure how to respond, not quite at a place where forgiveness came easily—and she wasn't the one who needed to apologize. I wasn't sure any apology would be sufficient. Not yet. It was too soon, too fresh. I glanced at the red marks around his neck, scars from the times his shock collar had been activated. How many times had that been? Would he ever tell me all the details? Did I want to know them?

We sat in silence for a few moments. Though I knew in my soul that Hollister cared about my mother and Leela . . . and me, on the surface he had one focus—to get back to Antonia—and the tapping of his foot, the bouncing of his knee under the table, only revealed his impatience. I could almost hear his internal dialogue: *Why are we just sitting here? Can these people help us? If so, then why aren't they? Where's Gibson?*

They obviously know him. We told them what we need. So, why are we just sitting here? I placed my hand on his knee to still him, to calm him, to let him know he wasn't alone in this mission. He stopped moving, looked at me, and grabbed my hand, giving it a squeeze. We were in this together.

Patrick finished his last bite and then said, "Well, we don't have a transporter. Phaedra took it with her when she returned to Antonia. But we can take you to see Gibson in the morning, to see if he can help."

"Can't you take us tonight?" Hollister asked, even though I could tell he was exhausted and needed sleep.

Standing and beginning to clear the dishes, Haleh said firmly, but with a hint of bitterness, "He won't be any use to you tonight. We'll take you in the morning. You can stay here tonight." Why wouldn't he be any use to us tonight? *He went a little crazy in the head*—that's what Curwen had said. Was he still crazy, or would he be able to help us? All we needed was a transporter. We didn't need Gibson.

Young Phaedra and I both rose, grabbing plates and glasses and following Haleh into the kitchen, while the guys put the chairs back in order and wiped down the tables. It was strange being there with them. Had Durham known we would find them there? Had he known about Haleh's life and whereabouts and never told her sister? Again, I wished Phaedra could have been there to see her twin and her niece. Family reunions had come to mean so much more to me now.

Once everything was cleaned and prepared for the next day, we grabbed our backpacks from the car. Then the lights were turned out, the doors were locked, and the sign was flipped from "open" to "closed." We followed the little family of three up a narrow flight of stairs, our backpacks rubbing against the walls, our feet heavy on each step. They lived in an apartment above the diner and store, simply decorated and cozy, a place that was inviting and warm, like our home, like Phaedra's home. Patrick showed the guys to a guest room and the couch, and Haleh assigned me to share with young Phaedra; she seemed excited at the prospect of having me all to herself. I'd only heard a few words from her mouth, so I was also interested in seeing what she would have to say away from the ears of her parents.

"If you need anything, just let Phaedra know, or I'm right next door," Haleh said.

I nodded at her. "Thank you. Thank you for your hospitality."

"It's no problem. We have guests often, though none quite so special and unexpected. Get some rest. Sounds like you'll need it." She smiled sadly, probably imagining the difficulties that were ahead for us, and then closed the door behind her.

The room had two twin daybeds covered with bright floral comforters. "That bed belongs to my sister, Marcella," young Phaedra explained, pointing to the one on the left wall. "She's away at college now, doing a summer internship." Two nieces, not just one. I plopped my bag down on it. "So, you've really met my Aunt Phaedra?" Her eyes lit up. "By the way, you can call me Phae. All my friends do."

I smiled; she considered me a friend.

"Yes, I have met her. She's wonderful, and I can't wait to tell her about you."

"What's she like? Mom doesn't say much about her."

"Hmm . . . " I thought about how to describe her. "Before I met her, Sheldon said she was the best person he had ever known. She's welcoming and open and kind and protective. She gives some of the best hugs too—the kind of hugs you don't even realize you need until she's got her arms around you and won't let go." My mother gives hugs like that. *Gave* hugs like that.

As she listened, her eyes became envious. "I can't believe you've been to Antonia!"

"But haven't you met a lot of people who've been there?" I asked.

"I've met a lot of people who are *from* Antonia. I've never met anyone from here who has traveled there and back. I've never met anyone who's been a slave, like Hollister. Well . . . except for Uncle Gibson. But he's Antonian."

"Why did your parents say Gibson would be no use to us tonight?"

She shrugged her shoulders, even though I could tell she knew the reason. "You'll meet him in the morning." Changing the subject, she asked, "So your sister really has the mark?"

"Yes, I guess so. We only ever thought it was an ordinary birthmark, though."

"Since Mom is Antonian, my parents said they were always so worried that Marcella or I would be born with the mark. They didn't want anyone to come looking for us. But . . . " She paused. "I guess you don't have to be Antonian to have the mark."

"I guess not." Talking about Leela made me worry about her again. I pulled the satphone out of my bag. "I've got to call my dad," I said as I stepped into the hall, shutting the door behind me. The conversation didn't need to be private, but something in me just wanted a moment alone. The lights were out, and the bedroom doors were closed. Only a dim light glowed above the kitchen sink, and I walked softly toward it.

The phone rang a couple times before my father's gruff voice answered. "What's wrong?" he asked. I had woken him up.

"Nothing. Everything is okay," I assured him and then briefly updated him on the situation. Finally, I said, "I just wanted to check on Leela. Has Annabelle drawn anything new?"

"No. Once she ate dinner, she fell asleep. She hasn't drawn anything. I'm sure Leela is okay. They seem to be taking care of her," he tried to be comforting. I hoped he was right.

As I turned around to return to the room, to sleep my cares away, I was startled by a dark figure sitting on the couch. *Curwen*. "Any update on Leela?" he asked quietly.

"No." I shook my head. "I just want to get back to her."

I never thought I would ever want to return to Antonia.

"Me too. We will," he promised.

CHAPTER 10

[LEELA]

Greer didn't give the three of us a chance to tell Phaedra goodbye, and there was never an opportunity to speak to Durham. Phaedra would have to fill him in on any details—not that we were able to share much with her. She had asked about Curwen, and Greer had answered bluntly, "He's been exiled for his actions." That's when she had excused herself, claiming she needed to check on things in the kitchen, but I knew she really needed a moment to cry and compose herself. And then we were forced to leave without telling her goodbye. Durham had watched us from the corner as we stood to leave; I wondered how Sheldon and Mara felt, being so close but not being able to talk to him. But he'd never struck me as a physically affectionate father—would he have hugged them even if he could have?

Back outside, I put my hat on, my only shield from the Antonian sun. Sheldon and Mara wore hats and sunglasses too, and they kept their heads down, trying to keep people from noticing the bruises and cuts on their faces. Greer hadn't even wanted to allow them in public until their wounds had healed, but Henley and Mara had insisted on this plan—to find the Ancient Ones—to keep me from marrying Gigandet. They didn't know how much time we had, how long he would wait before the wedding, and they didn't want to waste a single second. Did I believe their plan would work, that we would find an

Ancient One who would know of a different way to break the curse? No. Did I believe the curse was real? I still couldn't decide. But I had been able to use their belief in it, in the curse, to gain my family's freedom. That's what mattered. And going on this mission with them to find an Ancient One gave me something to do, gave my mind something to focus on—something other than the death of my mother, the separation from my family, and the impending marriage to a man I didn't want to marry.

We were headed to the black market where goods were smuggled into Antonia from my dimension and sold. Although it was technically illegal, Greer explained it was mostly overlooked due to the fact that guards and other government officials—the only ones with permits to travel—were the ones who smuggled the goods and profited from the sales. Corruption. Why did they think their society was so perfect, so much better than ours? Everywhere I looked, they had the same kind of issues and problems as us. It was like Sheldon had said the first time we met him, his reason for helping us: *People are people, no matter where they come from.*

Sheldon remained by my side in our group formation. I said softly to him, "I'm sorry you didn't get to talk to *your boss.*"

"He'll follow us." He was confident of that. Instinctively, I raised my head to look around, in search of Durham. "Don't look for him," he warned. "You'll draw attention." I returned my eyes to the ground. He was right; Greer was so attentive, constantly analyzing our surroundings—and us. Was Durham following us just so he could gain more information, or was he going to attempt some sort of rescue? I hoped he wouldn't try anything. Things were as good as they were going to get; if he attempted to free Sheldon, Mara, or me, I could only imagine what the consequences might be. Sheldon and Mara being returned to the dungeon and certain execution. Gigandet ordering my family to be retaken in order to make me compliant. The possible risk to Phaedra.

"He's not going to do anything, is he?" I asked, panicked at all the different scenarios running through my head.

He shook his head. "No. He just wants to understand what's happening."

I breathed a sigh of relief. "Do you think he knows I have the mark? Did you know? Had Curwen told you?"

"No. To all those questions. I think he's piecing things together, but he doesn't know that. If he did, he *would* do something."

"So, it's true that he had sent Curwen to find the one with the mark? What does he want with me?"

"To use you as leverage . . . to get Gigandet to agree to a more representative form of government," he said in an apologetic tone.

Just then, Greer cleared his throat. Had he heard us? The crowd around us was so loud, surely not, I hoped. But we didn't say another word. Henley and Mara were carrying on their own conversation as well; I couldn't make out their words either. They had become fast friends. Would I ever connect with them or have a good girl friend in Antonia?

We were approaching the end of a block where there was another gate, one that led to other parts of Antonia, places I hadn't been yet. Laney had seen so much more than me in the short time we'd been there. And now she was home, where I longed to be. I pictured that old country house with the wraparound porch and rocking chairs. I remembered sitting on the porch swing while my father rocked in one of those chairs. The kitchen window was open, and we could hear my mother inside, banging pots and pans, the aroma of good Southern food tickling our nostrils and making our stomachs growl. Corey was pushing Annabelle on the swing up the hill. Where was Laney? On a date with Hollister. They had driven to the city for the day. Home is where I wanted to be. But this was home now.

"Where are we going now?" I asked as Greer entered some codes into the gate keypad. They all seemed to forget that I wasn't from there, that I'd been there for less than a week.

"To the warehouses," Mara said. The warehouses where my father had been enslaved?

"We need to avoid the woodworking building," Sheldon said. "The guards will recognize me and Leela." *But they'll think I'm Laney.*

"We're going around the back," Greer said, opening the gate.

In front of us was a long, steep, narrow flight of stone steps. It reminded me of the stairs Greer had led me down the previous morning, down into the darkness. But these stairs led to a dirt path, just as Laney had described to me. We were exiting the city walls, entering the wild, natural places. I could see the forest in the distance; Laney had been there too. The stairway was only wide enough for us to go down in a single-file line; the city wall was on one side, and on the other side, there was nothing—no ledge, no railing—but the possibility of falling a hundred feet to the ground below.

"Leela, stay against the wall," Greer ordered.

"Yeah, because you wouldn't want me to die or anything," I quipped with sarcasm. I imagined plummeting to my death. The idea of dying wasn't funny. It shouldn't have been funny, but somehow, I couldn't stop myself from laughing out loud at the thought. To think about how long and how hard they had searched for me, the one with the mark, and how once they had found me, I had died before I could be used by any of them. What would they do about their curse then? It was a dark laughter, an ironic humor, and all of them looked at me like I was crazy. Except Sheldon; he just gave me a sad smile.

Henley and Mara went first, then Sheldon in front of me, and Greer behind me. I made sure to keep my one shoulder pressed up against the wall, staying as far from the edge as possible, and Greer kept a hand on my other shoulder. With the noise of the crowd behind us now, he decided to talk. "Sheldon, how did you get to the warehouses?" he asked. "Most citizens do not have permission or access codes to come outside the city gates."

"Why don't they have permission?" I asked instead, not allowing Sheldon to answer.

"For their own safety," Henley called back to me.

"What's unsafe out here?"

"*The bodies*," she said with attitude, like it was an obvious answer. *Slaves.* Not bodies.

"Are there not any slaves inside the city walls?" I asked. I could see her shaking her head in annoyance, like she was tired of my ignorance.

She didn't answer me, but Greer did, with a cutting tone, "Only when citizens rent them for the day." His remark was clearly aimed at Sheldon, an attempt to insult him for renting my father two days earlier, for trying to set a slave free him from his bondage. Sheldon didn't let it bother him.

We reached the dirt walkway at the bottom of the stairs. To our left was a row of warehouses, maybe a dozen of them, all with solar panels on their roofs. Several guards stood outside of each of them.

"Don't turn. Continue straight," Greer directed. "When you get to the back of the warehouse, then turn left. We'll go behind them. Sheldon and Leela, keep your faces down." We both pulled our hats lower over our eyes and watched the ground, my feet mimicking Sheldon's steps. My ribs had begun to hurt—deep breaths were difficult—and my head ached; the pain medication had worn off from breakfast.

When we turned the corner, to trail along the back of the warehouses, I could see there weren't any rear entrances. There were only a few guards here compared to the dozens out front. In our civilian clothing, I thought they would have stopped us, questioned us—what reason did we have for being there, if citizens weren't allowed outside the city gates? But they didn't. They simply nodded at us. They were corrupt, too. When we reached the seventh warehouse, there was a bunker door in the ground—one of them opened it for us; he knew where we were headed, knew it was illegal, yet he ushered us in.

There was a short flight of stairs—short in comparison to the two previous flights of stairs I'd encountered in Antonia—that led down into a massive concrete basement. It was cool and dark, with dingy fluorescent lights flickering throughout the place. Tables lined the walls and were organized into stations throughout the middle of the room; this was where the vendors set up their goods to sell. They did not lack for buyers either; their voices were loud as they bartered for lower prices. All the vendors eyed us, ready for fresh, new customers. On a table in the corner, I saw all kinds of candy from my dimension, including Skittles—like the ones Mara had used to bribe the slave into silence, the slave who had betrayed us as we tried to escape from the gardens with my mother. Mara had been here before, and she wasted no time usurping Henley's place in the lead. She knew who she was looking for; she knew how to find the Ancient Ones, or so she claimed.

In one corner, there was a television hung on the wall; an old American movie was playing on the screen, one I didn't recognize. A few people sat around watching, laughing, and drinking Sprite. Didn't they have anything else to do in the middle of the day? As we were passing by one vendor, I stopped at her table. It was full of books I recognized, all first editions. Sheldon came up beside me. "These are Curwen's books," I whispered. "They were in Gigandet's library yesterday. I thought he would keep them."

"The king must profit from his people," Sheldon muttered bitterly, picking one up and flipping through its pages. "I have no money to buy them back." When the vendor heard him say he had no money, she moved on to other customers.

"If you could buy just one, which one would you pick?" I asked.

His fingers walked across the books until he stopped on the one I had been secretly eyeing. It wasn't a book many had heard of, but it had been one of my mother's favorites. I'd been surprised when I'd seen it in Curwen's locked bookcase but hadn't noticed it on Gigandet's table the previous morning—otherwise, I would have asked to keep it as well.

"This one," Sheldon said, holding the fragile book with care. "It's the first one Curwen let me read. Actually, he insisted I read it."

"Put that down if you're not buying," the lady behind the table ordered him.

"Be careful with this one," he told her. "It's 120 years old, and it's worth more than you're asking."

Her eyes lit up, intrigued at the prospect of greater profits. "How do you know that?" she asked.

"We need to keep moving," Greer interrupted us. "Mara's waiting for us." He pointed in her direction. She was talking to a man who looked irritated, impatient, and intimidating. She'd told us last night that we had to make contact with a man named Yadriel—he would be able to connect us with the Ancient Ones. I'd wondered where she'd gotten her information but didn't question her in front of Greer or Henley; I didn't want to embarrass her or risk raising any mention about their resistance group. It was strange to imagine being the queen, being a part of the monarchy—because that would mean they would be against me.

As we advanced toward Mara, Henley, and the man, he appeared to become slightly more on edge. "I'll see if he has time for you," he said coolly as he disappeared down a hallway.

"What's going on?" Greer asked.

"Yadriel is in the back room," Henley explained.

"Then let's go." Greer began to walk in that direction, but Mara quickly grabbed his arm in a tight grip.

"Let's *not* draw attention to ourselves or make anyone angry," she said firmly, giving him a stern look.

He smirked, pulling his arm from her hand, and then nodded. There was almost something flirtatious in the way he smiled at her. I think she sensed it too; she shrank back from his direct gaze. Sheldon smiled at me; he had seen it too. But before I had too much time to analyze this interaction, the man was beckoning to us from the end of the hall. Mara and Henley went first, with the guys staying near me, protecting their precious *body* with the mark. The hallway was dark, illuminated only by the blue light pouring out of the open doorway we were approaching. There was red graffiti—spray paint, not blood, I assured myself—all over the concrete walls leading us there. My heart beat faster, and my breathing quickened. I would never have been in a place like this in my own dimension, a place with illegal activity, a place where it felt like bad things could happen at any moment.

Entering the room, I saw it appeared to be a place used for storage. Unmarked boxes and crates lined the far wall, and there was a metal desk in front of them. On the wall to the right was a black sofa, and on that sofa sat a young man—Yadriel, I assumed. He was watching a television hanging on the wall in the corner, but he had muted it in anticipation of our arrival. He checked all of us up and down, deciding how much respect he thought we deserved.

"So, you're here to buy some merchandise?" he directed his question to Greer.

"No," Mara replied, stepping slightly in front of Greer, making it clear that she was the one who had requested an audience with him. Hadn't she said two minutes earlier that we shouldn't make anyone angry? "We need to be connected to the Ancient Ones," she explained.

Yadriel scowled. "Are you serious? You're wasting my time on this?"

"No," she stated. "It is of the greatest importance that we make contact with them."

"The AOs don't exist anymore!" he hollered at her. He unmuted the TV and ordered the man to take us away. Greer stepped forward to protest. When he did, Yadriel pulled a gun out of his waistband. Although he didn't point it at any of us—he flashed it as a show of strength—we all raised our hands and stepped back. "That's what I thought," Yadriel said with an amused smile, pleased with his power.

"Where did you get that?" Greer dared to ask.

"Man, do you know where you are? Where do we get everything here?"

Greer continued, "Importing guns is one of the most serious crimes, immediately punishable by death."

"Don't preach the law to me. I'm not the one who imported them. I only sell them." He smiled again.

"Who imported them?" Greer demanded. He and Mara did not know when to quit. Why was he not afraid?

Yadriel scoffed. "A high-ranking official of the guards."

Whirl. I know we all thought his name at the same time.

"I'd like to purchase all that you have," Greer said. Was he crazy? I just wanted to get out of there. Sheldon grabbed my hand when he noticed me inching my way toward the door. He gave it a tight squeeze and shook his head slightly. I had to stay there.

Yadriel laughed. "You couldn't afford it."

"How much?" he challenged. He wouldn't quit. This was not what we had come there for.

"You see all those boxes?" He pointed at them behind the desk. "All of them are filled to the brim. I've got an armory here! No one but the king himself could afford them all. And even then, he would just be using the people's money. Now *get out of here*. And don't come back." When we all hesitated to move, he flashed his pistol again for motivation. We all backed out of the room and didn't turn around until we were safely in the hall with the door shut behind us. Yadriel turned the television up even louder.

There was a lady at the end of the hall; she seemed to be waiting for us. She seemed anxious, fidgeting. Mara, Henley, and Greer walked right past her, ignoring her completely, but I made eye contact with her and smiled. This gave her a boost of confidence, and she spoke to me and Sheldon. "Are you looking for the AOs?" she asked. We nodded, encouraging her to tell us what she knew. "The last known AO was Yadriel's grandfather. But he was picked up a couple years ago. . . . Last we heard, he was taken to the scientists. That's all we know. That's why Yadri acted like that."

Yadriel's man came out of the room at the end of the hall; even in the darkness, I could see he was glaring at us. "Thank you," I whispered to the lady. Then Sheldon and I hurried to catch up with the rest of our group. How could Greer have left me there? Wasn't protecting me his number-one priority? When we got outside, it was obvious that Greer had other things on his mind. He was fuming, furious about the guns; he punched his fist into the side of the building. The few guards nearby began to approach. Fearing any trouble from them, Sheldon quickly stepped forward, smiled, and apologized to them, grabbing Greer's elbow and pulling him down the dirt path. "Come on," he coaxed him. "Let's go." The rest of us followed them.

When we were out of earshot, I relayed to them the information the lady had given us. "The scientists have him," Mara said out loud to herself, letting it sink in. "Greer, how can we get into their facility?"

I could tell that was the last thing Greer wanted to think about; me not marrying Gigandet had become a secondary issue. He was far more concerned about guns being sold in Antonia, about who might get their hands on them and how they might be used. *Whirl.* His plan ran far deeper than Gigandet knew or imagined; he had underestimated his enemy. *My* enemy. *Our* enemy.

When we reached the bottom of the steep flight of stairs, Greer's phone rang, shaking us all out of our thoughts. He walked a few feet away from us. "Sir?" I heard him answer as he continued moving farther away, and I assumed he was talking to my future husband. I shuddered at the thought. Did he know the guns were being sold? He had sent Curwen's books there to be sold; how much did he know about the black market, and how often did he contribute to it? What if he was the one who'd imported the guns? *No.* He cared too much for the Antonian people to do that. If he didn't care for their lives, he would never have searched for the one with the mark. He would have let them die from the disease. *If the curse is real. Which it isn't. Please don't let it be real.*

Greer was coming back toward us. Had he told Gigandet about the guns? I tried to read the expression on his face but couldn't tell. I tried to meet his eyes, but he avoided looking at me. Before he could say a word, Mara spoke. "So, how can we get into the scientists' facility?" she repeated her question.

"There's no time," he said, still not looking at me. "Gigandet wants us to come back immediately."

Something wasn't right. My stomach felt sick. "Why?" I asked hesitantly.

"He wants to have the wedding ceremony tonight."

I ran a short distance away from them and threw up in the grass.

CHAPTER 11

[LANEY]

We all slept later than we wanted; Haleh didn't wake us because, as my mother used to say, *you don't wake sleeping children*, no matter how old they are. Patrick was in their kitchen cooking breakfast when we all emerged from our rooms. Curwen was sitting at the counter talking with him, and they already appeared to be old friends. Corey wasted no time making himself at home, going into their fridge without permission and pouring himself a glass of orange juice. When I apologized for my brother's poor manners, Patrick replied, "That's what it's there for. We don't have guests here." Corey stuck his tongue out at me as he sat down at the table. Patrick's response reminded me of the first time we had met Curwen—he'd asked me to pour him a glass of orange juice, but I had only stood there glaring at him, just before holding a knife to his throat and demanding that he get out of our house.

As though Curwen was remembering the same thing, he asked with a teasing smile, "Laney, want to pour me a glass?" This time I did, handing it to him with an eye roll. Hollister had come into the room and was observing us closely, but I couldn't tell what he was thinking. I used to be able to read him perfectly, but now it felt like there was all kinds of missing words, broken paragraphs, and poor grammar.

"Good morning," I said to him with a smile. He returned a tight-lipped smile as he sipped a cup of coffee, which I knew meant he had a lot on his mind—who among us didn't? And he was ready to be going—who among us wasn't?

"How long before we can go see Gibson?" Hollister asked Patrick.

"Curwen and I were just discussing that," Patrick said. "As soon as y'all are ready, I'll take over the Saturday morning breakfast crowd downstairs, and Haleh can step out to take you to Gibson. Hopefully he'll be sober enough."

Oh. That was why he had been no use to us the previous night. "He has a drinking problem?" I asked.

Patrick nodded. "But he thinks drinking makes his problems disappear."

"Don't they all . . . ," Hollister mumbled bitterly as he took a seat at the table and began putting pancakes on his plate. Hollister's father had been an alcoholic; he'd left him and his mother when he was eleven. He rarely ever talked about his father, mostly because he didn't need to—I had been there. I had known his father, had seen the way he treated his family, and had been so glad when he was gone. Patrick gave me a curious look, wondering what Hollister had meant by his comment, but with a sad smile, I just shook my head at him.

"Where's Phaedra?" I asked. "She wasn't there when I woke up." Her bed had been perfectly made though, and she had folded my clothes neatly, setting them on top of my backpack—that's something Leela would have done.

"She gets up early to help her mother with the store. Saturdays are busy, especially this month with all the summer tourists driving through. When y'all are ready, you can come down." He left us to go help his wife and daughter with the business.

Both Hollister and Curwen rushed us along, and we were ready in no time. As we were descending the stairs, Curwen in the front, he stopped suddenly, almost making all of us fall on top of him. Holding his hand up, he gestured for us to go back, to stay behind the wall that enclosed the staircase.

"What is it?" Hollister asked, annoyed.

"One of Whirl's guards is here," Curwen whispered. My eyes went wide, and dread filled my stomach.

"Where? Will he recognize you?" Hollister asked, peeking around the banister but pushing me back gently—for my protection—when I tried to do the same.

"At the counter. Talking to Haleh and Patrick. Yes, he knows me," Curwen explained, turning his face in the opposite direction, trying to remain unseen while still being able to see what was happening. Corey and I wanted to see too, but fear kept my feet rooted on the top steps, and I blocked my brother from getting past me.

I heard the man say something but couldn't make out the words. Then Haleh spoke loudly, as though she wanted us to be able to hear. "Well, if she's in her twenties, she's a woman—not a girl," Haleh corrected him. "We have many women with blond hair come through here. If you don't have a photo, we can't help you."

"Here," I heard the man say.

Curwen peered around the corner. "He's handing her a family photo—the one that was hanging in your living room," he explained.

"He's been to our house," I gasped and began to panic. Why were they coming after me? Hollister stepped up to where I was and pulled me close, wrapping his arms around me in comfort and—in a silent way—telling me he wouldn't let them separate us again.

"What about Dad and Annabelle?" Corey whispered in my ear.

"They're at the cabin," I said. *They're okay*. They had to be safe. I couldn't think of the possibility of anything happening to them. We couldn't lose them too.

"But what if he tracked them there?" Corey was scared too. He was speaking the question my mind was thinking. I stuck my arm out and pulled him into our embrace.

"Good-looking family," I heard Haleh say, "but we've never seen them before. Not that I remember."

"Thank you for your time," the man said. "May I get a cup of coffee to go?"

We stood frozen, hiding at the top of the stairs, holding one another until we heard the doorbell chime and Curwen gave the all clear. We still didn't move until Haleh came to us. "That was a close one," she said from the bottom of the stairs, her eyes still watching out the front windows. "I don't think he believed me."

"I'm sure he didn't," Curwen agreed.

"He's driving away. Let's get you out of here." She ushered us quickly toward a back door before turning back to tell Patrick, "I'll be back." There was concern in the look they gave each other. How often had they done things like this before? Did they help ex-slaves and exiled Antonians regularly, or was this something new? Haleh led us to a red truck parked in the rear; we all piled in, and she instructed me to sit in the back and keep my head down.

"He could recognize any of us," Curwen said. "Where are we going?"

"Thankfully, he drove in the opposite direction," she explained as she turned on the ignition. "We're going to an RV park not far from here. Gibson helps Patrick run and maintain the place in the summer months."

"Do you have the satphone?" Corey asked. "Can you call Dad and check on them?"

I pulled the phone from my pocket, in my scrunched-up position in the back, and dialed the preprogrammed number. With each subsequent ring, my heart beat faster. *Pick up. Pick up.* Finally, I heard my father's voice on the other end. "Are y'all okay?" I asked immediately.

"Yes. Yes, we're fine," he assured me. "What's wrong?" I breathed a sigh of relief.

"An Antonian guard was just here looking for me." I explained to him about the family photograph.

"We're good here. Don't worry about us. I'm just sipping some coffee and reading. Annabelle's drawing," he explained.

"What's she drawing?" I asked, suddenly worried about Leela again.

"Let me see . . . " I could hear him rustling with some paper on the other end. "What's this, Annabelle?" I heard him ask her. He wasn't skilled at interpreting her drawings yet; he would have had a hard time figuring them out before, when she hadn't been talking. But now she had her sweet voice—I could hear it in the background. My father cleared his throat and explained, "It's Leela in a fancy dress. She says she's getting ready for the wedding."

"Noooo," I said quietly, in protest. "Has it already happened?"

"What's wrong?" Hollister, Curwen, and Corey all asked in unison. Haleh eyed me from the rearview mirror.

My father answered, "No. Annabelle said she's just getting ready for it."

"What's happening?" Corey asked again.

I held my hand up, indicating that I would tell them in a minute. "Anything else?" I asked my father.

"No, honey. But she sure is spending a lot of time embellishing this dress."

"Because it's pretty!" I heard Annabelle exclaim.

"If she draws anything else, please call immediately," I said. He agreed and hung up. All the guys were staring at me, waiting to know. I sighed and said, "She's getting ready for the wedding."

Curwen's jaw clinched. "That was fast. He's not wasting any time."

"Engagements in Antonia are a big deal. With at minimum a two-week announcement and huge celebration," Haleh explained. "Why's he rushing it?"

"Something must be up," Curwen said, staring out the window. "And I'm sure it has to do with Whirl."

"Whirl?" Haleh asked. "Is he still around?"

"I wish he weren't." He glared out the window, his hatred for Whirl reflecting in the glass. "You really don't get any updates from the motherland?" he asked Haleh.

"It's been easier to adjust to life here without constantly knowing what's happening there."

"Were you ever tempted to go back?" Corey asked.

"Of course I've thought about it over the years . . . but I could never live in a place where people like Patrick, or Hollister, or even you, Corey, would be enslaved."

"Maybe it could change," Corey suggested optimistically. "Maybe if Leela is queen, she can change things."

None of us responded. None of us wanted Leela to become queen. *She* didn't want to become queen. How would the people accept a queen they believed should be a *body*? I was anxious to meet with Gibson, anxious to get back to Leela. Haleh drove around another curve and then flicked on the turn signal for a road on the left that was shrouded in trees and shrubbery. There was a wood sign for the RV park where she turned.

"Will Gibson be able to help us?" I asked. "Patrick mentioned his problem . . . "

"Yes, I hope so," Haleh said. "I called him early this morning to wake him and told him I'd be visiting. He should be up. His problem isn't constant; it's sporadic. This weekend just happens to be the anniversary of the death of his wife and daughter." My father had lost his wife and daughter too.

"He was married?" Curwen asked. He was interested in this man, this cousin of Durham's. "How did his family die?" Maybe he wanted to be able to tell Durham—if Durham didn't already know.

"Yes, for almost ten years," she said. "There was a car accident."

After about half a mile, the road opened up to the campgrounds. A small office building sat off to the right, and beside that was a trailer home—where Gibson lived when he was in the area. There were a dozen or more RVs parked there. Families were enjoying their day; some kids played a game of basketball while others were on the playground. It was the kind of vacation my family would have taken, traveling around for the summer, if we'd ever owned a camper. She parked next to the office building and told us to wait in the truck while she checked to see what kind of state Gibson was in, whether he was presentable for company. *We don't have time for this.*

"We don't have time for this," Hollister said. His men from barrack twenty-seven—had they already launched their attack? Part of me hoped they had so he wouldn't have a chance to be a part of it, to risk being injured, captured . . . or killed. Would Curwen help if he knew what Hollister had planned?

"Curwen, is ending slavery part of the resistance's agenda?" I asked. "Since Gibson went undercover as a slave all those years ago—was that part of their plan, to abolish slavery?" I could feel Hollister tense up beside me, unsure about me bringing up the subject, but I wanted to know the answer.

"It was definitely part of the plan when Gibson was there," he said. "And I think it still is, but when the rebellion was suppressed and the resistance went further underground, fighting the importation got forgotten in the midst of other issues."

"Importation?" Hollister was angry. "It's abduction and enslavement."

Before Curwen could respond, Haleh waved to us from the porch, telling us to come. The wooden steps creaked under our weight as she held the door open. Inside was dark and musty, with beige-colored walls and dingy, matted, olive-green carpet in the living room. A man came out of the shadows of the kitchen, stirring the contents of a coffee mug. He raised one hand to block the sunlight from his eyes. *Gibson.*

"So, what's this all about, Haleh? You tryin' to do some sort of intervention again?" he asked once we were all inside, the door shut behind us. *Again?* How many times had she tried to help him?

"Nope, I've given up on that," she replied dryly, examining the space around us, displeased with its condition.

"Then what's this about?" he repeated. Gibson didn't sound like an Antonian—not that they really had an accent—but he'd fully developed an Appalachian dialect. His salt-and-pepper hair was long and unkempt, and he had a full beard. His brown eyes were still bloodshot from binge drinking the night before. His clothes were disheveled, and he moved at a slow pace, which was an annoyance to all of us who felt an intense sense of urgency. *Just give us a transporter so we can go.* I expected Hollister or Curwen to blurt out an answer, to tell him everything so we could move things along, but to my surprise, they waited quietly, allowing Haleh to control the situation.

"These young people need your help," she explained. "They—" We heard a car door slam.

Curwen peeked through the blinds. "It's Whirl's guard."

"*Whirl?*" Gibson asked, his eyes wide. "Haleh, what kind of trouble are you bringing to my door?"

"I'll take care of him," Hollister said, his face so fierce I wasn't sure what he might do.

"It will require both of us," Curwen added. "He's stronger than he looks."

"No," Haleh ordered, her mother voice snapping us all to attention. "Gibson, you get rid of him." Her eyes warned him not to mess up as she ushered us down the hallway to a back bedroom, shutting and locking the door. The room reeked of alcohol, with overturned bottles, stains in the carpet, and an unmade bed. There was a muted television in the corner playing Saturday morning cartoons. From the expression on Hollister's face, I could tell it was bringing him back to his childhood, a place he had no interest in revisiting. I reached for his hand and gave it a squeeze, pulling him back from there. Corey grabbed my other hand. We were all silent, listening. There came a rap on the thin metal door.

Gibson opened it, and before allowing Whirl's guard to speak, he said in a gruff voice, "You need to go to the office if you want to rent a campsite."

"No, sir, I'm a private detective, and I'm looking for a missing woman," we heard the guard reply. There was a moment of silence. Perhaps the guard was showing Gibson our family photograph.

I whispered to Curwen, "Is there any way the guard could recognize Gibson?"

He shook his head. "The guard's too young to have known him—I wouldn't have known him."

"Plus, he looks very different now," Haleh added.

"Hmm. There's two of them, huh? Twins," Gibson observed. "How will you know if you find the right one?"

"Trust me, I'll know," the guard replied, sounding overconfident and threatening. Hollister gave my hand a squeeze. "Have you seen her?"

"Nope. Can't say I have. You better move along now. Don't disturb any of the campers with this either. Don't need them thinking girls go missing around here—would be bad for business. I'll be watching to make sure you leave." The man must have hesitated because Gibson added, "Go on now. Get gone."

A minute later, a car door opened and closed, and then we heard the engine rev. Curwen looked out the blinds of the bedroom window and then nodded at us. The guard was driving away—for now at least. "Gibson is standing out there on the porch, watching like he said he would," Curwen explained. "The vehicle is out of sight."

We heard the metal door close and lock, and then Gibson said, "All right, come on out here and tell me what this is all about. I ain't got time for no trouble around here."

Haleh led us back to the living room. She wasted no time. "Gibson, this is Curwen. He was raised by Durham. He's been exiled. This is Laney and her brother, Corey. And Hollister. They are from Tennessee, but Hollister just escaped from slavery. And they all—well not Corey—need to get back to Antonia to help Laney's sister, Leela."

Gibson was silent for a minute, looking around at each of us, weighing the information she'd given him. "So, you're the boy I gave Durham to raise?" he asked Curwen.

"What do you mean?" Curwen seemed confused. "He never said anything about that."

"Oh, no reason to, I guess," Gibson said quickly, almost like he was covering himself, like maybe he'd said something he shouldn't have. "Just that I found you orphaned and knew you needed a home. How's my cousin? How's Durham doing?"

"He was well, the last time I saw him."

"Which was when?"

"A few days ago."

"So your exile is fresh?"

Curwen nodded. "Yes."

"Why are y'all trying to go back to that awful place? Especially you," he pointed at Hollister. "What a body you would make!" He was impressed by Hollister's height and build.

"Yeah, you must have made an awful body," Hollister joked. They both laughed.

"Hey, I might be short and scrawny now, but in my prime, I was something to behold!" Gibson laughed. This was the Hollister I knew —his ability to strike up a conversation with anyone, to make everyone feel instantly comfortable. It was part of his charm. Where had it been? *Preoccupied with distrusting Curwen and plotting to get back to his men in barrack twenty-seven.* "So, why do you want to go back there?" Gibson asked again.

"My sister's still there," Corey explained, annoyed that Gibson hadn't heard that the first time. "She sacrificed herself to the king so Laney, Hollister, and my dad could be free."

Gibson moved to sit down on the old cream-and-green checkered couch, sipping on his coffee. "What does he want with her? That doesn't seem like a fair trade."

"She's the one with the mark," Corey said. "She's got to marry Gigandet to break the curse and save all the Antonian people from dying." It sounded so dumb when he said it that way. I doubted the curse was real. But that's what I had thought about lightning travel too.

"We need a transporter to get back there. Obviously mine was deprogrammed," Curwen explained. "Do you have one we could use?"

"Wait, wait." Gibson raised his hand. "Tell me more about . . . Leela? That's her name?" We nodded. "Y'all are identical twins?" he asked.

"Yes," I said. "Except for the birthmark."

"And she's planning to marry Gigandet?"

"That's how it appears," Curwen answered.

Gibson looked me dead in the eyes and very seriously warned, "You can't let her do that. You must stop her."

"I know. That's what we're trying to do," I said. *Wasn't he listening?*

"You don't understand," he said. "You *can't* let her marry him. She's not the one who can break the curse."

My stomach dropped. "What do you mean?" I demanded.

"Haven't y'all figured it out yet?" he asked, looking at us like we were stupid. "The curse says the king has to marry the *match* of the one who has the mark." We stared at him, waiting for further explanation, which he didn't offer. Curwen appeared to understand first; something clicked in his brain.

"Laney," he whispered.

"Exactly!" Gibson exclaimed, in a very loud voice. "Your sister is the mark, and," pointing at me, he said, "*you* are the match. You're the one who should be marrying Gigandet. If your sister marries him, she will not live."

Hollister grasped my hand strongly, possessively. I was his. He was mine. I couldn't look up at him. I couldn't meet his eyes. Leela was getting ready for the wedding. She thought that by marrying him she was going to save lives, but really, she would lose her own.

We had to stop the wedding. We needed the transporter. Did he have one?

Curwen shook his head in disbelief. "Are you sure, Gibson? I've never heard that interpretation."

"You've never met an Ancient One," he declared. "Have you?" Curwen shook his head. "That's what I thought. I'm telling you, if she marries him, she'll die."

His words, every one of them, felt like a separate punch to the stomach. *If she marries him, she'll die.*

"We need to get back there *right now*," I demanded. "Do you have a transporter for us?"

Gibson rubbed his bearded chin. "I do."

"Can we have it, please?" Curwen asked with a tone of impatience.

"What about Corey?" Hollister motioned to my brother standing beside him. We didn't have time to return him to the cabin, to our father.

"What about me?" Corey asked defiantly. "I'm going too."

I couldn't take it anymore—his attitude and the idea that he was ever going to set foot in Antonia. "You're not going anywhere!" I yelled at him, taking a step toward my little brother. He wasn't little anymore—I couldn't tower over him; he was nearly as tall as me, and it wouldn't be long before his height surpassed mine. But my eyes were stern, the way our mother's could be, as I stared him down, silently daring him to protest again. Glaring back at me, I could tell he wanted to.

Haleh stepped forward, putting a hand on Corey's shoulder. "We'll keep him with us," she said firmly, but with compassion for Corey in her voice. I imagined she knew what it felt like to want to see her sister, but she was also a mother who would protect her child from danger. "When it's safe, we'll return him to your father."

"No," Corey said softly, defeated, knowing protest was futile. "I'll never see Leela again. She's gonna die like Mom." My stomach sank. Was he right?

Curwen shook his head. "No. *She won't.*" He was determined to save her. "And *yes,* you will see her again. But we need to leave now." He turned to Gibson and repeated, "The transporter?"

"Right." Gibson nodded. "Let me get it." He disappeared down the narrow hallway. I took a step back so I could peer down the hall; he was rummaging around in his bedroom closet. Every second felt like a century. *She's getting ready for the wedding*, I heard my father's voice say. Gibson returned with a shoebox in his hand; it didn't seem to be a very secure storage location for such devices. He set the box on the counter and removed the lid so we could all get a glimpse inside—he had at least a dozen transporters. "I've collected them over the years from ex-Antonians," he explained in response to our questioning faces.

"They gave these to you willingly?" Curwen asked, reaching his hand into the box.

"Not all of them were so willing," Gibson said with a mischievous grin. He had stories to tell; maybe one day I would hear them. But now was not the time—a sense of urgency was rising in my chest, a pressure building. Curwen picked out the transporter that appeared to be the latest model, the one he was most familiar with.

"Haleh, please keep Corey in here until we are gone," he instructed her.

"Where will you travel from?" Gibson asked. "You can't do it here. I've got customers . . . "

"We'll walk a ways into the woods."

"They'll still see the light," Gibson argued, his face wrinkled up in disapproval.

"Look," Hollister asserted, "you don't seem to understand. There's no time for us to go anywhere else. Just tell your customers, if they ask, that it was heat lightning. Heck, tell them it's a UFO. We don't have time to worry about them." He reached into the box and grabbed a second transporter. "Just in case," he explained, sliding it into his pocket. *Just in case what?* I knew he really wanted it because he still didn't trust Curwen, or maybe he had plans for the men of barrack twenty-seven that I didn't even know about yet. "Let's go stop a wedding." He and Corey did their special handshake, and he warned my brother, "Don't do anything stupid. We'll see you soon."

"I won't hold my breath," Corey muttered, dejected.

"Good. 'Cause that would be stupid," Hollister joked. Corey rolled his eyes, in no mood to laugh.

I moved in to give him a quick hug. "No time for long goodbyes," I said apologetically.

"I know. Hurry up!" he ordered, pushing me away. "Leela needs you. So, go!"

"Okay." I squeezed him one more time. "I love you."

"Yeah. I love you too," he mumbled without feeling. But I knew he meant it.

"Thank you, Haleh," I said. She simply smiled and nodded her head toward the door, silently telling us to leave. Just before the door shut behind us, I saw her wrap her arms around Corey's shoulders—to comfort him, but mostly to keep him from chasing after us. Gibson pointed us in the direction we should go, away from the camp, away from his customers. We started out walking at a brisk pace, but once we were out of sight, we began running. I could hear my heart pounding in my ears, a new determination spurring me forward; I overtook Curwen and Hollister, challenging them to run faster. *My sister is waiting.*

I kept running until Curwen shouted from behind for me to stop. "This is a good place," he said. The trees had given way to a small clearing. I walked back to them as Curwen examined the transporter in his hand, turning it on and figuring out how to input the necessary data. "This one's different than the ones I'm used to, but it can't be more than a few years old. I wonder who he got it from."

"Wonder later," Hollister said, almost as impatient as I was. But there was no lack of urgency in Curwen's actions; he wanted to get back and save Leela too—he just showed it differently, silently. I could tell from his demeanor; I was learning to read him. He ignored Hollister, focused on the transporter.

"Ready," he announced, not looking up. I grabbed Hollister's arm and placed my other hand on Curwen's shoulder. Suddenly, I was filled with an intense dread—I never wanted to return to Antonia—and it competed with the sense of urgency in the pit of my stomach. *Think about your reason for doing it*, I heard my mother advise. *Love*. Leela, the one I looked like, the one I sounded like, the one with whom I had shared our mother's womb—she needed me.

CHAPTER 12

[LEELA]

The entire way back to the palace, Henley continued to complain about why Gigandet was pushing the wedding forward. "We need more time. What's the rush?" she asked Greer. "What exactly did he say?" she kept asking, trying to analyze their conversation and figure out what Gigandet meant by every single word.

Eventually, Greer told her to stop asking because he had nothing new to tell her. Gigandet had simply demanded to know where we were and why we had left the confines of the palace, and then he had ordered Greer to bring me back immediately because the wedding would take place that night. There was no explanation why. "He did say we need to be on high alert," Greer instructed. "All of us stay close to Leela and get her back safely." Sheldon and Mara were on each side of me, Greer behind and Henley in front. "Leela, keep your head down," he added.

"Why high alert?" Henley asked. "Is somebody looking for her? Do they know she's here?"

"He didn't say," Greer replied bluntly.

"*You* didn't ask," she accused. Why were we on high alert? Who else was looking for me, other than Durham? He already knew where to find me; he was probably still following us, observing us, as Sheldon had said he would. Everywhere we went, I felt like eyes were watching me, eyes that could see right through me. All the guards stationed along the way—were they loyal to Gigandet or to Whirl? Were they watching me too? Did they recognize Greer in his civilian clothing? Some of them seemed to nod at him as we passed.

My head was spinning. I inhaled and exhaled deeply to blow away the nausea. Their bickering voices faded into the background as I focused on putting one foot in front of the other. I still had the taste of vomit in my mouth; even though I'd chugged all of my water bottle and some of Sheldon's, no amount of water could wash it away. It was late afternoon—the sun was high, the heat intense, and I could feel it burning my skin through the fabric of my shirt. It was an almost pleasant feeling, one I could get used to. A small part of me wished there was a quicker way to get to the palace, to get this over with, but a bigger part of me didn't want the long trek back to end, didn't want to become that man's wife.

As we walked through the meeting quarters, I noticed the crowds had died away, and I felt a little more freedom to raise my head and look around. The sidewalk we were on was enclosed on both sides with tall, white brick walls—they were bare and tidy, not a speck of dirt on them or green vines trailing up them. But then I began to notice them sporadically spaced, stuck into the cracks and crevices, poking out from places they didn't belong. *Red flowers*—the symbol of the resistance. *There's one.* Ten steps later, another one on the opposite wall. Did anybody else see them? From the glances exchanged between Sheldon and Mara, I could tell they had. What about Greer and Henley—had they noticed, and if so, what did they think? He was behind me, and she was in front; I couldn't see their faces.

We came to the end of that path, entering the grand avenue—the one with two long, rectangular fountains down the center of it, lined with beautiful trees and benches in their shade. As we entered the avenue, I saw more of them—the red flowers were spaced evenly along the outer ledge of the fountains. In both directions, as far as the eye could see, the fountain to the left and the fountain to the right were surrounded by the red flowers. It was impossible not to notice; it was also impossible that somebody could have done it without being seen by the guards. The placement of the flowers was conspicuous; it was poetic; it had meaning. But what did it mean?

What did Greer think? He was constantly analyzing and paying attention to every detail. Did he know what the flowers represented? Without the crowds, he had fallen back some, a safe enough distance away that I risked whispering to Sheldon, "What's going on? What's with the flowers?"

"The boss is making sure we know we're not alone," he said. Mara nodded, smiling with confidence and a sense of pride. Was that really what it was—Durham letting us know that he hadn't abandoned us? Or was it a threat—a threat from the resistance against the crown? The floral display was beautiful, but it didn't give me the same comfort or assurance that it gave Mara and Sheldon. What was Durham doing? Where was Whirl? And what was Gigandet's plan? There was a game being played with too many players, and I couldn't fit the pieces together with limited knowledge. But I could appreciate a beautiful flower; I wanted to scoop up a handful of them as we walked by the fountains but resisted.

This time, as we approached the palace, we didn't go through a side door but instead went to the front entrance, up a dozen chiseled limestone stairs to a large terrace. A guard was pacing back and forth on the landing; his eyes went wide when he recognized us, and then he sighed with relief. "Glad to see you're back without incident," he said to Greer. "You're all to go immediately to the king's library." Two other guards nearby opened the massive double doors for us. They stared at me in an odd way as we went by them. Did they know who I was? They weren't supposed to—nobody was. *For now, it is best kept secret*, Greer had said. For peace among the people. For my own protection.

I still gasped in awe at the splendor of the grand hall as we passed through—the gold floors that shimmered, the jewel-encrusted stone walls that glimmered with rubies and emeralds, sapphires and topazes, diamonds and rose quartz, all shapes and sizes. The evening sun cast a beautiful glow throughout the space, cascading through the enormous glass windows that looked out over the quiet city below. Floral arrangements had been set up down each wall, thousands of white flowers in large ornate vases. People were arranging them, and there was a photographer taking pictures of everything; thankfully, they hadn't noticed us come in—I didn't want the camera turned on me. Large candles had been lit, leading up to the throne. No. There were two thrones now. A crown was set on each throne seat. One was Gigandet's. The other would be *mine*. I didn't want it. I imagined myself running to it, picking it up, and casting it down on the gold floor, watching it shatter to pieces. I couldn't appreciate its beauty—I didn't want it to be mine.

Sheldon saw where I was looking. "Are you okay?" he whispered.

"I don't want to do this." I felt myself begin to panic. *Don't throw up again.*

"Me either." He put his hand on my shoulder. "You don't have to."

Greer came between us, breaking us apart and grabbing my upper arm tightly. "*Yes*, she does." He walked on, pulling me along, the group following close behind. The cameraman finally noticed us, but we disappeared down the dark, narrow hall, making our way to the king's library. Greer gave three rapid knocks and then opened the door without waiting for a response. We interrupted a moment between Gigandet and Elodie; he was holding her face in his hands, and she had been crying. I sighed with annoyance—I wanted to feel sorry for them, but I could only feel anger. She needed to go away.

"I'm going," she said, as though she had read my mind. Again. She stood on her toes to kiss Gigandet's cheek and then turned away without meeting his eyes. Approaching me, she added, "I'll only come back if you summon me, if you need me for anything." Would I need her? She had been preparing for this role for a long time; I'd never even seen the script. I simply nodded, unsure what to say. Henley put her arm around Elodie's shoulder, throwing a hard look at me before walking out the door with her friend. Was Henley going to leave now too? One could hope.

"Where have you been?" Gigandet demanded. Hadn't he already asked Greer that same question on the phone? Was he going to make us give account of ourselves again? *I can't live with this man for the rest of my life. I don't want to be his wife.* As Greer was about to answer him, Gigandet waved his hand. "Never mind, I don't care. We need to get this wedding over with." Glad to know he felt the same as I did. "Whirl knows we have the one with the mark. Dr. Brandon told him. We have to move quickly before Whirl makes his next move, before he comes for her."

"Wait a minute," I said. "What does *Whirl* want with me?" His evil, menacing face flashed across my mind, dread filling every single nerve in my body. "I thought he was only trying to find me for *you*." They all stared at me. All of them knew something I didn't, something I hadn't pieced together. Sheldon and Mara too.

Eventually, Mara explained, "He wants to prevent you from marrying the king."

Prevent how?

"It doesn't matter," Greer said. "Because we aren't going to let that happen."

"Right! Right," Gigandet assured me. Or was he trying to convince himself? How strong was his army? How many guards were still loyal to the crown? "Go upstairs and get ready. There will be people to help you get dressed, and a photographer will take pictures before the ceremony. We need to document the event to share in the announcement that will be circulated immediately. By morning, everyone will know."

By morning, everyone will know. What would they know? That I married the king or that I was prevented from marrying him? What did Whirl want to do with me? Imprison me? Exile me? . . . Kill me? Three days earlier, he'd me in his grasp, already imprisoned in the dungeon below our feet, but he had failed to examine me for the mark. How embarrassed—and angry—he must have felt when he found out. I'd barely escaped, but was he coming for me? *Stupid Dr. Brandon.*

Just then, Allen entered with several guards; Mara pulled me to the side so they could pass by us. How did Gigandet know which guards he could trust, which ones weren't under Whirl's command?

Gigandet nodded at Greer. "You all can go. We have security measures to discuss."

"Sir, I'd like to speak with you privately," Greer said to Gigandet. So he could tell him about the guns?

"Come back in twenty minutes," Gigandet ordered. Then, he turned to speak with Allen.

Greer grabbed my arm again, less roughly this time, and led me out. Henley was waiting for us at the end of the hall. Why couldn't she have gone with Elodie? The photographer who had spotted us earlier was waiting there also, but Greer quickly ordered him to leave, to wait until the ceremony.

We began to make our way up the wide spiral staircase, the red carpet reminding me of the resistance—it was the same shade of red as the flowers that had been taunting us on our walk, the same flowers they put in the windows of their safe houses. If I found a way out of the palace, would I be able to find a safe house? Would I be welcome at a safe house? Were the flowers in the avenue only to give encouragement and show solidarity with Sheldon and Mara, or with me too? I hadn't been back to the living quarters, but I had seen the entry gates on our excursion today. The gates—how would I know the codes to open them? How could I get my hands on Greer's access card? *Still need the codes.*

"You agreed to this marriage in exchange for your family's freedom. So, stop looking like you're walking to your death," Henley said, interrupting my scheming thoughts. "There are photographers around every corner. Thousands of women would be happy to be in your position." Would they? *Really?*

"Greer, you can let go of me," I demanded, snatching my arm from his grip, nearly falling down the stairs at the same time. Sheldon steadied me. "Greer, why are you so insistent I must do this?" I demanded. "Ask Gigandet for more time. There could be another way." Did I really believe that, or was I just searching, grasping for any other option? Did the Ancient Ones truly know something that could help us?

Greer sighed and then said, "Maybe there is another way. But we don't have time to figure it out. Whirl could come at any moment. And . . . my brother called me yesterday and told me that my niece and nephew are beginning to exhibit some of the early symptoms of the disease. I know to you the victims of this disease, whatever it is, may seem very distant, like an abstract concept. But they are real people." He was right—*they are real people*. But so were the *bodies* they enslaved. How could he not see the hypocrisy? *You don't care about something until it affects you personally, until the problem becomes your own*, I heard my mother's voice say.

"Are the *bodies* real people?" I challenged him. Again, like the previous morning when I had asked him about my worth—would I have less value if I didn't have the mark—he remained silent. There were two extra guards stationed outside my living quarters; they opened the carved wooden double doors for us. Henley ordered me to take a shower, to wash any remaining blood residue from my blond hair. When she began to remove the stitches from my head wound, Mara saw how rough she was being and offered to take over the task, working with more care and gentleness. Henley left us in order to get some food. Sitting on the bench at the end of the bed—*my* bed—I could see Greer and Sheldon were in the living room. Greer had just returned from his private meeting with the king. He and Sheldon sat on opposite ends of the couch, both silent, both of them staring into the flames of the burning fireplace. What were they thinking?

Mara whispered in my ear, "Sheldon said we can try to get you out of here, if that's what you really want."

Was that what he was thinking about? I gave her a quick side-eyed glance. "How?"

"The underground tunnel system."

I shivered at the thought of returning to those cold, pitch black tunnels.

“What about the shock collars?” I asked.

“I still have the release codes up here.” She pointed at her temple. She had removed my mother’s collar with the memorized codes. But were they the same?

“But are the codes the same?” I countered.

She shrugged. “Worth a try. Just trying to give you another option. There’s no good decision to make now. Everything is risky and will probably lead to all of us dying.”

“That’s encouraging,” I quipped. We laughed quietly, bitterly together.

Henley entered the room with a tray of bread, cheese, and grapes. “In a better mood?” she asked sarcastically. I stared blankly at her without saying a word. “Good,” she said with a fake smile. “The lady is here to do your hair.” She asked Mara to step back and invited the middle-aged woman into the bedroom—*my* bedroom—while giving her instructions. “Braid it to one side so the mark on her neck is clearly visible, and right here,” she pressed her fingers hard into the places my stitches had been behind my ear, causing me to tense up in pain, “make sure to place some flowers or jewels to keep this wound hidden.”

“Oh my,” the lady said in shock as she looked at the side of my head. “What happened?”

I’m not Antonian. I should be a body. The guards arrested and abused me.

“Just an accident,” Henley answered for me. “She tripped and fell down some stairs. But she’s fine—just clumsy.” She smirked at me, pleased to make me look foolish. The lady accepted her explanation without question and began to comb through the tangles of my wet hair, remarking on how she had only ever worked on half a dozen other blondes in her career. *That’s because I’m not Antonian. That’s because you don’t work on bodies.* “Yes, it’s a wonder they haven’t gone extinct yet,” Henley quipped. I was becoming numb to her remarks, trying to emotionally detach myself from the situation I found myself in, from the reality of what was happening.

"Oh, but look at this mark!" the woman exclaimed, touching my neck and examining it closely. *Too closely*. "It's perfect. Do you know how many girls have wanted to have this mark?" she asked me.

"I'd gladly give it to them."

She came around in front of me so she could see my eyes. "What . . . you mean you don't want to be queen?"

Before I could answer, Henley quickly gave her a warning look. "Remember, no questions," she reminded the woman. She must have been given prior instructions about her interactions with me. That was fine; I couldn't tell her anything that was true, and I despised small talk. The woman seemed ashamed at being chastised by Henley; she became silent and focused on her task.

There was a knock at the door, and Henley sent Mara to answer it. The guys had stood up, on alert, but when they saw who it was, they sat back down. Sheldon caught my eye and gave me a wink and a smile as I winced from my hair being pulled. Was he trying to think of a way to get me out of there? I couldn't come up with an option that wouldn't endanger my family, that wouldn't lead to all of us dying. My father and Laney, but mostly Corey and Annabelle—they were the only thing keeping me there. Corey and Annabelle. How had they responded to the news about our mother? My insides ached with the desire to hug them, to pull them near. *They were—are—real people too.*

My hair was finally complete—a braided crown around my head with jeweled pins throughout. I turned my head to examine it in the mirror. The wound wasn't visible; she had hidden it well. Henley looked pleased, and she dismissed the woman with a nod of her head. Mara returned with a zipped dress bag, hanging it on a hook on the wall across from me. I'd only ever looked at the magazines with Laney as she dreamed about being a bride and becoming Hollister's wife—I'd never imagined my own wedding dress. But there it was in front of me. Chosen for me. It felt like everything for the rest of my life would be chosen for me.

Henley shut the bedroom doors and began unzipping the bag quickly, almost impatiently, like she wanted this all to be over with too.

Would she leave me alone then? "This was supposed to be Elodie's dress," she explained, taking it out of the bag. Gigandet was supposed to be hers too. The dress was a bright white—the color of the Antonian city, the color of their royalty—with an intricate and unique white lace overlay. There were button details on the shoulders and down the back; the buttons were tiny jewels, all different kinds. They reminded me of the grand hall. The skirt flared out slightly, and the train seemed a manageable length—hopefully, I wouldn't really trip and fall and prove to be *clumsy*. The gown was beautiful, simple, and elegant. *Like Elodie.* Once the dress was on, I stared at myself in the mirror, examining every detail. Was this who I was now—a queen? I could appreciate the beauty in the mirror, but I didn't want it.

"Okay, it's time," Henley announced. *No*, my heart protested.

She had her hands on the door handles, but I pleaded, "Wait. Let's go to the scientists. Let's talk to the Ancient Ones. Let's find another way."

She paused, almost looking at me with kindness. "I'm sorry. I wish we could, but there's no time. You're in too much danger. Gigandet needs to stop the disease from spreading." She threw open the doors and ushered me out.

Sheldon turned to look at me over his shoulder, his eyebrows raised in surprise and a goofy grin on his face.

"Close your mouth," Henley ordered him. "This is your future queen. As much as it pains me to say that."

"Yeah." Greer kicked Sheldon's foot with his. "Don't make me move you to another service."

"Might be a good idea with how close they've been today. You can't trust a body and a traitor," Henley added, watching my face to see how I would react to her harsh comment. I remained stoic, refusing to give her any satisfaction. But my first move as queen would be to remove *her* from my service. "Come on," she ordered everyone. "The king is waiting." *He can keep waiting. I don't want him.*

She had given me gold shoes to wear. I clutched the train in my hand, and with each step, I focused on the shoes, the way they contrasted against the plush red carpet on the curved staircase and the way they blended in with the floor in the grand hall once we reached the bottom. I could see Gigandet standing near the thrones—because there were two now instead of one—speaking with another man. There were guards lining both walls and several against the front entrance. Was the danger as bad as Henley said? Beside the banister stood another large vase, like the ones I'd seen the florist setting up earlier with white flowers. But this one was full of the red flowers, the petals falling to the floor, each one silently announcing that the resistance was somewhere among us.

Gigandet noticed us standing there and raised his hand, waving us to come forward. *It was time.*

CHAPTER 13

[LANEY]

"Are you ready?" Curwen asked a second time. Ready to be struck, to travel back to Antonia.

Hollister confirmed that he was. All I could muster was a slight nod of my head. Curwen pressed the button, and the bright white travel light shot down from the clear daytime sky. The campers would definitely be asking Gibson for an explanation. I squeezed my eyes shut tightly, remembering Curwen's instructions from before, and this time I tried to see if I could feel any of the pain Leela had felt the first time. But all I could feel was a warm tingling—nothing like what she had described as her body burning from the inside out. Was it because she had the mark?

"Laney, we're here," Hollister said. Mere seconds. I slowly blinked my eyes open. It was dark, and we were in a place I didn't recognize, but still outside the living quarters, beyond the outer wall of Antonia. Sheldon had told me there were security cameras that had caught us on video last time; *next time you can travel to a different location, without cameras*, he had said. I'd forcefully declared that there wouldn't be a next time.

The heat, though. How quickly I'd forgotten the heat. *It doesn't get cooler at night*, Curwen had said. He was almost right. It did feel a couple of degrees cooler but was still barely bearable. There was a gate nearby that Curwen led us to, and he began to input a series of access codes. Without us asking, he explained, "I'm entering Durham's codes. Mine would be on the banned list and would alert authorities."

"Are we going to find Durham to help us?" I asked.

Curwen didn't answer for a long moment, but then, with shame, he said, "I don't know if Durham wants anything to do with me now . . . now that I've betrayed him."

"But you did what was right," I argued in his defense.

"Not in his eyes. But let's not talk. We don't want to draw attention," he warned as he peered inside the open gate. He looked both ways to make sure it was clear and then ushered us inside. Even though every house looked the same—white washed stone exterior with black solar-panel-shingled roofs—I recognized the street as the one we had been marched down when we—Curwen, Sheldon, my dad, and me—had been arrested. The people had stood watching us, most in fear and curiosity, but a few in solidarity—the few who had red flowers in their windows, the few who belonged to the resistance.

From where we stood, I could see the outline of the white palace against the dark blue sky, sitting atop a plateau. *We just need to get there*. Curwen took us to the right, down the narrow white stone street. We tread lightly, trying not to let our steps make a sound. Most of the houses had dark windows, their inhabitants having retired for the evening, but a few still had a light on—one of those had a red flower in its windowsill. Who lived there, and would they help us? I had a tiny urge to knock on the door, to try to recruit more people for our cause, which should have been their cause too. Our team was larger before, and look what had happened to us. Enslaved. Imprisoned. Exiled. . . . Dead. What could the three of us do, and would the king listen to us?

I would *never* willingly marry him. Was I walking into my own forced marriage? Would I have to replace Leela at the altar? My heart ached for the man who was walking behind me, the one who should be my husband. Hollister and I hadn't had a moment to discuss Gibson's new revelation. He wouldn't let someone else marry me, would he? Antonia—slavery—had changed him. I knew him, but I didn't know him. We needed time. *You do not need to doubt that I love you and that I still want to marry you. Those two things will never change.* I continued repeating his words to myself, for assurance, for a small bit of confidence. I reached my hand back without looking, hoping he would grab it. The seconds felt like an eternity. But then his fingers interlocked with mine, and he took a step forward to walk beside me. My lungs released the breath they'd been holding captive.

We were approaching the end of that street; at the corner, we could only turn left. When we did, there was an old man sitting outside one of the homes. I couldn't make out the details of his face because he sat in the shadows, but he immediately looked in our direction. My first instinct was to panic—what if he alerted the authorities to our late-night activities? *Maybe that wouldn't be so bad.* Maybe it would get us brought directly to the king. But, perhaps it would only get us thrown in prison until after the wedding had taken place. *If it hasn't happened yet.*

"It's past curfew," the man warned us in a deep, gruff voice.

"Yes, we know," Curwen said, not stopping. "We're going home now." We kept walking, picking up our pace, probably increasing his suspicions. We didn't have time. We just needed to get there.

"You don't live on this street," the man called after us. "I saw the light! Where did you come from? You're not government officials! Where'd you get permits to travel?" He was shouting at us. I was afraid he would bring more people outside. We were running now, desperate to get out of his sight, off of his street. Curwen had been leading us down the fastest route, but the old man forced him to take us a different way—left, right, right, left—until we finally found ourselves on the path that led to the meeting quarters.

At first, I didn't notice them in the dark, too focused on reaching the connecting gate, but Hollister pointed them out. Single red flowers stuck, sporadically spaced, into the cracks in the walls on both sides of us.

"What does it mean?" I asked Curwen.

"Durham must be making a move," he said.

"What kind of move?" I asked anxiously. "Is he going to hurt Leela?"

"No, he wouldn't hurt her. The only person we need to worry about is Whirl." Every time he said that name—Whirl—disgust dripped from his tongue, and anger welled up inside of me. Hollister gave my hand a squeeze. Just then, I saw a flash of light, silent but bright, from the direction we had come; someone else was traveling too. Who?

"Curwen," I whispered.

"I saw it," was all he said. We kept walking until we finally reached the gate, and he began inputting some codes. It always amazed me how many codes he and Sheldon had memorized. Were they the same for every gate or different? I had never been good with numbers, so I had never tried to watch over their shoulders to peek at the buttons they pushed, but I saw that Hollister was watching closely. Curwen did too, but he didn't seem to care; he wasn't hiding anything anymore. A change had come over him also; I recognized a new willingness in him to offer up information rather than making me pull it out of him.

"Why does it keep saying that?" Hollister asked.

I stuck my head between them to look at the keypad. "Saying what?"

"We can't get past this gate. All access has been denied," Curwen explained. I could tell he wanted to punch something, his frustration building, frustration at his own limitations. I felt it too.

"Aren't there usually guards at the gates?" I asked, remembering my march to the palace.

Curwen nodded. "Something is very different tonight. Whirl must be making a move too."

Hollister raised up on his tiptoes; he was almost tall enough to see over the top of the gate. "If there are no guards, let's just climb over," Hollister suggested.

"If it were that simple, I wouldn't be standing here," Curwen said in annoyance. "You'll get electrocuted and activate the spikes."

Hollister and I glanced at each other.

"*Spikes?*" I asked for further explanation.

"Yes. They eject from the top of the wall."

"Can't you call Gigandet?" I asked, remembering his phone conversations with Durham. The transporter could be used for communication also.

"No." He shook his head. "This older model doesn't have that technology."

"What about this one?" Hollister asked, pulling the extra transporter from his pocket.

Curwen started laughing. I had never seen him laugh so hard; it was both startling and amusing. Hollister didn't think so as he continued holding the transporter and glaring at Curwen. Finally, Curwen took a breath and said, "That thing is even older than I am. Why do you think Gibson didn't care if you took it?" Hollister shoved the transporter back into his pocket—I knew he was determined to make it work when the time came to use it. Curwen suddenly became serious. "I heard something," he whispered.

We were all quiet, straining to listen. "I don't hear anything," I said after a moment.

"We can't stay here," he said softly, still convinced there was a sound. Before I could protest, he added, "We'll find another way."

"She could be getting married this very second!" I protested anyway. "We can't find another way! She could already be married . . . or be *dead*."

"She's not dead," Curwen stated firmly, but it sounded like he was trying to convince himself, not me.

"Laney, you would know if she was," Hollister tried to encourage me and give me hope. But he was wrong.

"No. I wouldn't! Leela and I have never had that kind of connection." I shook my head, desperately wishing we *did* have a supernatural twin telepathy.

"You have more of a connection than you realize," he countered.

Curwen sighed. "We don't have time to argue about this. It's not helpful."

“Obviously!” I turned and walked away from them, taking the lead, heading back the way we’d come.

They followed in silence, but Curwen instructed me, “At the end, take a right.”

As I obeyed him, turning right, a dark figure came from the other side, from behind the wall; his strong arm grabbed my wrist, pulling me close from behind. It was a man, a guard, and he wrapped his arm tightly around my waist. I kicked against his embrace until I realized in his other hand, he held a gun, and it was pointed at me. *That is one of our strictest laws—guns are not allowed to be brought into Antonia*, Curwen had told Corey. What was it doing here?

Hollister and Curwen were frozen half a dozen feet away; my eyes searched theirs frantically, trying not to cry out, not to draw more attention. “You thought you’d outsmart me,” came the guard’s voice over my shoulder, his breath hot and repulsive on my neck. What did he mean? I hadn’t seen the guard at Haleh’s store or at the campground—the guard who was searching for me—so I didn’t know what he looked like. Though I hadn’t seen his face, his voice was familiar. Was he the same one? Was he the flash of light we’d seen five minutes earlier, coming after us from the other dimension?

“Let her go,” Hollister demanded, taking a step forward.

“Don’t come any closer. Stay where you are,” the guard warned, raising the gun a little higher, its metal glimmering in the light from the corner street lamp.

“Why do you have a gun?” Curwen asked in a steady voice. “It’s against the law. You’ll be executed for that.”

“The law has changed now,” the guard replied. “Who do you think gave me the gun?”

“What do you mean?” Curwen asked. It was clear he was buying us time—time to find a way of escape. But Hollister and I were already silently plotting with our eyes. He’d taught me all the right self-defense moves a few summers before. I flashed back to that moment in our living room; it started because Leela was studying anatomy and ended with me pinning Hollister to the floor. Replaying the movements in my mind, I formed my plan of action and waited for the right moment.

The guard didn't answer Curwen's question but instead sneered at him. "I should shoot you right now, but I know Whirl wants to finish you himself."

"Whirl is nothing but a coward," Curwen attempted to provoke him. It worked—the guard took the gun off me and aimed it at him. Hollister gave me a slight nod. I swiftly stepped on the guard's foot, elbowed him in the ribs, twisted out of his grasp, and struck his nose upward with the heel of my palm. In the struggle, the gun went off, but Hollister wrestled it from his grip and knocked him hard over the head with it—the guard fell to the ground, unconscious. Hollister and I stared at each other for a moment before he pulled me into a fierce embrace, crushing me to him. My ear pressed against his chest, I could hear and feel his heart beating fast. The same as mine.

Curwen came closer, and I could see that his arm was bleeding. "The bullet only grazed me," he brushed off my concern. I pulled away from Hollister in order to examine the wound anyway.

We heard more footsteps and looked up to find the same old man, standing on the corner, the streetlight illuminating his features this time. "What have you done?" he asked, taking in the scene. In his eyes, we looked like criminals, the ones who had done wrong. "I've called the guards," he said. "They'll be here soon." Then his eyes landed on the gun in Hollister's hand; the man's eyes got wide with fear, and he raised his hands in peace as he backed away from us.

Hollister slowly set the gun on the ground, raising his hands in the air. "We're not going to hurt you," he explained to the man. But the words were barely out of his mouth when the old man turned and ran as fast as he could, disappearing down his street, out of sight. The guard was stirring; he groaned and rubbed the back of his head, the place where Hollister had hit him. The lights came on in the windows of the nearby homes; they had heard the gunshot. *I've called the guards. They'll be here soon*, I heard the man's words echo in my head. I imagined us being marched back through the streets, straight to the fluorescent jail cells. But this time, we wouldn't be taken to a field to be given our freedom; this time, we would receive our final punishment. Because *the laws have changed now.*

"Let's go. Now," Curwen ordered, snapping me to attention. He took off running in the direction he had instructed me to go earlier. Hollister and I were close on his heels. We turned so many corners, there was no way I could keep up with the directions, especially in the dark.

"Where are we going?" I asked, out of breath.

"To a safehouse."

"Will they welcome us?"

"There's at least one who will."

"Who?"

"Muriel," he called back to me.

Muriel. The old woman I had met with Sheldon; the woman with the wrinkled, sun-leathered skin; the woman whose eyes were ancient, beautiful, wise, and blind. The woman whose hand had felt like rose petals when she'd insisted on shaking mine. The woman who had smiled and hoped my mission would be a success.

• • •

Curwen knocked on the door, a special kind of knock, but very softly, and I was sure there was no way the old woman would hear us. In my panic, I wanted to rap on the door and call out for her to hurry, but that would alert the neighbors, whose windows were dark—they were still sleeping soundly, oblivious to whatever was happening up the hill, at the palace. What *was* happening? The guard had said *the law has changed now*. What did he mean? Was Leela okay? The people slept safely in their beds, not realizing they were actually locked inside the living quarters, unable to leave if they wanted, unable to help their king if they knew he was in trouble—that is, if they wanted to help him. How many of them knew about the resistance? How many of them were aware of Whirl's army? How many of them belonged to either group?

In the middle of Curwen's second attempt at knocking, the door flew open. Muriel, the little old lady, stood there. Her blind, cloudy cataract eyes appeared frightening in the dark; there was only a small table lamp casting a faint glow behind her. "I'm blind, not deaf," she chastised in a whisper. "Come inside quickly!" She invited us in, shutting and locking the door behind us. "You three, have a seat. Catch your breath. I'll fetch the tea I prepared. I've been waiting for you." How did she know there were three of us? It must have been our footsteps or our breathing. Those were the things that had allowed her to recognize my presence before, the first time we had met. My legs suddenly felt very weak, the after effects of adrenaline, so I sat on the sofa like she had instructed.

"How did you know we were coming?" Curwen asked as he took a seat in an oversized armchair. He fell into it as if he'd done it a million times before; he was comfortable here. Every piece of furniture in the small room was oversized, each piece touching the one beside it, which created a cozy and intimate atmosphere, even more than at Phaedra's house.

"Curwen, you know I have the ability to see things others can't." She must have known him by his voice. We'd never said who we were. "I know Laney is here—don't look so surprised," she warned me, chuckling softly, "but who is the other young man?"

"My name is Hollister, ma'am," he introduced himself, taking her hand in both of his.

She smiled, patting the top of his hand with her free one. "Welcome to my home, Hollister." She smiled into the air, but then her nose wrinkled up. "One of you is bleeding. I can smell it. Is it urgent, life-threatening?"

"No," Curwen said. "The bullet just grazed my arm."

"Bullet?" she asked with alarm. "You can tell me after I get the tea and cookies. Go clean the wound. You'll find bandages in the cabinet." She went to the kitchen, and Curwen disappeared down the dark hallway. How well did he know this home? How often had he been here before? If Phaedra was like his mother, was Muriel like his grandmother?

Hollister took a seat beside me on the couch, and I was suddenly very nervous to be alone with him. We hadn't had a minute to process anything—the fact that I had just been held at gunpoint or the idea that I was supposed to marry another man. My fingers fidgeted in my lap, my hands unsure what to do with themselves; they wanted to touch him, to hug him, to hold his hand at least. But I stopped them because I couldn't risk him pulling away or pushing him away. I was too fragile to face rejection in that moment; at any second, I felt like I could burst into tears thinking about what had just happened, remembering the cold metal of the gun pressed against my skin and his hot breath in my ear. And realizing we were no closer to helping Leela. Instead, we were further away from her. I clasped my hands tightly together, the way my mother had taught me to pray when I was a little girl. *Here is the church, here is the steeple, open the doors, see all the people*, I heard her voice reciting the nursery rhyme while I mimicked the movements with my fingers.

Hollister noticed what I was doing, and he copied me, his skilled fingers adept and never clumsy. I looked up at him, finally meeting his eyes, and he smiled a soft, reassuring smile. "Laney, I got you," he affirmed. "I got you," he repeated more firmly. I exhaled slowly, deeply, as a single tear rolled down my cheek. He wiped it away with his thumb, like it had never been there, like there was no reason to cry.

"Here's the tea," Muriel sang as she entered the room, interrupting us. She stopped directly in front of the table, as if she'd memorized the number of steps so she wouldn't run into it. Hollister wasted no time grabbing a cookie from the plate and complimenting her on how amazing they tasted. Curwen returned a moment later, his arm bandaged tightly a couple inches above his elbow.

"Muriel, you said you are able to see things that others can't," I began. "What did you mean by that?"

"Oh, I have visions occasionally. They come less and less the older I get," she explained nonchalantly. "But they are strong in moments of urgency, like tonight—I knew you would need shelter from some kind of danger."

"How did they begin?" I asked. "When did they start?"

"Why so curious?" She wasn't offended by my questions, but she didn't understand why it mattered to me.

Annabelle. I looked at Curwen, silently asking if it was safe to tell her about Annabelle. He nodded; it was clear from his demeanor that he had not yet made a connection between Muriel and Annabelle, that he hadn't thought about it before that moment. "My little sister," I told her, "has begun drawing all kinds of visions in the past few weeks."

Her face lit up in surprise. "How old is she?"

"Four."

"Has she been exposed to the travel light, in close proximity? She's *seen* it, but not traveled through it?"

Hollister and I looked at each other, remembering the day he had been taken, and then I replied, "Yes."

"She saw me get struck," Hollister added.

"Is that what happened to you?" I asked. What I really wanted to ask was: *is that what caused your blindness?* Would Annabelle become blind too?

She nodded softly—not in a sad, self-pitying way, but in a confident way, as a woman who'd accepted herself long ago. "I had weak eyes from birth. I was already losing my sight, but seeing the light caused it to happen sooner. My father was going to be traveling for a long time, for work, and my mother took me with her to tell him goodbye. It was forbidden for young children to be taken to the travel fields, for their safety. But I don't think anyone understood the effects of travel light exposure back then—my mother certainly didn't. And for whatever unexplainable reason, it doesn't seem to affect adults in the same way. So, she took me with her. And a week later, I was drawing pictures, things I couldn't explain. And my eyesight was fading. I traded one kind of vision for another."

Curwen cleared his throat and asked, "Do you think that's what's happened to Annabelle?"

She shrugged. "That's the only explanation I can give, what I know from my own experience."

"Do you only get visions of things that *will happen* or things that *are happening*?" Hollister asked.

"When I was young and inexperienced, it was mostly just things as they were happening. As I got older and tried to have the visions—rather than just waiting for them to happen—I began to see things that would happen in the future. Like your visit here tonight."

"So, even though you can't see, you still know what we look like because of your visions?" Hollister asked.

"Oh, yes." She chuckled. "And you are a very handsome young man. Those green eyes—oh my!" She whistled. Hollister blushed. I suppressed a snicker.

"Only Muriel can say things so unabashedly," Curwen said with a teasing smile.

"Being blind makes you bold," she quipped. "I don't have to see the way you react to my words."

"Will Annabelle go blind too?" I asked, suddenly in a panic at the thought of it.

She shrugged. "If it hasn't happened yet, then probably not." Then with an edge to her voice, offended by the sound of concern in mine, she added, "But, even if she does *go blind too*, it's not the end of the world. She can still have a beautiful and useful life."

"I'm sorry," I apologized quickly, ashamed. "I didn't mean any offense."

"Nobody ever does, child." She gave a small smile. "I forgive you." It was silent for an awkward moment before she spoke again. "So, this bullet—tell me about it! Does that mean the guns are being used publicly now?"

"What do you mean?" Curwen asked. "You *knew* about the guns?" He was clearly upset, his voice saturated with accusation, like *how dare the blind old woman not do something to stop the guns*. She had been offended by my tone, but she didn't appear to be fazed by his.

"I didn't know," she corrected him. "You know my neighbor, Baron, who lives next door—he's a member of the guard. I kept hearing these faint popping sounds, for several weeks now. I eventually pinpointed the sound to the basement of the house next door—I could hear them loudest from my basement. Other people probably wouldn't have noticed the sounds—they were barely audible—but, you know, my hearing is better than most. I've never heard a gun before, so I didn't know what it was. When Baron's wife brought me a meal a few days ago, I asked her about the noises coming from her basement; she said she didn't know what I was talking about, that she hadn't heard anything . . . but I could tell in her voice she was lying. The sounds ceased after that. When Durham stopped by this afternoon, I told him about it, and he explained that Whirl has been importing guns, that I had probably heard the guards practicing with them in a sort of makeshift firing range. One of our affiliates had reported to Durham that he had taken part in a target practice in another guard's basement."

I shuddered in fear. Not because of the guns—I had been around guns my entire life, and it was hard to imagine any place existed without them. No, I shuddered because *Whirl* had armed the guards with guns. Because now they had weapons that could be instantly fatal, weapons they had little experience with. Because they took their orders from Whirl. And because one of them lived next door.

"How long has Durham known about the guns?" Curwen asked, again with a tone of betrayal, like *how dare he not tell me about them*.

She shrugged. "He didn't say. I didn't ask." She was too old to get worked up about things, very different from the three of us. I remembered my grandma had been like that as she aged. *You get too old to care*, she had explained to me years earlier.

"Did he say anything about me?" Curwen asked. I could tell from his voice he was worried, like a son trying to find out if his father was mad at him. Was Durham angry with him for his betrayal, for helping us when he should have simply turned Leela over to the resistance?

Curwen wanted, needed to know where he stood with his father, his boss.

"Of course we all knew about you getting marched through the streets when you were arrested, so I asked him how you were, if you were okay. But he wouldn't tell me what had happened. He simply said you had made your own decisions," she explained.

Curwen's chin dropped to his chest.

Just then, there came a loud rap on the door. "Muriel," a deep voice called.

"It's Baron," Muriel whispered, suddenly alert, her demeanor changing. "You three go out the back, through the kitchen." When none of us moved, she added fiercely, "*Now.*" We rose and began to tiptoe toward the kitchen; she stopped me and, handing me the tray of tea and cookies, said, "Put this on the counter. Silently." Silent. My father had taught me how to be silent when he'd taken me on his hunting excursions. I glanced back to see her straightening the couch cushions—without sight, how did she know they were wrinkled—as there came a second, louder pounding on the door.

There were no lights on in the kitchen. I realized Muriel must have prepared the refreshments in the dark—she didn't need the light. There was a rear door, which Hollister already had open, so it wouldn't make noise, exposing us to the man at the front door. We paused to listen as she opened the door to him.

"Good evening, Muriel," we heard the man—Baron—say. "One of the neighbors say they saw three people come to your door this evening. Do you have any visitors?"

"No, sir, there's nobody here. But who do you have with *you*?" she asked.

I could tell we were all holding our breath in anticipation, in dread.

"I'm searching for three fugitives, ma'am," came the voice of the man who'd held me at gunpoint. I was frozen in place, my blood like ice, as if the gun were still pointed at my head. How had they found us so quickly? Was it really the neighborhood watch that tipped them off or secret surveillance cameras, the ones the people knew nothing about, the ones Sheldon had access to on the monitors in his hidden closet? Hollister was impatiently motioning me toward the door, but I shook my head at him; I needed to know what else the guard would say.

"I'm sorry I can't help you," Muriel replied. "There are no fugitives here." It was clever the way she lied. To her, it was the truth—she didn't define us as fugitives.

"Are you sure about that? Then you won't mind if we look around?" His voice was louder now, as if he had come inside. I was desperate to look around the corner of the other kitchen entrance, the one that led into the dark hallway. Curwen beat me to it. There was a grandfather clock blocking our view—blocking the guard from seeing us—but we could get a tiny glimpse of the foyer between the clock and the wall.

He turned back to us. "He's inside, and he's got the gun on her. You two, go!" he ordered us in a whisper.

"We're not leaving you," I argued. Hollister was already trying to pull me toward the door, but I jerked my arm from his grasp. "Come with us, Curwen," I pleaded. "They won't hurt her if we're not here, if she's telling the truth."

"I'm not leaving her," he said, waving us toward the door, but my feet were planted to the floor. I could not move from that spot; perhaps, like Hollister, I had also found things—people—I was willing to die for. I squeezed past Curwen and peeked around the corner this time, closing one eye so I could see clearly through the slit behind the clock. The guard had Muriel in his grasp now, much the same way he'd had me earlier. She was shorter and physically weaker than me, but her face showed no fear. It was hard like steel with tightly pursed lips; she had nothing more to say. Curwen was pressed up against me so he could also see what was happening, but Hollister continued to wait beside the open back door, ready to flee when the moment came.

"Come on out, Curwen," the unnamed guard taunted him as he stepped farther into the house. "This doesn't have to end badly. We just want Laney." A shiver went up my spine when he said my name. Why did they want me? Were they aware that I—not Leela—was the one who could break the curse by marrying Gigandet? If so, that could only mean they wanted to kill me, to prevent the marriage from happening, to usurp the throne.

"Come on, man," Baron tried to persuade him from the open doorway. "You don't have to do this. She's just an old lady who's been kind to us for years."

"Just do your job," the guard ordered him while taking another step forward, another step closer to us. He twisted Muriel's arm behind her back in an unnatural way; she cried out in pain. I couldn't watch anymore.

I pulled back into the kitchen, pushing Curwen out of the way, and looking at both men, I told them, "I'll go." Everything was happening so quickly, I couldn't comprehend how I was suddenly willing—like Leela, like Hollister—to risk everything for someone I barely knew. But it didn't feel right to simply stand there and watch. Immediately I knew, from the expression on his face, that Hollister would never allow it. But could he stop me? I weighed our positions. All I had to do was take two big steps and I would be in the hallway, in full sight of the guard, hands raised in surrender. But all Hollister had to do was reach out his long arm to grab me, to pull me out the back door.

Curwen was also considering our options. "No," he concluded. "*I'll* go. This mess is all mine." Before I could protest, he took a step backward into the hallway, giving me a nod of assurance. Tears immediately filled my eyes. He turned to face the guard, calling out to him. "Anderson, let her go."

"Where's Laney?" Anderson—that was his name—asked. I wanted him to stop saying my name. Hollister shook his head at me and reached out a hand to hold my wrist, not taking any chance that I would also step into the hallway.

"She's not here," Curwen replied. "She and her boyfriend left me. They just used me to travel here so they can get to her sister at the palace."

Anderson laughed. "Her sister won't be at the palace for long." What did he mean? Where would she be?

"What do you mean?"

"Don't worry. All of Antonia will know by morning."

I watched through the sliver between the clock and the wall, one arm being held tightly by Hollister, as Curwen walked into the foyer. "Just let Muriel go, and take me to Whirl," Curwen ordered with frustration, tired of Anderson's games.

"Baron," Anderson said, "cuff him. We're taking him to the scientists." Baron reluctantly entered the house, grabbed the cuffs from Anderson's belt, and walked cautiously toward Curwen. He seemed to let out a sigh of relief when Curwen didn't resist, his hands secured behind his back. "Put a collar on him too," Anderson added, gesturing to the backpack he wore. Baron fumbled around with the zipper but quickly returned with the shock collar for Curwen's neck. The tears were streaming down my face now. How could Hollister let this happen, especially when he knew how it felt? Why wouldn't he fight for them? *Because he has others to fight for, others he's willing to die for.* In anger, I tried to jerk my wrist loose from his grip, but he wouldn't let go this time.

Baron activated the collar, and immediately Anderson ordered him to shock Curwen. The first shock barely fazed him. "Higher," Anderson ordered. "Much higher."

Baron shook his head. "Come on," he protested again. "We don't need to do this. He's not resisting arrest. Let's just take him and go." But Anderson was sadistic like Whirl, his eyes holding the same kind of cruelty. He demanded Baron give him the controller, and he turned the dial up to its highest level; I could see Curwen's shoulders tighten as he prepared for what was about to happen to him. Turning my head away, I squinched my eyes closed—I couldn't watch. But I heard it—Curwen's body convulsing before he hit the floor.

When I opened my eyes, he was just lying there, but I heard him faintly utter, "Let. Her. Go."

Anderson smiled wickedly. He let her go and took a step away from her. I breathed a sigh of relief. They would just take Curwen, and we would figure out how to rescue him. "She harbored a fugitive and lied about it," he said. And then, without warning, he swiftly, without hesitation, raised the gun and executed Muriel.

I let out a shriek, partly drowned out by the gunshot and partly drowned out by Curwen's cry of protest and anguish as he watched Muriel's limp body fall to the floor beside him. Anderson looked in my direction, at the clock. Hollister instantly had one hand over my mouth and one hand around my waist, lifting me from the ground, taking me out the back door. There was a gate leading to a different street. He set my feet on the ground and ordered me to run. My mind kept replaying what I had just witnessed, in shock, tears pouring down my face as I ran. It was hard to catch my breath, my shoulders heaving as I sobbed. Hollister stayed right behind me; instinctively, I understood that he didn't take the lead because he wanted to be my shield, in case any bullets flew at me. But I was angry with him. No. I was livid. I was filled with a hot fury. She had been killed with the gun we'd left behind; we'd allowed him to keep his weapon.

That situation didn't have to happen like that.

We *all* could have done something differently.

We didn't even try.

Had she seen in her vision that she would die tonight?

Had she known that inviting us inside also welcomed her death?

Had she known and done it anyway?

CHAPTER 14

[LEELA]

With every step nearer to the thrones, nearer to Gigandet, I felt more nauseous. These weren't the kind of butterflies a bride should feel on her wedding day; their wings should tickle with excitement, not flap violently with dread. As Henley had been helping me dress, she'd been explaining the order of the ceremony, instructing my every move, but my mind had been preoccupied—mostly it had been plotting ways to get out of it, thinking of Mara's offer to help me escape or, at the very least, to postpone the wedding, to gain some time to get to know Gigandet better. I didn't expect to ever love him—or for him to love me—but perhaps I could like him more than I did.

Every time I saw Gigandet was like meeting him for the first time because I could never sketch a clear picture of him in my mind—he was an unremarkable, average-looking man with forgettable features. He wasn't ugly—I just could never decide if he was attractive. I think he was most attractive when he was beside Elodie, when her presence and her beauty animated his face with love. *Love makes people come to life*, my mother'd said once when we were watching Laney and Hollister together, cheeks flushed, acting silly—acting like fools, I had thought—with their laughter filling the air. I'd argued with her that people can come to life without being in love. She'd quickly agreed, explaining that *all kinds of love give life, not just romantic love.* So, as I looked at

Gigandet, knowing we would never have a romantic love, I wondered if we could have a kind of love that could still give life.

Gigandet had waved us toward him, beckoning for us to come forward, but he was deep in conversation with an older man I had not seen before, and he did not immediately acknowledge us.

Henley grabbed my arm to stop me from approaching them. "You do not speak to him first in public spaces," she instructed me.

"Even when we are married?" I asked.

"Yes, even then."

It was a social formality I knew I was bound to break several times before I learned. I almost laughed out loud thinking about how much harder it would have been for Laney to obey that rule if she were in my place. We'd been taught to speak our minds whenever we had something beneficial to say, but my twin was far less skilled at holding her tongue or waiting patiently to be addressed. Better me than her.

"Does the rule apply for the queen too?" I asked. "Will people not be allowed to speak to me first in public?"

She stared hard at me, annoyed. "Yes."

I smiled. "Oh, well then I'll make sure that you and I will be in public spaces all the time," I joked. So long as I didn't talk to her, Henley wouldn't be able to say anything to me. *That* was one thing to look forward to.

There were people all around us. A couple of them, the photographer and her assistant, were working on lighting. There were at least fifty guards plus Greer, Sheldon, and Mara. There was another man with a notepad, constantly jotting things down; he must have been the one who would write the announcement, the one that all of Antonia would receive in the morning. How much of the truth would he be allowed to share? Would he interview me? *Please, no.*

There was a middle-aged woman with ash brown hair fussing with a bunch of flowers. She caught me looking at her—perhaps she took that as permission to approach—and she walked toward me, a bouquet in her hands. The bouquet was beautiful, consisting of a few big white peonies, but in the center was a single large red and white dahlia. It looked as if it were transforming from white to red, the red slowly seeping into every petal, red ink soaking into thin white paper. Was this more symbolism, strategically placed there to send a message? As she handed it to me, she curtsied and glanced up at me, meeting my eyes with an intense stare—was she trying to tell me something? Was she the mastermind behind all the red flowers we'd seen that evening? Or was I simply on high alert, as Greer had instructed, looking for signs everywhere?

"Thank you. It's beautiful," I told her, giving a slight nod. When she walked away, I turned to find Sheldon or Mara to ask them if they knew her, if she was part of the resistance, but they were no longer near me. Greer had positioned them at opposite sides of the great hall, waiting in the wings. Only Henley—the one I didn't want—remained by my side.

"We're ready," the lead photographer said loudly, directing his remark to the older man with Gigandet, but it was obvious he meant for the king to respond.

Gigandet cleared his throat and finally turned to address me, walking a few feet in my direction. "Leela, I'd like to introduce you to a member of my council. This is Tad. He'll be performing the ceremony tonight." Tad had silver hair and thick black eyebrows and some of the brightest blue eyes I'd ever seen, but his skin was wrinkled and tan from too many years in the Antonian sun. I simply smiled and nodded at him, unsure how to speak to any of these people because they hadn't told me who I was supposed to pretend to be, how much of my true self I could reveal.

"It's okay, Leela. I know the truth. You can be yourself," Tad said, as though he had read my mind, just like Elodie. "I'm Elodie's uncle," he added with a broad smile.

"Oh," was all I could mutter. The presence of Elodie hung around me like a heavy weight; I realized I would never escape it. Her best friend beside me. Her groom in front of me. Her uncle set to marry us. Gigandet's face showed that he thought I was being rude. So, I added with a slight smile, "It's nice to meet you."

Gigandet cleared his throat again. "It's tradition to take separate portraits before the ceremony and then one together afterward," he explained. "I'll go first so you can see how it's done." He abruptly turned and walked up the few steps to the thrones where the photographer waited.

"Excuse me, dear," Tad said. "I must take my leave to prepare." I smiled and nodded, grateful I wouldn't have to make small talk with the rightful bride's uncle. I watched Gigandet for a moment, since he wanted to show me how it was done. Like I'd never had my portrait taken before. The photographer was tedious and monotone.

"Remember all those young women who have dreamed about having the mark and marrying the king?" Henley whispered in my ear. I nodded. "Well, pretend you're one of them. Smile like you're one of them. Let your eyes sparkle like this is the happiest day of your life." What she didn't know, what any of my siblings could have told her, was that I was horrible at pretending, at faking my emotions. She was gifted at it, though, flashing her beautiful smile—one I had never seen before—at everyone in the room, acting like she was so pleased with what was about to happen. I turned away from her and the thrones, my eyes scanning the room.

"My dear, you are not the one?" I heard the photographer's assistant ask Henley. "When I saw you come in earlier, I thought surely you were the one. I thought the light-haired one was just a body!" she exclaimed with laughter. Didn't she know I could hear her loud, obnoxious voice?

Henley gave a fake, polite laugh. "No. Leela is your future queen," she said with a hint of correction. I should be a *body* though. In that moment, with a false smile plastered across my face, I almost wished I was one.

My eyes fell on Sheldon. His olive skin contrasted with the white uniform they'd been instructed to wear for the ceremony. The only flaw on his smooth skin were the bruises on his face, but they weren't noticed in this crowd—the guards were used to seeing a man who'd been in a fight. Did they know that it was Whirl who had inflicted the wounds? Whirl hadn't shaved Sheldon's head like Mara's, but Greer had made him cut his dark hair; he looked older now. There was no question whether I thought he was attractive. Not like with Gigandet.

I stared at him long enough that his light green eyes finally met mine. He nodded toward the rear, behind the thrones, to the doors I had entered my very first night here. He was still offering me a way of escape—if I wanted it. I began to list all my reasons for doing this, for *choosing* to marry this man. Annabelle. Corey. For their protection. Laney. Hollister. My father. Curwen. Sheldon. Mara. For their freedom. Greer's niece and nephew. The Antonian people who were sick and the ones who would become sick. For their health. For all of our lives. I slightly shook my head at him. No—I would have to see this through.

"You're up," Henley said, pinching me, drawing me back to reality.

Scowling at her, I rubbed the back of my arm where her pinch still lingered. I lifted my heavy skirt to climb the three marble steps where the photographer was waiting; Gigandet had moved off to the side again, back in discussion with Tad, who had returned. The throne actually looked inviting, as I longed for a place to sit, but I vaguely remembered Henley explaining that I was not allowed to sit there until *after* the ceremony.

I looked up and caught Sheldon staring at me this time. It made me blush, reminding me of the way he'd looked at me upstairs earlier, his mouth agape in awe. No man had ever looked at me like that—none I had noticed—though I'm sure Laney would argue with me about that. He gave me a sad smile and nodded toward the rear doors again, enticing me with an impossible escape plan. This time, I didn't give an answer but simply turned away from him, away from the temptation, focusing on the directions of the photographer with a big smile permanently etched across my face. Remember, *this is the happiest day of your life*.

After she finished photographing me from behind, ensuring some good shots of the mark, there was nothing else to postpone the ceremony. Gigandet came forward to take my hand and lead me down the steps, where we waited for Tad to take his place. Though the king also had a smile plastered on his face, I imagined he felt much like I did; this was not a celebration—it was a time for mourning our losses.

"Are you sure about this?" I whispered to him.

"There's no other choice, and there's no more time," he replied firmly, trying to convince both of us. "We know that Whirl is making his move in the next twenty-four hours, and, thanks to your excursion today, we know that he has an armory full of guns."

"You didn't know?"

"Of course not." He seemed offended I would think he did. "What kind of ruler do you think I am?"

"I couldn't say. I don't know you," I replied bluntly. Neither of us were smiling now, but the camera was still taking pictures. What kind of looks was it capturing between the bride and groom, and how would those looks be interpreted by posterity? Tad cleared his throat; he was ready. It was time.

Nervously, I glanced around, meeting Mara's eyes as she stood in the wings. Her stare was blank, not sympathetic. She wasn't offering me a way out like Sheldon had. Perhaps this marriage would make her happy; she wouldn't have to worry about love growing between me and Curwen—even though no love existed, and she only thought it did. Sheldon was behind me, in the wings opposite Mara, so I couldn't look at him for an encouraging smile or wink. Greer stood only a few feet from me, and Allen was a few feet behind Gigandet. Other than the photographer and her assistant, the fifty guards lining the walls were our only audience. It felt like an elopement, an arranged marriage, and a destination wedding all at once.

"Let's begin," Tad said with a smile at each of us. I was replacing his niece. How could he smile?

He began to speak again. But then there was a loud boom. I knew the sound. A rifle.

While the guards' heads whipped around, searching for the sniper, my eyes fell on Tad. He'd been the target. He'd been shot in the head.

Executed. A direct hit in the middle of his forehead. The muscles in his face relaxed, his smile disappearing as he began to fall.

I caught him in my arms as he fell toward me, but his weight was too great, and we both began to sink. Gigandet grabbed his shoulder, guiding his body to the floor. His head lay in my lap, his glazed eyes staring up at me. With my hands, I put pressure on the entry and exits wounds, attempting to stop the blood—even though my mind knew he was already dead. He had died instantly. Did his death mark the beginning of a war, or would this be the only battle? Would we all die here? Whirl would succeed in preventing the marriage.

I looked at Gigandet, whose eyes were wide with fear, anger, and defiance as he frantically scanned the room, trying to find the gunman. Because my father and Corey had taught me these things, I knew from which direction the bullet had flown; it had come from the top of the staircase. "The balcony," I told him as we both strained to see the recessed, partially hidden balcony. Whoever had been there, whoever had shot Tad, was not immediately visible. Guards were rushing to surround us, to protect us, shoving Gigandet down to the floor beside me; it was like slow-motion, silent chaos. They stood like a wall around us, obstructing my sight. I struggled to see between them.

First, I saw his shadow on the wall, flickering in the candlelight, and then I saw his feet as he stepped out from his hiding place. I knew who it was, and his perfect aim indicated that he had been shooting guns much longer than he had been importing them. The guards encircling us had no distance weapons to use against him or his army. But we hadn't seen the army yet. Just the one man, Whirl, now appeared before us, his presence sending shivers through me. His light-brown, graying hair was disheveled, and his blue eyes piercing as he glared down at us. "GIGANDET!" Whirl yelled like a madman. "What happened to my invitation?"

"Are you hit?" a voice asked, drawing my attention away from the balcony. It was Sheldon. I hadn't realized he was crouched beside me.

"What?" I asked absentmindedly, unable to focus.

"Are you hit?" he repeated in my ear, pointing at the blood on my dress.

"No," I shook my head. "It's not my blood. It's not my blood. It's not my blood." Red staining white, like the flower in the bouquet that lay in shambles beside me. Greer was also beside me now; he pushed Tad's body off of me.

"Sir," he said to Gigandet, "we need to get you both to the safety." Gigandet was frozen, unsure, silent, in shock. He hadn't expected Whirl so soon. He wasn't prepared, but they were coming for us, and they were armed.

Above us, we began to hear the rhythmic sound of marching, of heavy boot steps on the floor. They were upstairs. His army was coming. How had they gotten in? *Through the tunnel, through the vaulted door.* Allen ordered the king's guard to form a line across the hall, a barrier between us and them. It felt like they were simply lining up for the firing squad. There would soon be a bloody massacre.

"Oh, Allen, don't make it easier for me!" Whirl hollered down to him, laughing.

And then a gunshot, and another one. Two men fell to the ground.

"Let's go," Sheldon ordered, not waiting for instructions. He grabbed one of my arms, Greer grabbed the other, and they lifted me to my feet. Allen did the same for Gigandet, who finally seemed to be coming around, able to grasp the situation and give instructions.

"Greer, you know the way. Lead us," he demanded. We all dunked our heads as we ran for cover, toward a part of the palace I hadn't been to before. More gunshots rang out, more bodies fell to the golden, jewel-encrusted floor. The rear doors, the ones Sheldon had motioned to earlier, had guards standing outside of them—but they weren't the king's guards—they were Whirl's, and they each had guns of their own. One of them caught a glimpse of us; he came inside and began shooting, but his aim was too poor for moving targets. We kept heading toward a metal door; I didn't know where it led. Just twenty more feet, and we'd reach it.

But then, behind us, we heard Allen cry out. Gigandet had been hit. He was on the ground, but he shouted to us, "Go! Don't stop!" Greer still seemed to hesitate, not wanting to leave his king behind. But Sheldon and Mara—I hadn't noticed she was with us—continued to pull me toward the door. Only after Gigandet yelled one more time did Greer follow us. He opened the door and hurried us through, shutting and locking it. We were in the kitchen.

"Sheldon, help me," he said. They moved the industrial freezer in front of the door. Then they shoved the fridge against the freezer for extra assurance. "Come on, to the pantry," he ordered. We followed without hesitation. As he opened the walk-in pantry door, Elodie was standing there, clutching a butcher knife.

"What's happening out there?" she asked, her eyes fearful as she scanned my—her—wedding dress.

Greer grabbed her wrist and removed the knife from her grip. "What are you doing here?" he demanded. What *was* she doing here? Had she snuck in to watch the wedding? Or to protest against it?

"I was told to come here. To let somebody in," she said, glancing down at the floor beside her. As if on cue, there came a banging from beneath the floor boards. There was a trap door, and it was locked. Who was she supposed to let in? More of Whirl's soldiers? They were entering through the tunnel system.

My eyes narrowed into slits as I tried to comprehend her betrayal. "You're helping Whirl?" I asked softly, unable to believe it.

"No! No." She shook her head, her eyes becoming even wider, more afraid that I would accuse her of that than of what was happening out there. "I'm here to help you!"

"Who told you to come here?" Greer asked in anger.

Mara followed with, "Who are you letting in?"

"I don't know his name," Elodie explained quickly. "He only signs his notes with a 'D.'" *D is for Durham.* "My father used to receive notes from him, but when he died, they ceased. Until this evening. He told me I had to come here and unlock this door if I wanted to help Gigandet. Where is Gi? Why's he not with you?"

None of us wanted to answer that question. There was banging from beneath the floor again. And then banging on the outer door, the one barricaded by the freezer and fridge. They were trying to get in. We were surrounded. *D is for Durham.* I was sure of it. Had he sent the resistance fighters to help against Whirl? We needed to open the trap door. I rushed past Greer before he could stop me and flipped the lock.

Greer pulled me back just in time for the door to be thrown open without hitting me. A young man's head of dark curly hair popped up. "What took so long—" he began in annoyance, but when he saw me, his face changed to concern. "Is she okay?" he asked instead.

"Jace?" Sheldon recognized him. "What are you doing here?"

Greer sighed. It was obvious he was becoming more and more frustrated; he must have felt like an outsider in this group, like someone who was no longer in control of the group he was supposed to lead, like the only royalist in a group of dissenters.

"Durham sent me to help you," Jace explained, remaining down in the hole. "He's been monitoring the situation. He knew Whirl was attacking tonight. Hurry! We need to go."

"Wait." Greer's eyes were full of suspicion. "Why should we trust this Durham? He shouldn't even know about this tunnel entrance."

"He's our . . . father, and you can trust him," Mara assured him. "His goal is to keep Leela alive. We all have the same goal."

"But is it worth it?" I said without feeling, in a state of shock. Was it worth it? Was it worth keeping me alive? They all stared at me in silence, half of them thinking I had lost my mind, half of them questioning if the risks were really worth it. The game had changed. Guns had become a part of it, weapons they were unfamiliar with in every way. There was renewed banging on the metal door as Whirl's guards attempted to get inside.

"We don't have time for this," Mara argued, heading for the trap door.

"Wait," Elodie pleaded. "Where's Gigandet?" She was going to cry. I could see the desperation in her eyes.

They began shooting at the metal door. "He's out there," I told her, pointing in the direction of the gunshots. "You need to come with us."

Immediately, vigorously, she began shaking her head. "I won't go." She began pushing the fridge away from the freezer. "You all better go now. Because I'm going to unlock this door in a minute," she warned us. I expected Greer to stop her, but he didn't. He was letting her choose for herself. But he hadn't let me choose for myself. "Go on now," she encouraged us. The fridge was out of the way; she was now struggling and straining with the freezer. The gunshots had ceased, but the banging continued.

"I'm not dying today. Are you coming?" Jace demanded, his patience decreasing as his fear increased. Mara had already disappeared into the hole. Sheldon took my hand to help me descend the stairs, the dress and skirt hindering my movements.

Greer grabbed Sheldon's arm and firmly warned him, "We're only going with him for now. We're not staying with him. I will not seek help from rebels."

Sheldon jerked his arm free and declared with anger, "Those *rebels* may be the only ones left to help you."

We were going down into the darkness again, down a flight of stairs into the depths of the earth, into the cool, damp ground—a place where only the dead, not the living, should go.

CHAPTER 15

[LANEY]

There was nothing but the sound of our heavy breathing and feet on the concrete. In unison, our feet thumped, our muscles pumped. One, two, one, two. We'd been running for several minutes. Running in circles, it seemed, with every street and every house looking the same as all the others. It had been hard enough in the daylight to visualize and memorize a mental map of the living quarters; at night, it was impossible. I just kept turning right, then left, then right, then left, trying to get as far away from Muriel's home as possible. We'd not seen or heard the guard—Anderson—following us. Perhaps he had not heard me scream. Perhaps he was too busy cleaning up the mess he'd made—Muriel's body and blood. Perhaps Muriel's neighbors had come to see what had happened to her.

And Curwen. We'd left him behind too. I barely knew him, but viscerally, deep down, I felt he would never have left me behind. Hollister had completely disregarded Curwen. And I had let him; I hadn't fought hard enough. It all had happened so fast. There'd not been enough time to formulate a better plan. *Excuses. Nothing but excuses.*

I couldn't run anymore. My sides ached; my muscles burned. I led us into a dark alleyway between two houses, leaning against one of the walls, gasping for air.

Also trying to catch his breath, Hollister asked, "Are you okay?" His hand was on my shoulder.

I shrugged him off and pushed him away. "Please don't touch me."

He stepped back, his face confused. Even I was confused at the words I'd said. I'd never felt that way toward him before. But *don't touch me* was all I could think.

"You're angry with me," he stated. It wasn't a question; he knew.

"Yes." *And with myself.* "We shouldn't have left the gun behind."

"You're right." He looked at the ground, silent for a long moment, knowing there was nothing that could be said to change anything. His eyes remained downcast. "I'm sorry. I'm sorry that happened, and I'm sorry you had to see it."

I glared at him. "That? That was *murder*. And you didn't see it. You didn't even look to see what was happening!" I shouted in a whisper.

"Because I needed to get us out of there!"

"We could have helped!" I argued. "We could have done *something*."

"No." He shook his head. "There was nothing we could have done. There were two of them. We were lucky to get away the first time. I wasn't going to risk your life again." At the mention of it, I imagined Anderson's hot breath in my ear, the muzzle of the handgun against my skin. I shivered in disgust, shaking the thoughts away. Hollister reached out to pull me into his embrace. I resisted, half-heartedly, wanting comfort but still so angry and too tired to fight it. With his chin resting on my head and his arms wrapped tightly around me, he said, "We can't help anyone if we are arrested or dead."

Excuses. More excuses. The things we'll tell ourselves to justify our actions, to help us sleep at night, to make ourselves feel better.

Where did we go from here? We had to stop the wedding. We had to get Curwen back. We needed help.

"Laney," came a deep whisper. I pulled away from Hollister. Who had said my name? Was it Anderson, still searching for me? Was it foolish to have stopped here?

"Did you hear that?" I asked.

"No." He shook his head. "What did you hear?"

"Someone called my name."

His eyes narrowed as he turned around and searched the area with only a dim, faraway streetlight to help him. He took my arm and led me farther into the alleyway, into the dark shadows of the houses.

"Laney," came the voice again. Louder this time. From the house across the street. The door was open, and someone was standing in the dark doorway. "Get in here," the voice ordered, stepping into the light so I could see his face.

As my feet began walking toward him, Hollister held me back. "It's okay," I said, removing his hand. "It's Durham." *Durham.* How could I tell this stern man, a man I didn't like very much, that his son had been arrested? That Muriel had been executed? Part, most, of me wanted to run away to avoid that conversation, but my feet only obeyed the sound of his voice. My feet were tired, and they wanted to rest. They made the final decision.

As soon as we entered the house, I recognized where we were. It was Sheldon's home; I'd been there twice before. The first time, Sheldon had let me watch the hidden surveillance monitors to see if Hollister was okay in the slave barracks. The second time, we had been searching the system to find out what had happened to Leela and Mara when they tried to rescue my mother. It was the place where I had found out about my mother's death, the place where my father and I had wept in each other's arms. Why was Durham here?

Durham quickly closed and locked the door behind us. He didn't have any lights turned on, but I could see the glow of the computer monitors coming from the secret room inside the kitchen pantry. "Laney, what are you doing here?" he demanded.

"You told me to come inside."

"Not, *here*. I mean, what are you doing in Antonia? Why did you come back?"

"For Leela," I said softly.

He shook his head, annoyed. "Where's Curwen? I saw you three on the monitors. Why are you two by yourself now?" He motioned to

Hollister but did not introduce himself, and Hollister didn't say a word, choosing instead to observe.

I hesitated before asking, "How much did you see on the monitors?"

"Not enough." He sounded frustrated. "I can't figure out how to navigate between the cameras. Sheldon was supposed to teach me."

"When did you see us?" I asked.

He led us into the pantry and pointed at one of the monitors. "Here."

Hollister and I both peered more closely. It was the entry gate, the place where we had first entered the living quarters. He hadn't seen anything that had transpired since then. One of the other monitors was still turned to Hollister's slave barrack—barrack twenty-seven—but it was empty. It should have been full of men—slaves—*bodies*—but there were none. I glanced at Hollister to see if he had noticed it yet. He hadn't. His eyes were squinting at another monitor; I followed his gaze. It was the one with the hospital records, the one that had revealed my mother's status as *deceased*. Her status had been updated—*cremated*. I grabbed the chair in front of me; I had to sit before I fell down. Hollister's hand squeezed my shoulders as he stood behind me.

Durham watched us staring at the screen. "Yes!" He pointed at it. "Why is this important? I have been trying to figure everything out for days, and this still doesn't make sense. Please, tell me everything so I can help get my children back." I'd never heard him plead for anything from anyone; he was always the boss, always demanding. But now his weakness was visible, for a moment at least. "Where's Curwen?" he asked again, more urgently.

"Number 3126 was my mother, and she died three days ago," I said without feeling, like I was simply stating a fact, detaching myself from any emotion. "She, my father, and Hollister," I pointed at him, "were enslaved here. Curwen brought Leela and me here so we could save them and bring them home. What Curwen failed to tell us was that Leela is the one with the mark. So, when our plan failed and we were all arrested, Leela traded herself to Gigandet so all of us could go free. We came back tonight so we could stop the wedding."

We have to stop the wedding. We couldn't be distracted. We couldn't afford to waste anymore time. The night was wearing on—surely the wedding had already taken place. Would Leela die immediately? She was immune to the queen's disease, so how would she die? Would I instinctively know when she was gone? Would I feel it in my twin soul if the one with whom I'd shared a womb no longer had life or breath?

We had to stop the wedding, but I didn't tell him that I should be the bride, that Leela would die if she married Gigandet. Did he already know that? Did he know that part of the legend—that I'm the match of the one with the mark? Gibson knew, so maybe Durham did too. If he did, his face didn't reveal it.

He was stoic; I couldn't read him. Curwen seemed to have kept so much from him. So, how much could I share, *should* I share? How could I stress how urgent it was to stop the wedding without also telling them that I was supposed to take her place? I didn't want to tell him. I didn't want to tell anyone. I didn't want it to be true. Hollister also wasn't offering up the information. *He doesn't want it to be true either.*

"Can you help us stop the wedding?" I asked.

"The wedding has already been stopped," he stated, brushing off my concern. "But tell me, where . . . is . . . Curwen?"

"What do you mean *the wedding has already been stopped*?" I demanded, my eyes narrowed, examining him. Was he telling me that Leela was clear of danger, for the moment at least? Who'd stopped the wedding? What had happened? I wished I had access to Annabelle's drawings right then.

Durham eyed me with suspicion also, both of us waiting for the other one to tell us what we wanted to know. We were holding out on each other. Keeping our secrets. Because we didn't trust each other, not fully. "No, no," he finally said, shaking his head at me. "I've eased your anxiety about Leela. And I'll tell you more. But first, tell me where Curwen is."

I couldn't bring myself to say the words. I was sitting in the same seat Sheldon had been in when he'd turned to my father to deliver the news of my mother's death. He hadn't been able to say the words either, not until my father had ordered him to. It was as though Hollister understood my struggle because, after a long pause, he answered for me. "We went to Muriel's because we'd had a run-in with an armed guard who was trailing us from our dimension, a guard who works for Whirl. The guard showed up at Muriel's. He arrested Curwen. And . . . " He hesitated.

"And what!" Durham demanded. He sounded like my father. *Just say it, son*, my father had said to Sheldon.

"The guard shot and killed Muriel."

Hearing the words out loud caused tears to stream down my cheeks again. It replayed in my mind. The gunshot. Curwen's guttural scream. The blood splatter. Her body falling. I covered my eyes, rubbing hard to make it go away. If I had been blind like Muriel, I wouldn't have seen a thing. Or had she seen it in her vision? Did she know she would lose her life? That question would haunt me forever.

Durham's face remained expressionless, hard to see with only the faint glow from the computer monitors and a dim fluorescent light above the kitchen sink. Whatever emotions he felt at hearing this news were hidden from us; the only change I could detect was an increase in his blinking, perhaps to hold back tears.

Just then, there was a soft knock at the door. My blood ran cold. *Anderson*. He'd found us again. Durham saw the fear on my face. "Stay here," he said, closing the pantry door, shutting us in the tiny closet. My hand reached for Hollister's; he squeezed mine tightly. We held our breaths to listen. Seconds felt like minutes, but we finally heard a woman's voice. It was Phaedra.

"I didn't want to be home alone, knowing what is happening out there," she said. "I knew you'd be here, so I brought some food."

"You shouldn't be out tonight. It's not safe," Durham reprimanded her. He tried to sound harsh, but he was only worried—worried about Phaedra being in danger. And she knew it, so she ignored him, offering him a sandwich instead. She was in the kitchen. I wanted to throw open the pantry door, to throw myself into her mother arms and weep into her shoulder. If Durham didn't reveal our presence soon, I would.

"It's Phaedra," I whispered to Hollister, releasing his hand as my anxiety faded away. It wasn't Anderson.

"We have visitors," Durham announced loudly as he opened the pantry door.

I did exactly what I'd wanted to do; she wasn't able to utter a word before my arms were around her neck and my shoulders heaved with sobs. Her big hand patted and rubbed my back as she soothingly repeated, "Hush, hush, everything will be okay." She couldn't know that. She didn't know what had happened, what was happening. But the sound of her voice, the confidence in it, made me believe what she said. *Everything will be okay.*

Durham cleared his throat, clearly uncomfortable with the emotion. Phaedra pulled back and held my face in her hands, wiping my tears away with her thumbs. She took a deep breath, indicating I should too. "Good," she said, nodding, as I exhaled. "Now, introduce me to this very tall, young man." She smiled up at Hollister as he towered over her. She wouldn't be smiling when she heard the things we had to tell her. I didn't want to tell her.

Swallowing hard, I managed a tight-lipped smile. "This is Hollister," I said, stepping back so he could come forward. He stuck his hand out to shake hers, but she pushed it away and went in for a hug, the way she had hugged Curwen and Sheldon, like a son—a kind of affection I had witnessed nowhere else in Antonia. It was like she was one of the only ones allowed to be so free without fear of consequences. Like Muriel.

"You're very different from Haleh," he said quietly.

Her eyes went wide; she and Durham looked at each other before turning to us with questioning looks. "You know Haleh?" she asked him, her eyes glossed over. It was her time to cry, hopefully happy tears. This was probably the only thing we could tell her that would make her smile.

"We met her and stayed at her house last night," I explained. "She helped us get back here."

She was quiet for a moment before asking, "Is she okay?"

"Oh, yes." I nodded. "She's married to Patrick, and they have two daughters. One of them is named after you." The words flew out of my mouth. Because it was the only good thing I had to tell her, I wanted to share it.

"Sit," she said. "Let's eat, and you can tell me all about it."

I didn't have an appetite. Instead, I felt sick. Sick from the cookies Muriel had served us. No. Not sick from the cookies—sick from the fact that Muriel, who had served them with a beautiful smile, was no longer alive. Had Phaedra known her well? How would she react to the news? I didn't want to find out yet. So, I shared the good news first. Sitting, I was keenly aware that I had chosen the same chair I'd been sitting in when Sheldon had told me about my mother, when he had said the words *I'm sorry, but she's deceased.* Were those the words I should use to tell Phaedra about Muriel?

Avoiding it, we told her about Haleh. We told them about our last three days trying to get back to Antonia. I didn't tell her that Haleh had been angry with her for leaving without saying goodbye. I didn't tell her that Curwen had shared her story with Haleh so her sister would understand why Phaedra had disappeared without a word. I didn't want to bring it up, to embarrass her or hurt her, because it was the one thing she'd never been forthcoming with, the one thing she had previously avoided talking about.

She was most intrigued to hear about her niece, her namesake. We told her all we could from the twelve hours we'd spent with them. And then Durham, who I could tell had been trying hard to be patient and quiet, finally asked, "So, how did she help you get back here?"

"She took us to meet Gibson," I revealed. We—Hollister and I—had had the privilege of meeting the two people that they—Durham and Phaedra—hadn't seen in twenty-five years. Their family. Her twin. His cousin.

"How is he?" Durham asked earnestly.

Hollister and I looked at each other, unsure how to answer.

"He's okay," Hollister offered. "He could be better, but it seems like Haleh and Patrick take care of him." He turned to Phaedra and changed the subject. "Earlier, you said you didn't want to be home alone, knowing what is happening out there. What did you mean? What is happening out there?"

"Chaos," Phaedra said with a sigh.

"Whirl staging his coup," Durham expanded on her words. "Bodies attacking their guards. Guards killing civilians."

"The slaves revolted?" Hollister asked, his eyes wide. He was too late.

"Who have the guards killed?" Phaedra demanded. She didn't want to know.

"He's staging his coup?" I asked, panicked. Was he the one who had stopped the wedding? Where was Leela? Would she end up like Muriel?

He decided to answer me first. "Yes, Whirl has put the city on lockdown and taken his army to attack the palace and stop the wedding. He found out about Leela having the mark. One of my undercover guards let me know about the impending coup this afternoon. Everything has developed very quickly. That's why Gigandet rushed the wedding."

"Is Leela . . . " *Dead*—I couldn't bring myself to say it. "Not alive?"

"She's alive. She got out safely."

My entire body relaxed, the tension dissipating as I let his words wash over me. *She got out safely*.

"But who have the guards killed?" Phaedra demanded again.

"If my reports are correct, Whirl opened fire on the king's guard at the ceremony. And another one, according to Laney and Hollister, killed Muriel and arrested Curwen." He said it like a news report, without feeling, just stating the facts. Phaedra sat in stunned silence for a minute before rising and leaving the room. I was about to follow her, to comfort her, but Durham shook his head at me. "Just give her a few minutes."

Whirl had opened fire during the wedding ceremony. How could Durham be sure Leela was safe?

"The slaves?" Hollister repeated. He wanted news about his men from barrack twenty-seven.

"Yes, there was a barrack of slaves who attacked a group of guards very early this morning. I'm assuming, from your reaction, that was your barrack?"

Hollister nodded. "Yes, I was supposed to be with them, to help them. What happened to them?"

"You couldn't have helped them. Gibson couldn't do it twenty-five years ago, and he knew this place better than anyone. Your friends have all been taken to the scientists' facility."

"That's where the guard said he was taking Curwen too," I offered, remembering Anderson's threat. "We can go there together and get them all back." Hollister was nodding at my suggestion.

"Yes, we can," Durham agreed. "But we need to meet up with Leela first."

I gasped. "You have her?"

"My people have her. They are hiding out right now, but soon we can meet up with them."

She got out safely. She's alive.

CHAPTER 16
[LEELA]

I didn't want to go into the ground again, into the dark. I kept fearing that I would trip over my mother's dead body. But her body was no more; she had been cremated. She was ashes, dust. I kept imagining, like in my nightmare, Whirl's face appearing in front of me, lit up with an evil sneer. He had just been before me, in the grand hall—his eyes had been wild, full of hatred, drunk on power, excited by the fear he created in others, delighted at the life he had carelessly, flawlessly taken.

With each step downward, my legs felt heavier, weighed down by the wedding dress—the one Elodie should have worn—and my eyes burned with unshed tears and images I rapidly blinked away. Tad had been smiling at us, ready to proceed with the vows. Then his body had been crumpled in my lap, my fingers covered in warm blood, and Whirl's face had been crazed with madness. The images flashed before my eyes as I stared into the blackness in front on me. Nothing felt real except Sheldon's hand holding mine, warm flesh and bone—living, not dead.

When Greer closed the trap door behind him, darkness fell upon us. I didn't want to be in the dark again. There was too much darkness in Antonia. Darkness and death. They tried to hide it with the brightness of their sun, the whiteness of their houses. But it was a dark place.

Jace had only a weak flashlight to guide us, and he didn't know how to keep it steady, the small circle of light constantly bouncing around. We walked in silence for several minutes. Greer kept a hand on my shoulder so we wouldn't lose each other; we were a slow-moving human train passing through the tunnel, keeping our ears alert for any sounds not created by us. Whirl's guards had entered the palace through the tunnels. My body shivered, not just from the cold, but from the thought of running into them.

Then, as if my thoughts made it happen, we saw a light ahead in the distance, a lantern like the one Greer had used when he took me to the morgue. To see my dead mother. *Her body, not her.* Were we about to see more dead bodies? Was the person with the lantern a guard? Was he armed? *Please, don't have a gun.*

The lantern was coming toward us; whoever carried it was running in our direction. Jace clicked the flashlight off. "Back up quickly," he ordered. "We just passed a tunnel on the left." We felt our way along the wall until it gave way to the other tunnel; we hid ourselves there, hoping whoever held the lantern wouldn't turn that way and find us huddled there.

The light from the lantern got brighter, closer, and the hurried steps became louder. "Just leave me alone!" he begged. "I did what I was supposed to do!" The voice was familiar. Who was this man, pleading for his life? He was being chased, hunted in the dark. Who was following him? And what had he done?

He was approaching, his footsteps nearer, louder. As he passed us, he looked back, his face twisted in agony, trying to see how close his attacker was. And then his eyes met mine as he saw our group illuminated by his lantern. *Dr. Brandon.* He opened his mouth to say something. He tried to slow the momentum of his body, perhaps to turn and join us in our hiding place, but his feet stumbled. We'd distracted him. Then a shot rang out, reverberating in our ears. Mara immediately stifled a scream by covering her mouth. Dr. Brandon was hit in the back, and he fell to the ground fewer than ten feet away from us. My initial instinct was to go to him, to assess his wounds, but Sheldon stood like a firm wall in front of me, blocking me, and Greer kept me in place, his hands holding my upper arms.

Dr. Brandon had betrayed us to Whirl—that was what Gigandet had said. Dr. Brandon had told Whirl about the mark on my neck and that I was in the king's possession. He had, at least partially, set this entire evening in motion. Several people were dead because he couldn't keep quiet, and how many more lives would be lost? But I took no pleasure in his death, especially if there was a chance he could be saved. I would be a doctor like him, one day—if I survived, if I ever got to go home. They couldn't keep me from helping him. As I went to force my way through, to get to the fallen man, we heard more footsteps approaching. The hunter was coming to examine his kill, to assess his marksmanship.

"Take. Him. Down," I demanded quietly in Sheldon's ear. He nodded his head. Greer must have heard me—or he just had the same idea—because he pushed me behind him as well, stepping forward into position beside Sheldon. Greer tapped Jace on the shoulder; he glanced at them and quickly realized what they were planning. Their fingers were wrapped around the end of the electric batons in their belts. Mara reached for hers as well. All of them had weapons. I didn't.

The guard came into view. The doctor's fallen lantern still lit the scene for us. If he looked to his right, he would see us all. But he was intently focused on Dr. Brandon in front of us, just past where we were hiding. He nudged Dr. Brandon in the side, to see if there was any reaction; when he groaned softly, the guard raised his rifle to shoot again, to finish the job.

Greer gave the signal. All four of them—Greer, Sheldon, Mara, and Jace—attacked the guard with their electric batons. His body convulsed violently from the shock, and his finger pulled the trigger as his knees buckled. The shot was almost deafening. Greer removed his baton from the guard's neck and struck his head with a swift blow, knocking him to the ground. When it was certain that he was unconscious, I rushed forward to check on Dr. Brandon. He had groaned. Maybe he could be saved.

"Leela, don't!" Sheldon tried to grab my arm as I passed him, falling on my knees beside Dr. Brandon.

Sheldon had wanted to spare me. The doctor couldn't be saved. I couldn't help him. The second shot had been fatal. Why had they murdered him? He had given Whirl the information he wanted. Why was his lifeless, blood-soaked body lying before me? Anger welled up in me, and I glared up at Greer, at all of them, and asserted, "You should have gone after him sooner. Before he had the gun aimed. This man didn't have to die."

They accepted my blame in silence, their eyes downcast. I glanced at each of them as I slowly stood up, becoming increasingly aggravated with the dress. Then my eyes fell on the motionless guard. It was the same guard from the king's garden, the one who had arrested me on the day my mother died. The same guard who had kicked me in the ribs and banged my head into a brick wall when *I* was unconscious, the one Greer had said wouldn't go unpunished.

Pointing at the guard, I accused Greer, "You said he wouldn't go unpunished!"

Mara took a closer look at the guard's face in the dim light. "It's the one from the garden," she said, recognizing him. He'd arrested her too.

Greer floundered. "He was punished. He was fired from his duties."

"So, then he just went and joined Whirl's army!" I whispered bitterly, throwing my hands in the air. I bent down and reached for the rifle, gripping the stock and picking it up.

"What are you doing?" Mara cried in fear.

"Taking the gun with us," I declared.

"No. We should leave it here," Jace argued. Everyone else stood around staring at me—I must have looked frightening in the glow of the lantern, my wedding gown and hands stained with blood as I held a weapon they had never held before, a weapon that had just been used to kill several people right in front of them. Trying to persuade me to put it down, he implored, "Please, leave it. We don't know how to use it."

They feared what it was capable of. They feared what they didn't know. "It's okay. I do," I assured him, pulling the bolt handle, ejecting the cartridge, and turning on the safety.

He gasped, and his eyes went wide. Slowly, he asked, "Are you not from Antonia?"

"No." I shook my head. "I'm from Tennessee."

Shocked, he glanced around at the rest of the group, trying to see if he was the only one who hadn't known. Durham hadn't told him everything—perhaps Durham didn't know everything. Sheldon was certain that Durham had been following us that morning, but had he been able to piece it all together, from the moment he met Laney and me until now?

Grabbing the radio and picking up the lantern, Sheldon ordered, "Jace, lead the way."

It felt wrong to leave the doctor behind. Like my mother, he would soon be ashes too.

As we began walking, Greer fell into step beside me. "Remember," he warned me, "it's better if people don't know where you're really from." He didn't like that I'd told Jace the truth.

"It doesn't matter anymore," I said. "I'm not going to be their queen. Their king is dead."

He grabbed my upper arm roughly and growled, "Don't say that." He didn't speak in anger though; he spoke in denial. My words had spoken his fear out loud. His dark eyes pleaded with mine, silently asking me to retract my statement, hoping my words weren't true. I hoped they weren't either. I didn't want to be queen, but I didn't wish their king dead; I took no pleasure in the death of anyone. *But Whirl does. And he has the wounded king in his hands.*

"Okay," I agreed softly, patting Greer's hand until his grip loosened and his shoulders relaxed. He needed someone to believe, to hope, with him. He needed to know that he'd done the right thing by leaving his sovereign behind, by obeying Gigandet; he needed to know that his actions hadn't been in vain. But I couldn't tell him that.

"We're here," Jace announced.

"Where's here?" Mara asked.

Sheldon held the lantern higher, its light revealing a door. Jace unlocked it and pushed it open. "This used to be a rest area for guards when the tunnels were being built," Jace explained as he flipped a switch. The fluorescent lights flickered on, and we all squinted as our eyes adjusted. "Come in quickly." He waved us through, then shut and locked the door behind us.

There were lockers to our right and cots lining the wall to our left. Jace grabbed a blanket from one of them and stuffed it at the bottom of the door we had just entered, ensuring no light would escape into the dark tunnel, alerting others we were there.

"Did you know about this place?" Sheldon asked Greer.

"I've heard about the rest areas, but I've never seen one," he said. "If Durham is your father, why didn't he tell you about it?"

Sheldon shrugged. "It's a need-to-know relationship. And Durham is a man of many secrets."

"Right." Greer rolled his eyes. "Are you sure we're safe here?" he asked Jace.

"Safety is an illusion," he said matter-of-factly. "But this is our best option for now."

Safety is an illusion. He was right. Safety was illusive, not real. It was *elusive*, something that could not be grasped. Not in Antonia. Not for me. Feeling unsafe, *being* unsafe, was normal.

Jace opened one of the gray metal lockers. There were several sets of clothes on hangers, some black guards' uniforms as well as civilian outfits. "Durham had me stock this place with the things we might need," he explained. He pulled out a few of the guards' uniforms, handing them to Mara, Sheldon, and Greer; they were each a perfect fit.

"How did Durham know . . . ?" I began.

"I told you he was watching us this morning," Sheldon softly reminded me.

"He told me to have two sets of civilian clothing, though. One's for you," Jace said, pointing at me. "But there was supposed to be another woman with you. . . . "

Henley. My stomach dropped, and I felt instantly sick. I had to sit down on the bench to keep from falling over. In the chaos, I hadn't thought of her. We'd left her behind. Had she been captured or . . . killed? I didn't like her, but I would never want her dead. I took no pleasure in the death of anyone.

I tried to remember the last time I'd seen her. After the photographer had finished taking my pictures. She'd instructed me on where to stand and had reminded me about the vows. But when I'd scanned the grand hall, before the shot rang out—the shot that killed Tad—I couldn't remember seeing her. She should have been nearby; she should have come with us when we ran. *Where was she? Where* is *she?*

Sheldon squeezed my shoulder. "It's okay. Breathe."

"She's okay. I'm sure of it," Mara said firmly, attempting to convince herself. She *did* like Henley. They had clicked and could have become good friends. They were the same, with hard exteriors protecting their soft spots, refusing to be vulnerable, using sarcasm to keep people at a distance, letting you in for a second and then quickly shutting the door.

This time, Greer put a hand on her shoulder. "I'm sure you're right. She is okay. She's a fighter. She knows the palace well and has probably found a good place to hide."

Was he right? *Please, let it be so.*

Jace handed me one set of clothes—some khaki pants and a cream blouse. "There's a bathroom with showers through that door there," he said, pointing to a doorway in the rear on the right. "Oh, I almost forgot," he added, reaching to pull something else from the locker. "Durham wants you to color your hair." He held the hair color box in the air—dark brown. It was from my dimension; he'd probably bought it at the black market. "You're too noticeable with blond hair. We won't be able to smuggle you out of here."

"You're not smuggling her anywhere," Greer contended, staring Jace down and tossing a sideeye at Sheldon.

Before it could escalate into an argument, I snatched the box from Jace, and I set the rifle in the corner, warning the guys not to touch it. Mara followed me into the bathroom. I didn't need any assistance applying the hair color; I'd helped my mother cover her grays many times, even though I had never dyed my own hair. It'd been tempting though, sometimes, when I had wanted to look different than Laney, to declare my own identity separate from her. But I could never bring myself to do it, to follow through. Now, it was necessary.

After the events of that night, I was altogether a new person. There was no going back.

The water ran black as I washed my hair. Even though it was only seconds, it felt like forever before the water flowed clear, pure. The blood was gone from my hands too. I marveled at the way the water could make things clean. Only the physical, though. It couldn't cleanse my mind, heart, or soul.

Mara found a comb and gently brushed through my tangled hair. My dark hair.

"It's not too bad," she said, her way of giving a compliment. "It makes your blue eyes stand out."

My eyes, my blue eyes, observed her in the mirror. Her thick waves of black hair were gone; Whirl had taken them from her and left her with razor cuts on a bare scalp. But she didn't need hair to be beautiful. Her dark, almond-shaped eyes glanced up and caught mine, glaring at me until I looked away. She wouldn't be pitied. She wouldn't be vulnerable. When she finished, I turned around. "Do you remember the codes to unlock the shock collar?" I asked.

"Of course."

"Tell them to me, so I can take yours off."

She hesitated. "Greer won't like that."

I examined her. "Are you abandoning me or our mission?"

"What's our mission?"

We stared at each other for a long moment before saying it at the same time: "*Whirl.*"

"Now tell me the codes," I demanded, pulling her shirt collar down so I could get to the tiny buttons on the shock collar. After I input the final numbers, we both held our breaths until we heard a beep and it clicked open. I pulled it off and set it on the counter. "There. That's better."

She smiled, rubbing her neck. "I didn't think the codes would be the same."

I rolled my eyes. "Yeah, there's a lot of incompetence around here."

Entering the locker room, I quietly closed the door behind me when I saw Greer was asleep on a cot.

Jace was sitting on one, continuing to eye the rifle in the corner; he didn't feel safe with it there. But *safety is an illusion*. He had been raised to fear guns—having one in your possession was treason. No. Antonians liked to maintain control and inflict punishment in a clean way with electric batons, stun guns, and shock collars—things that would cause no damage, no mess, no blood. Until now. Until Whirl.

Grabbing a blanket from an empty cot and wrapping it around me, I went to the front, where Sheldon was sitting guard.

"Hey," he whispered when he saw me. I sat on the bench beside him, our backs leaning on the wall. Without explaining to him what I was doing, I began inputting the codes into his shock collar, setting him free. His hand reached up to stop me, but I shook my head at him.

"You're not wearing this anymore," I said firmly.

It beeped and clicked open. I pulled it off and handed it to him.

"Thank you," he said, his mouth against my ear. "You should try to get some rest."

Pulling away, I looked him in the eyes and nodded. Then I found a cot in the farthest corner to curl up on.

But I wouldn't get any sleep that night. I couldn't close my eyes without seeing dead men.

• • •

"Leela, stop it." Someone was shaking me. My head felt groggy, and I couldn't fathom how I'd actually fallen asleep—a fitful sleep, though, with my brain trying to process. Peering through my eyelashes, I saw Mara on the cot beside me, her arm outstretched, touching my shoulder. "You're talking in your sleep. You're keeping me awake," she complained.

"So sorry to inconvenience you," I muttered. Annoyed and glaring at her, I rolled over, away from her, to face the concrete wall, placing my palm against its cool, rough surface, the cot creaking beneath me. My fingers danced across the wall, tracing all the ridges. We were sleeping in a concrete box beneath the ground, like a catacomb under the city. Buried alive. How much longer would we be alive? If they found us, if this place wasn't as secret as Jace suggested, we would be at their mercy. *They don't have mercy*. Whirl wouldn't let us live.

I tried to imagine what was happening out there. Were they frantically searching for us, or were they too consumed with clearing away the bloody mess they'd created? Had the guard regained consciousness and reported Dr. Brandon's body yet? Was Gigandet still alive? How was Whirl going to spin the story when he revealed it to the Antonian people? What would he tell them, and how would he justify his actions? Would they follow him? Or would there be more bloodshed to suppress them?

Greer should have purchased those guns from Yadriel at the black market when he'd had the chance. He should have forced the issue. Searching for the Ancient Ones had distracted us from the real danger; while we were trying to preserve the love between Gigandet and Elodie, we should have been preserving our lives. Gigandet should never have allowed Whirl so much freedom and power. He'd underestimated him. He'd turned out to be a weak monarch, too disconnected from what was happening in his own land.

Now, we were all paying for it. Like a family suffers when a father fails to lead well.

I turned to my back, unable to get comfortable on the cot, and stared up at the dim, flickering, fluorescent lights. The dark-green blanket was scratchy and thin as paper. Who had used it before me? Who had rested on these cots? Jace said this was a rest area for the guards, but had the *bodies* ever been allowed to rest here, to take a break from their hard labor? *No.* I knew the answer was no. *We are weary and find no rest*, I imagined their voices crying out, lamenting. Like my mother—she'd been weary, so weary, but she did find rest, eternal rest.

Everyone else was sleeping; I could hear their steady breathing. Jace had taken Sheldon's place near the door, his turn to be on watch. But his head was hanging to one side, leaning against the wall; he'd fallen asleep on guard duty. It might have been comical if it weren't so sad that he, a young man of barely eighteen years, was our first line of defense. How many young lives had Durham acquired for his purposes? Was Jace another one of the orphans he'd collected? Just then, the phone in his pocket started ringing and buzzing; it startled him awake, which almost made me laugh out loud as he jumped up, struggling to get the phone out of his vest. I sat up, and my ears perked up, intent on listening. But I couldn't hear anything—he was too far away and spoke too softly.

When he flipped his phone shut—it was a brief conversation—he looked in my direction and saw that I was awake. He motioned for me to come forward. I stood slowly, unsure what he wanted with me, especially with everyone else still unconscious. Walking past the cots, past Mara, then Sheldon, then Greer, I couldn't understand how they hadn't been disturbed by the phone ringing. My sleep-talking had prevented Mara from falling asleep, but once she had drifted off, no sound could wake her. Like when we were in the prison cell together, she'd never woken up when I left with Whirl. I felt abandoned by them as I took my final steps toward Jace.

"Who was that on the phone?" I asked quietly.

“Durham. He wants us to meet up with him as soon as possible. I need to check the tunnels, to see if it’s safe for us to go now.”

“Safety is an illusion,” I reminded him of his own words.

He smirked. “Well, I need to find out what kind of activity is happening out there. Are you good to sit guard, or do you want me to wake up Greer? You have the gun. . . . ”

“You should take it with you,” I said, lifting it and holding it out to him.

He raised his hands and stepped back. “No.” He shook his head. “I don’t know how to use it, and I don’t want to kill anyone.” He shook his head again, emphatically.

“Okay.” I returned the it to the corner. “Yes. I’m good to sit guard.”

“Good. Don’t open the door for anyone. I’ve got a key. And please don’t shoot me when I get back.” He smiled like he was joking, but there was still trepidation in his eyes as he glanced at the rifle.

“What if . . . ” I hated to say it, hesitated to ask it. “What if you don’t come back?”

My question didn’t faze him, though; he was used to planning for the what-ifs. “There’s a map of the tunnel system in that locker.” He nodded at one behind me. “There’s also a good supply of food in the cabinets and fridge to last for a couple weeks.” My face must have expressed the dread I felt at the prospect of being stuck there for two weeks because he quickly added, with confidence, “But I will be back.” He peeked his head out the door to make sure it was clear before slipping through. He was gone. I replaced the blanket at the bottom of the door, to keep the light from seeping into the darkness, revealing our location to our enemies. Alone. Silence except for the hum of electricity to the lights and the tick of the wall clock. Two in the morning—I’d slept for almost three hours, minus the amount of time it took me to doze off. Sitting on the bench, my head leaning against the cold, hard wall, I stared at the clock, ticking away the seconds, wondering how long it would be until he returned . . . or how long we should wait if he didn’t return.

The map of the tunnels—I decided to pull it out, to study it, to memorize it. The locker door squeaked open, but none of my companions budged from their sleep. Antonians slept too hard, as if there weren't a million reasons for them to be alert, on edge, restless. Spreading the map on the floor, my eyes went wide, amazed at how extensive the tunnel system was. It took a while to find our location because it wasn't marked. We weren't far from the hospital, even though it had felt like we had been traveling in the opposite direction earlier that evening. Perhaps Dr. Brandon had been coming from the hospital. Perhaps, with regrets, he thought he would try to warn us before it was too late. Perhaps that's why they killed him.

The minutes felt like hours until I heard the key in the latch. Finally, Jace was back. Or was he? I grabbed the rifle just in case. He had to push hard against the door because of the blanket stuffed at the bottom, but before entering, he immediately whispered, "It's me. Don't shoot."

Lowering the gun, I waited for him to slip inside and close the door behind him. "What took so long!" I exclaimed, relief washing over me. But Jace didn't look okay. "What's wrong?"

He shook his head. "I ran into a couple guards. They made me help carry that man's body to the hospital."

"That man? You mean Dr. Brandon?"

"You *knew* him?" His eyes went wide. I nodded. "Well, he's being cremated. They're hiding the evidence."

I sighed. How would the people really know what happened here tonight unless we told them? We had to get out, to get the truth out.

"So, is it clear for us to leave?" I asked.

"Yes, we need to go now. Whirl is having a victory rally in the palace courtyard, and all the guards, with the exception of a few, are required to attend. They tried to get me to go, but I slipped out of the morgue when they weren't looking."

"Did they say what happened to Gigandet? Is he alive?" I desperately wanted to know.

"They didn't say. I didn't ask. I didn't want to raise their suspicions. Time to go, though; it's our best opportunity." We stared at our team, jealous of their undisturbed sleep. He grinned mischievously at me and then ran down the line, shaking all of their feet, yelling, "Wake up! Wake up!" All three of them shot up, ready for a fight. "Come on, we need to go now," he repeated to all of them.

After they'd had a minute to wake up, Jace explained everything to them, everything he'd just told me. I folded the map back up and tucked it into my waistband; it would be useful for something. Jace opened one of the lockers, and I saw the blood-stained wedding dress hanging inside, stuffed inside. He grabbed a couple of backpacks and handed them to Mara and Sheldon so they could fill them with food and drink supplies. Greer appeared unsure; he had to do exactly what he didn't want to do—rely on the *rebels* for help. He was going to meet the leader of the rebels. How much did he actually know about the resistance? Gigandet had been unaware of the extent of Whirl's actions, so I assumed he was oblivious to Durham's also.

Five minutes later, we were in the dark again, following Jace's tiny, faint orb of light. I hated it. It was like being blind, only seeing blackness. We felt our way along as before, but this time, we didn't run into any of Whirl's soldiers. His army was celebrating. Would his party be loud enough for the sleeping city to hear? Would the people awake from their dreams to discover the nightmare, their new reality? We had to, somehow, ensure that Whirl's victory was short-lived. But how? Did Durham have a plan for this, a way for the resistance to restore peace and order? It was the only thought that offered me any hope. Mara and I had agreed Whirl was our mission.

After making a couple of turns, suddenly a light appeared in the darkness. There was a doorway far in front of us, on the right. What if somebody saw us? But Jace did not stop or show any alarm; instead, he headed straight for it. He stopped before it and peeked inside to see if the coast was clear, and then he ushered us past it. I recognized where we were—the basement of the hospital, the morgue. This was where I had seen my mother. This was where Jace had brought the doctor. Only their bodies, though—not them.

“This is where I leave you,” Jace said.

“You're leaving us?” I asked. “Why?”

“Yes. I will exit through the hospital. I've completed my part of the mission. You cannot risk being seen, though, so the rest of you need to continue to the end of this tunnel, then turn right and take that to the end. You'll come to an opening, to a metal gate. Durham should be waiting for you there.”

I visualized his directions; if we followed them, we would end up outside of the city, according to the map now etched in my mind. We all—even Greer—shook hands with Jace, thanking him for his help. When we heard distant voices coming from inside the hospital, Jace gave Sheldon his flashlight and urged us to go, to hurry away.

It wasn't much farther, and thankfully, it was uneventful. After we turned right, I could see the sky—a deep velvet blue with uncountable, glowing stars—at the end of the second tunnel. It really did open up; I was going to escape from this concrete coffin, to breathe fresh air. I couldn't stop myself from running, passing all of my companions. They called for me to slow down, but I wouldn't, I couldn't. I was swimming for the surface, my lungs burning for oxygen. They caught up with me, Sheldon beside me with Greer and Mara on our heels.

But then I slowed down several yards away. There were three silhouettes outside the gate, three figures waiting in the dark for us, illuminated by the moonlight. If one of them was Durham, he wasn't alone. But what if they were Whirl's guards, ready to capture us? One of them was very tall, intimidating. We walked the final distance, cautiously.

"Who's there?" Sheldon called out, shining the flashlight at them.

"Son, what took you so long?” It was Durham. There was an audible sigh of relief from three of us—Greer was still not onboard with this plan.

"Leela! Are you okay?" a voice cried. My own voice. Laney's voice. Why was she here? That meant the tall man was Hollister. Why were they both here? I wanted to be glad, but my cheeks flushed hot with anger. I had done all of this, been through all of this, so they could go home. What were they doing here?

"Why are you here!" I demanded when we reached the gate. "Why did you come back here?" They should have been home with Corey and Annabelle. That was what they should have been taking care of; my siblings and my father were their responsibility now.

"We came back for you!" she yelled defensively.

"You shouldn't have." We stared at each other through the metal bars, waiting for somebody to open it. Greer pushed me to the side so he could access the keypad.

"Wait." Durham warned him, "Don't use your codes. Then they'll track you in the system."

Greer stopped, clearly annoyed, and asked, "Then whose codes would you like me to use?"

"Jace's," Durham replied, unfazed by Greer's attitude.

"He didn't give us any codes!" I panicked, beginning to fear I would remain trapped in the tunnels.

But Durham's voice remained calm, steady. "What did he give you?"

"Only this," Sheldon said, shining the flashlight in their faces again.

"There it is," Durham said. "Look at the light." Sheldon held it up for us to see; Jace had glued a piece of paper over the lens, a piece of paper that contained the access codes. That explained why the light had been so dim. Sheldon called the numbers out so Greer could enter them. The gate finally beeped open, and I rushed through first.

Laney threw her arms around my neck, tears instantly falling from her eyes. I couldn't muster any of my own, though. The expression of her emotions made me contain mine. That was how it'd always been. One of us—usually me—had to be in control so the other could fall apart. She finally pulled away and looked at me. "Your hair," she whispered, grabbing it in her hands. "Did Gigandet make you color it?"

"No, I did," Durham answered. "For her protection. And I would have done the same with you if we'd had the supplies and the time." She grimaced at him as I shook her hands away from me and stepped back. Hollister squeezed my shoulder and gave me a wink.

Durham had just been reunited with Sheldon and Mara, the children he'd raised, but he didn't show them any affection. Only his eyes and a handshake revealed that he was relieved to see them again. Sheldon introduced Greer to everyone, and Laney introduced Hollister.

Then Sheldon surveyed the group. "Where's Curwen?" he asked, suspicious and concerned. Where was his brother, his best friend? I glanced at Mara to see her face was painted with worry. Where was the man she loved?

"He's been arrested," Durham explained. "We need to go to the scientists' facility to get him."

"No," Greer protested. "You can go to the scientists, but we've been ordered to keep Leela safe."

"What's your plan for her safety then?" Durham challenged him, the older man testing the younger. Greer remained silent, but I couldn't tell if it was because he didn't have a plan or if he just didn't want to share it with the leader of the resistance. "Everyone in favor of going to the scientists?" Durham asked for a vote. All of us except Greer raised our hands. Greer shook his head in defeat, hating that he was getting sucked into something, but knowing that he wouldn't be able to protect me by himself. He needed the rebels' help; his pride and his loyalty despised that.

Durham was pleased. "Good. Besides, we need to protect both of them. Whirl has his guards searching for Laney now too."

"Why?" many of us asked at the same time.

"Not sure." He shrugged. Then, pointing at the rifle tucked under my arm, he said, "I see you have a gun."

"Yes, Leela lifted it from one of the guards," Sheldon explained.

"After he murdered someone," I added.

Durham nodded. "Good. It will be helpful."

I looked questioningly at him and then asserted, "The safety is on. We're not shooting anyone . . . "

" . . . Just scaring them," Laney finished my sentence and smiled at me because we sounded like Corey.

"Maybe after we get Curwen, we can look around the place for the Ancient One," Mara suggested, still holding onto the idea that we could break the curse. It couldn't be broken *if the king was dead*. I didn't say that out loud though, not wanting to disturb Greer again. Laney and Hollister looked curious about the Ancient One, but nobody responded to her, almost as if they didn't take what she said very seriously or consider it a worthwhile plan. She was back at the bottom of the chain of command; she and Henley got to lead their own expedition yesterday, but now it was time to follow orders again.

"Who's been to the scientists before?" Durham asked, looking at Greer expectantly.

But he shook his head. "Not me. Wasn't my jurisdiction."

"So, we're going in blind," Durham concluded.

"No." Hollister stepped forward. "I've been there. I'll take the lead."

CHAPTER 17

[LANEY]

Leela was angry with me for returning. She'd get over it. I was too relieved to see that she was okay, that she hadn't married Gigandet, that she hadn't died, to care about her attitude. She could have an attitude—it meant she was alive. I fell into step beside her. Durham and Hollister in the lead, Sheldon in front of us, and Mara and Greer behind. We were outside the city walls, whitewashed walls that towered high above us. Durham said there were usually guards on the walls, but we couldn't see any tonight. The city was quiet; all the activity was taking place up the hill, at the palace. In the distance behind us, it was lit up with lights.

"What happened in there?" I asked Leela when I saw her looking back at it.

"Whirl's army invaded the palace just before the ceremony." She paused. "I don't know how many he killed. We didn't stay to find out. Gigandet underestimated Whirl."

"Did he kill Gigandet?"

"He got shot by one of the guards, but I don't know if it was critical." After another pause, she asked, "Why did you come back here, Laney?"

"Because I couldn't let you marry Gigandet."

"That was *my* choice," she argued. "Who will take care of Corey and Annabelle? Are they okay?"

"Their father," I replied. "And it was *my* choice to come back here." There was barely any light—just the stars and the moon and the occasional spot light shining in our direction—but I could see her face was defeated. We'd both seen death tonight. "Corey and Annabelle are okay. Dad's taking care of them. Well, Phaedra's sister is taking care of Corey at the moment." She gave me a questioning look, and I filled her in on almost everything that had happened in our dimension on our journey to get back to her. Almost everything. But not Gibson's revelation. I didn't want anyone else to hear it—at least, that's the reason I gave myself.

We remained against the wall, walking toward the warehouses, the woods, the fields—places I had been before. I imagined the barracks must have been beyond the fields; they wouldn't allow the *bodies*, the slaves, to live too close to the city. The scientists must have been located near the barracks, near their test subjects. I had gathered that there were three goals for our journey to the science facility. One: rescue Curwen. Two: rescue the men from barrack twenty-seven—although this one was still a secret between me and Hollister. Now that Leela was by my side, I could pay some mind to Hollister's main mission. And three—the one I was most confused about—searching for an *Ancient One.*

Venturing to ask my twin another question, I whispered, "Who is the Ancient One?"

"I think he's just some really wise old man," she said. "But Mara thinks he knows how to break the curse without me having to marry Gigandet."

"At this point, I don't care about the curse. Let them all get sick and die," I said. "Then they can't enslave or kill anyone else." Even as the words came out of my mouth, I knew how heartless they sounded. I immediately regretted them even though I was filled with so much rage by what had been done to Muriel.

"You don't mean that," Leela said softly. "What about Curwen, Sheldon, Mara? Phaedra, and Muriel?"

Muriel. She had never met Muriel; I'd only told her about the sweet, old woman. I hesitated, my eyes on the ground, before saying, "Muriel is already dead. *They* killed her. And arrested Curwen."

I told her everything that had happened in *this* dimension since we'd returned. Her only response was to sigh heavily, like someone carrying a huge weight in her chest. It was clear she desired silence. She always did want the opposite of me; I just wanted to talk about every single detail—except Gibson's revelation—since we'd been apart, to ask her a million questions. I didn't get an option, though—Durham told us to be quiet as we approached the end of the wall. We now had to run across the field of tall grass and wildflowers between the city and the woods without being caught by the spotlights from the guard towers. Were the guard towers unmanned as well, like the walls? Were they attending Whirl's victory rally?

"Stay low," Durham instructed us. "When the lights approach, crouch down and be still." Hollister and Sheldon dropped back with us, allowing Durham to take the lead on this part. Curwen had taken me across this way in broad daylight, in the scorching sun, and he had instructed me to walk tall, like I belonged there, so the guards wouldn't question us. This time, we were bent low, in the dark, in hiding. We didn't belong there.

But except for a spider web in my face, we made it through without incident. We'd reached the trees. Being in the woods felt like home. We remained just off the dirt path, the same way Curwen had taken me before, but this time we followed the path to the right rather than the left. It was so silent, so still. Whirl was so stupid to leave all the posts unguarded for the sake of his celebration. He thought by putting the city on lockdown nothing could happen. Gigandet may have underestimated him, as Leela had said earlier, but Whirl had also underestimated us. He'd only sent one guard to track us down, my confident inner voice boasted. *But that one guard killed Muriel*, whispered my doubting voice.

I could hear the rush of water as we approached the river, the river I'd only seen from a distance, winding its way down from the purple mountains. Crouched behind a fallen log, we peeked out at a long, narrow bridge. At the far end was a guard house, shining a yellow glow, and inside, there was a lonely guard.

"I got this," Greer said, standing and walking out onto the path before any of us could protest. It took the guard a moment before he noticed Greer's dark figure walking across the bridge; he probably heard his footsteps before he saw him. My heart was pounding in my ears, but all of my companions looked ready to attack. Even Leela, who'd said we wouldn't shoot anyone, quickly had the rifle resting on the log, aimed and ready to fire.

The guard came out of his tower and approached Greer cautiously, but I couldn't hear the words they were exchanging. They spoke for a moment before the guard turned to reenter the tower; Greer took this opportunity, with the guard's back turned, to put his stun gun to the guard's neck and hold it there, catching the guard's body as he slowly sunk to the ground. Sheldon and Mara jumped up and ran toward them. The guard was not unconscious—I could hear him yelling words of protest—but he had been stunned into submission. Greer and Sheldon handcuffed him to the bridge while Mara found something—a bag—in the guard tower to put over his head, so he couldn't see us. They waved us forward. How quickly it'd happened; I was stunned in place too.

"Let's go," Durham said to us. Leela switched the safety back on before tucking the gun under her arm again. Hollister grabbed my arm and helped me rise from the ground. Then he took my hand as we ran across the bridge, our boots pounding across it like thunder. The guard was furious and continued to flail around in rage and shout threats into the air through the cloth bag. Durham stopped to crouch down in front of him. Reaching into the guard's pocket, he pulled out his access card and held it up for someone to grab; Leela took it. He also removed the radio from the guard's shoulder. The guard kept shouting for help, so Durham slapped his cheeks through the bag—

slap and then backslap. "Be quiet," Durham ordered, but the guard refused. "Be quiet." Durham gave him another chance.

The guard threatened, "You won't get away with this," before continuing to scream for help. But the rush of the water beneath us drowned him out. Quickly, Durham formed a fist and socked him hard in the face, knocking his head back so it hit the bridge railing. Leela and I both scrunched our eyes shut, recoiling from the sounds—fist to face, head to metal. *Now* the guard was unconscious.

"Was that necessary?" Greer demanded.

"This *is* life and death, right?" Durham asked, allowing us to draw our own conclusions about his actions and not caring about our opinions either way.

On the other side of the bridge were more woods. We veered off the path again, keeping to the right, keeping ourselves hidden among the trees. I assumed both areas—the slave barracks to the left and the science facility to the right—would be more heavily guarded than the rest of Antonia. Whirl had to protect his assets. Hollister was leading us to the place where he'd been tortured, or at least that's what I imagined had happened when they'd taken him there in the middle of the night. He had never given me any details; I had never asked, afraid to hear, but also not wanting to press him, to force him to talk about things he didn't want to relive. Perhaps I imagined it worse than it was. Perhaps it would be better if he just told me. Now, I would see for myself.

We didn't have much farther to travel. I could see lights up ahead through the branches. Finally, the trees opened up to a clearing, but we remained hidden behind them, crouched in the grass, observing the place—this place we'd heard so much about but had never seen. In the center of the clearing was a two-story building unlike any I'd seen in Antonia. It wasn't bright white, but instead a gray stone without any windows, like a large concrete block. It reminded me of an old prison or mental institution tucked away in the woods. Two massive stadium lights, one on each side of the building, taller than most of the surrounding trees, lit up the area with their intense beams. Large white signs with red letters read: *RESTRICTED. DO NOT ENTER.* I couldn't imagine anyone would *want* to enter.

To my surprise, there were only two guards patrolling the front façade. They appeared to just be hanging out with each other on the steps, joking and laughing, not on guard, not concerned about doing their jobs. The door behind them was metal with only a small sliver of glass to see inside—not that I could see inside from such a distance. It was a distance I knew Hollister was comfortable with—if he wanted to, if we were going to shoot people, he could hit each of them with perfect aim. But *we're not shooting anyone.*

"They don't have guns," I pointed out.

"Whirl doesn't have enough for his entire army," Durham guessed.

Greer quipped, "He will when he gets the ones from the black market."

"Oh, he won't be getting those." Durham smiled smugly. "I had a talk with Yadriel after you left him." I didn't understand what they were talking about, but Greer looked stunned *and* impressed.

"You've really never been here?" Leela whispered to Greer.

"No," he replied. "Why would I come here?" He nodded at Hollister. "Why has *he* been here?"

"Because I was a disobedient *body*," Hollister stated bluntly without glancing at any of us; he continued to assess the situation in front of us. A look of understanding washed over Greer's face—it seemed he hadn't realized Hollister was a former slave.

"So, tell us what you know about the place," Durham prompted him. Hollister hesitated. These were the things he was supposed to tell the men in his barrack, the things that could help them escape. Would he tell us everything or only as much as we needed to know?

"Here's the thing about this place," Hollister began. "You'd think it's heavily protected, but—there are no guards inside. They assume the fear of the disease will keep people away. The guards only enter the lobby when absolutely necessary. They don't want to risk being infected. If they are ordered to go to other areas, they must wear biohazard suits."

“What about the scientists?” Mara asked. “They can get infected too.”

“They always wear biohazard suits,” he said. “At least the ones that I saw.” He’d seen the scientists. What had they done to him? I would have to ask him when we were alone.

After a long moment, Leela concluded, “So only Hollister, Laney, and I can go inside. We’re the only ones immune.”

“No. We can *at least* go into the lobby,” Sheldon argued. “You’re not going in alone.”

“No, I think Leela is right,” Durham countered with authority. “A large group would be too conspicuous. The four of us can cause a distraction, to draw the guards away from the entrance. Take this.” He handed Leela the radio he’d stolen from the guard. “And Sheldon and Greer, give them your stun guns.”

Greer seemed like he wanted to protest as he handed his weapon to me. He gave in and asked, “Why are we doing this—risking so much for Curwen? He’s a criminal, and he shouldn’t even be here. He’s been banished.”

Everybody answered him at once.

“He’s my son.”

“He’s my brother.”

“He’s my friend.”

“He’s risked it all for us.”

Finally, Leela asked him, “What were you willing to do for your family? For your niece and nephew? You were willing to force me into marriage. Well, *this* is what we’re willing to do for someone *we* care about. You may call him a criminal, but he is so much more than that.” He didn’t respond; she had silenced him.

Hollister seized the moment to take the lead. “Y’all need to circle around to the other side.” He pointed across the way. “Then do something to draw the guards’ attention so we can sneak in the front door.”

Durham snickered under his breath. I couldn’t help but smile also because I knew what he was thinking; I’d seen what he’d packed in his backpack—a box of firecracker poppers, which I now assumed he'd purchased at the black market. "Once they realize you're inside, you'll probably only have twenty minutes before more guards arrive. So be quick, and meet us in the woods around back when you've completed the mission," Durham ordered.

What about Hollister's secret mission? Would he attempt to find and free all the men from his barrack? Would Durham be surprised by the amount of men we returned with, if we were successful? Where would we go from here? The thought almost made me panic, but I couldn't. *Focus on what's in front of you*, I heard my mother say.

Durham led his three soldiers away, two of them used to following his orders, but Greer seemed to resent it. They had to circle all the way around the building, staying in the tree line, remaining hidden. Hollister, Leela, and I followed them for a short distance, wanting to be closer to the side of the building so we could run and hide against it until it was clear to enter the front door. We stopped at the right spot, and the other four continued on without us. Only Sheldon glanced back to give Leela an encouraging nod.

But I wasn't encouraged. As we waited in the underbrush for the right moment, both of them could tell I was beginning to panic, my breathing becoming rapid. The length between us and the building seemed too great, too lit up, too visible. What if the guards *were* armed with handguns we couldn't see, like the guard who'd held me at gunpoint, who'd shot Muriel? Leela grabbed both of my arms, forcing me to turn and look at her. "Just pretend we're running the bases," she instructed me. "One base at a time. Right now, we've just gotta get to first. We've got this. We're the fastest runners on the team, remember?"

I nodded. Yes. This was our softball field lit up by the stadium lights. *We just gotta get to first.*

"Ready?" Hollister asked. "Go." We ran across the patchy grass in a single file line, our feet light and nimble, executing our stealth mission. When I felt the hard stone against my back, leaning against the building, I exhaled in relief. We were near the corner; Hollister peeked around to observe the guards, but I pulled him back.

"Don't do that," I ordered. "Just wait for the firecrackers."

"Firecrackers?" Leela asked.

"Yes. Durham has some in his bag. It will be a great distraction."

"Ooooh. The black market," Leela said, understanding. "I remember seeing them there."

We could hear the guards speaking now, only periodically being able to make out their words. Mostly, they seemed to be complaining that they weren't invited to Whirl's rally. It felt like we stood there for an hour, sweating beneath the stadium lights, but it couldn't have been more than five minutes before we heard the firecrackers begin to pop. It did take forever for the guards to react, though—neither of them wanted to investigate, both of them scared, unsure if that was what gunshots sounded like. But as the noises continued, their fear of Whirl—what he would do to them if they let something happen—overcame any other fears, and they both headed toward the woods on the opposite side.

"It's clear," Hollister said. "Let's go."

"Second base," Leela whispered. We took off running. It wasn't more than fifteen yards to the side steps. One, two, three, up the concrete steps to the front entrance. Hollister tried the door; it was locked. "Here," Leela said. She was out of breath and fumbling with the access card in her fingers. She slid it through the card slot, the door beeped, and we slipped inside. *Too easy*.

The lobby—more like a foyer—was a small rectangle the size of a large elevator with slate gray tile and white walls. In front of us was another set of double doors. Above those doors was a security monitor; it showed the front entrance. "There are cameras," I pointed out the obvious.

"There've been cameras everywhere," Leela said. "Didn't you notice them? I'm sure they know we're here. Let's hurry."

She tugged on the next door. It was also locked. She slid the access key through. A warning popped up on the screen next to the door. It asked, *Are all persons properly attired in biohazard suits?* Leela clicked *yes*. The door beeped, and Hollister pulled it open for us.

Now we were in a proper lobby with a small fountain and two benches in the center. The tile flooring had an intricate design, as did the wallpaper—a busy and dizzying room. There were four sets of double doors, two sets on each side, two toward the front and two toward the rear.

"Since Curwen was brought in a few hours ago, he's probably that way," Hollister said, pointing to the set of double doors on the front right and a sign that said *INTAKE*. Leela and I headed in that direction, but Hollister didn't follow.

"Aren't you coming?" I prompted him.

He shook his head. "I'm going to find Rick."

"What's are you talking about?" Leela demanded. "We don't have time to change the plan now." But there hadn't been a change in plan —she just didn't know the whole plan.

To save time, I blurted, "Rick Stover is here, along with the rest of the men from Hollister's barrack—"

"The ones who are still alive," Hollister interjected.

"Yes," I continued, "and we need to see if we can help them too. Not just Curwen."

"Okay," Leela immediately agreed. She, without question, valued their lives equally. She would have made a good queen—if it wouldn't have killed her. "Y'all do that," she ordered. "I'll find Curwen. Meet back here in ten." I was going to ask if she was sure, if she felt comfortable splitting up, but she disappeared behind the double doors before I could get the words out of my mouth. What if I never saw her again? Our lives seemed to be a constant potential last moment. That's what every second was—*a potential last moment*. Any minute could have been the end.

Hollister grabbed my hand, pulling me toward the doors on the rear left; a sign indicated that we were headed to the laboratory. "Is this where they took you before?" I asked, glancing up at his side profile. His jaw tightened, and he gave a slight nod; he didn't want to talk about it. I would see soon enough.

CHAPTER 18

[L E E L A]

The door closed softly behind me as I held the handle so it wouldn't slam. It felt like Antonia again; everything was bright white—the walls, the floors, the lights. A sterile environment for such dirty work. The hallway was quiet, no one in sight, no doors or windows. At the end, I could only turn left; I paused at the corner to see if it was clear. That's when I saw third base.

Down the next hallway, there was a large plexiglass window in the middle of the wall. Through it, I could see a man curled up on a cot, facing the wall. The lights were still on in the room, even though it was four in the morning—they didn't want to let him sleep; they wanted him to lose track of time. From the golden-brown color of his hair, I knew he was Curwen. They hadn't shaved his head like Mara's. In Whirl's world, the men got to keep their hair, untouched; the women had theirs forcibly removed as a means of coercion or dyed as a means of protection.

There were cameras in every corner. Whoever, if anyone, was watching the monitors already knew I was there. Part of me was constantly shocked at the lack of security, but most of me understood that Whirl's ego required as many people as possible to celebrate his victory. His *massacre*. His revelry would be momentary, though. I'd somehow—I didn't know how—make sure of that. Would the card in my pocket grant me access to his cell? Did Laney and Hollister need the card to complete their part of the mission? *No time to waste*. I walked twenty paces to the door, praying the entire time that the card would open it. As I slid it through the scanner, to my relief, it beeped and the light turned green. I entered quickly, leaving the door open.

"Curwen," I whispered, reaching to shake his foot. "Curwen," I repeated more loudly, touching his shoulder.

He shrugged me off, annoyed. "You've done enough. Leave me alone," he demanded, without rolling over. What had they done to him? *Enough*. What was enough?

"Curwen, it's me," I said gently. "Leela."

This time, he turned to look at me. "Leela?" He asked through squinted, groggy eyes. "What happened to your hair . . . it's dark . . . "

"Yes, it's me," I assured him. "I've come to get you out of here."

"I'm not dreaming?"

"You're not dreaming."

Once I said those words, he immediately sat up, grabbing both of my elbows to steady himself. His nearly black eyes, full of remorse, stared into mine as he said with deep conviction, "Leela, I'm so sorry. For everything."

His eyes glistened with unshed tears, and he looked like someone whose soul carried a heavy burden, weighed down by the things he'd done wrong. I took his face in my hands, the way my mother used to do when she wanted to make sure we *really* heard her. Smiling softly, I said, "I forgive you. We've all made so many mistakes. You don't need to apologize. Okay?"

He hesitated and then nodded. "Okay."

"Now," I said, moving my hands to his shoulders, "we don't have much time. Can you move? Are you hurt? Are you weak?"

"No, Leela." He removed my hands, pushing me away from him. "But they've injected me with the disease."

"What?" My mind wouldn't believe his words.

"When I got here, they called Whirl, and he ordered them to inject me with the disease," he explained again. "As punishment for all my crimes. You shouldn't be here. Just leave me to die. You need to go now before they capture you too."

He'd said his crimes were punishable by death. He'd said that Laney and I would be the death of him. Now he had received his punishment—a prolonged death, death that would come in stages. Now I *needed* to marry Gigandet, if only to save Curwen. I needed to marry the king to break the curse—if it was real—but was it even possible to marry him? Was he still alive?

"No." I shook my head, refusing to accept it. "No. You're not going to die in this place. We're getting out of here together." I pushed his chin up and to the side so I could easily see the tiny buttons on his shock collar, and I began inputting the codes Mara had taught me, the ones I had memorized just hours earlier. When I snapped open the collar and took it off, he had inflamed red welts on his neck. Laney had told me about how they'd shocked him at Muriel's house. Examining the welts, I was sure that wasn't the only time. Either he'd put up a fight or they'd shocked him just for their own amusement. Like Whirl. How many of Whirl's soldiers were like him?

On a table next to the bed was a surgical face mask. We had to prevent Curwen from spreading the disease to anyone else. I wasn't even sure if it was airborne, but Greer had worn a mask in the morgue. "Here," I said, handing it to him. He put it on, covering his nose and mouth. "Ready to go?"

But just then, a woman appeared in the open doorway, tall with long, black hair tied up in a bun, wearing a white lab coat and a face mask. She was too shocked at first to say anything, struggling to comprehend the situation. But when she understood, or thought she understood, her eyes narrowed, and she demanded, "What are you doing here? You can't be here. Who are you?"

Curwen and I glanced at each other, and then our eyes landed on the shock collar on the cot beside him. We had to do something fast before she ran away, before she alerted someone else. I raised the gun, aimed at the woman, and ordered her, "Come inside, and don't say a word."

She glared at me, attempting to appear defiant, trying to hide her fear, as she stepped into the room. Curwen stood and walked toward her; I could see her hands trembling at her sides. The gun's safety was on, and I knew I would never hurt her, but I hated doing this, hated creating fear in another human being, tears building up in my eyes—but *this is life or death, right?* I heard Durham justify.

"Please don't remove my mask," she begged. The thought hadn't occurred to me. *I wouldn't do that.*

"Why?" Curwen asked. Would he do *that*? "You don't want to be infected?" She shook her head, her eyes becoming more alarmed as he stood right in front of her. I circled around so I could be behind her, between her and the door, the gun still raised. "But it was okay to infect me?" he demanded, rough and furious.

I gasped quietly, a quick intake of breath. This young woman was the one who had injected him, infected him. I had only thought of our enemy as men who looked like Whirl, those who wore the black uniform. But here was a young woman, like me, in a lab coat like the one I would wear one day—if I lived, if I became a doctor. I wanted to see her whole face, to make sure I could recognize her if—when—I saw her again. *But I won't remove her mask.*

"You've committed crimes . . . ," she offered in her defense.

"This entire facility is a *crime*," I countered, bothered by her ignorance, nudging the muzzle of the gun into the small of her back. She let out a high-pitched, brief yelp. *We're not shooting anyone, just scaring them,* Corey's phrase repeated in my head.

Curwen held the shock collar in his hands. "No, please . . . no," she begged as he began to put it around her neck. He snapped it closed, tightening it to the right size.

Then he stared her down, and reaching into her coat pocket, he pulled out her access card. "Now, go sit in the chair," he ordered her, pointing at a chair in the opposite corner, one I hadn't even noticed. She hesitated, but I poked her with the muzzle again to get her moving. She walked to the chair and perched on the edge of it, as if she were afraid to pick up any germs from it.

"Now you can stay here and think about what *you've* done," Curwen said as he pushed me out the door and closed it behind us. Instantly, the young woman was at the window, banging her palm against it and screaming, but we heard nothing. The room was soundproof. She must have known that, but she cried for help anyway.

I had to turn away from the sight of her and swallow my tears. They weren't for her.

"Are you okay?" Curwen asked from behind me.

"No. But let's go." *No time to waste.* I knew I should have headed back the way I came, returned to the lobby, but something drew me in the opposite direction, toward the next set of double doors at the end of the hall. The sign above them read *ASSESSMENT*. What were they assessing? *Who* were they assessing?

Curwen didn't question me but followed closely. I attempted to open the double doors with the guard's access card, but it made a different sound and the light turned red, not green. Curwen tried the card he'd lifted from the woman—it worked. We passed through quickly, and the door clicked behind us. The fluorescent overhead lights were out on this wing; it was dark except for a few wall sconces.

On both sides of the hallway were large windows so we could see into the rooms. The scientists seemed to delight in observing their subjects. The lights were on in both rooms, but they were much dimmer than the ones where Curwen had been held. Like night-lights, they were conducive for sleeping and keeping the monsters away. The rooms were full of children in bunk beds—the children from my town, the ones I had babysat since infancy, and many of them, I knew from experience, were afraid of the dark. The tears I had choked back two minutes earlier began to flow. These were the children I knew and loved. In the faint light, squinting into the room, my face pressed against the glass, I could only make out a couple of their faces. But I knew they were all from our town. These were Corey and Annabelle's classmates, their friends. I hadn't thought about them being separated from their parents until that moment. I had only thought about *our* parents being taken from *us*.

We can't leave them here. "We can't leave them here," I whispered firmly. Curwen nodded; he agreed, but there was doubt in his eyes. Where could we take forty children in the dark, in the woods, when we didn't have a transporter to take them home? "Try her access card," I said, motioning toward the door, having absolutely no idea what I would do if it opened.

But instead of beeping green or red, the keypad's speaker began repeating, "Unauthorized entry attempt. Please enter your passcode." Curwen tried entering several codes, anything to silence the machine, but it continued to say, "Invalid code." After the fifth attempt, the entire wing lit up with red flashing lights and ear-piercing sirens.

"We have to go now!" Curwen yelled over the noise.

"We can't leave them!" I protested. But I knew we had to.

"We can't help them now! We'll come back for them!" His eyes promised it. "Let's go!" He waited for me at the next corner as I still hesitated. He grabbed my arm and pulled me into motion. I took one last glance over my shoulder at the large window; at least a dozen children's faces were staring out of it, confused and scared, trying to figure out what was happening. One of them—ten-year-old Eden—stared directly at me with her palm pressed against the glass. Her big eyes pleaded for me not to leave them, but Curwen would not let me go back.

This *was* life or death.

We'll come back for them.

We would make sure they get *life.*

CHAPTER 19

[LANEY]

Hollister made sure the heavy door closed silently behind us. We stood motionless, listening for any noise, any signs of people. The hallway was dark, but there was a room farther ahead on the right that had light pouring out an open door. There was a man's voice coming from inside the room. We stayed close to the wall, tiptoeing closer so we could make out his words. We stopped just outside, and I wrapped my arm under Hollister's, holding on to him for my own comfort. At first, it sounded as if the man were talking to himself, but I soon realized he was recording his notes.

Most of what he said didn't make any sense to me, until he began talking about the children. "All of the Tennessee children under twelve years are continuing to be monitored and assessed to determine which of them will be privately placed with parents among the Antonian population and attend school with the advanced ones. Those lacking high intelligence will be subjects in the inaugural youth trial. Dr. Bassa and I are currently developing a method and procedure for this trial. It is our goal to commence soon." The man stopped talking. We heard the rustling of papers. Hollister glanced down at me, that same intensity in his eyes again. He was ready for a fight.

What do they do with the children, when they're struck? I had asked Curwen. He'd said, *It's prohibited for children to be struck*; he'd said he didn't know what they had done with the children from our town. But now we knew. I felt sick, all my nerves tense. This was their first batch —*the Tennessee children*. Annabelle could have been a part of the group; she would have been if we'd been in the town square that day. I knew the names of every one of the Tennessee children, the names of their parents and grandparents too. They were my people. Where were the children? Could we liberate this entire place? Hollister's fight was beginning to take root in my soul; I could feel it like a fire shut up in my bones. Until that moment, it had only been a spark, something I couldn't focus on because Leela had been my aim. But she was here; she was okay. Soon the children wouldn't be. *Soon*.

The man began to speak again. He stated his name, the date and time, as if beginning a new recording. "Almost twenty-four hours ago, we received twenty-nine male bodies, enough to begin a new trial. A lottery was drawn to determine which of them would continue as living subjects and which would be deceased subjects. The lottery was not without bias, though, as Whirl asserted his authority in determining that one subject—body 1027—who was drawn as a deceased subject would instead continue as a living subject. Whirl determined that 1027 was the leader of the revolt in barrack twenty-seven, and therefore decided that he would remain living for the trial. Subject 1027 is currently undergoing the first blood-swapping phase in this trial. We are recording the process and will report the results."

From the anger on Hollister's face, I had to ask. I mouthed to him, "Rick?"

He nodded. Body 1027 was Rick. If Hollister had been here to lead the group in their attack, he would be the one undergoing the . . . *blood-swapping*. But it was Rick Stover, one of Hollister's closest friends and business partner. They'd ended up in the same barrack together; they'd planned to break free together. Rick's wife and baby were the only other people from our town who hadn't been struck. Instead, their picture had been printed in the paper next to the names of everyone else who was *missing*. But they had never been missing. They'd been kidnapped and enslaved. And now Rick was being used in a science experiment—something called *blood-swapping*. The term itself made me weak. Blood made me faint.

The man continued talking, but Hollister had heard enough. He peeked around the doorframe to see if we could pass. He nodded at me and motioned for me to follow him. I glanced over my shoulder as we went by the open door; the doctor's back was to us as he sat at a computer, wearing headphones, speaking into a microphone. He couldn't hear us anyway. We moved to the other side of the wall, making our footsteps light and silent as we left the doctor behind. As we turned the corner at the end of the hall, there was another set of double doors. There was an access keypad; the numbers were lit up in a yellow glow. "We need the access card from Leela!" I cried with concern. We shouldn't have split up.

"No. It wouldn't have worked," Hollister said. "The guards don't have access to this area. Only the scientists can bring them back, if they need assistance. That was something the guards complained about when they had to wait for a scientist to arrive to let us in. There are no access cards for heightened security, but I watched them enter the codes." He was already entering them while he explained it to me. These were the things he'd wanted to share with his men, to help them be better prepared for their attack. But they'd proceeded without him.

We heard the door unlatch, and Hollister pushed it open, checking inside to make sure it was clear. The hall was still dark, but ahead, on our right, there was a large observation window with harsh, bright-white lights illuminating our path. Was this the same room where Hollister had been taken? My legs trembled with each step as we approached the window, afraid of what we might observe. I ordered my legs to stay under me; I required it of them—fainting was not an option. Hollister looked into the window first, to see if it was safe. I watched his face to see how he reacted to what he saw. His eyes widened, and his jaw tightened, but he moved aside, clearing a space for me beside him. Two young men were in the room. One of them was 1027.

Rick was lying on a bed, restrained, his head turned to stare at the wall. A few feet away, on a second bed, was another young man who looked deathly sick. Did he have the disease? If so, he seemed like he was in the last stages, ready to pass away at any moment. He was not restrained but looked as if he was resting peacefully, his eyes closed. He must have voluntarily taken part in this experiment. They were both connected to tubes, tubes filled with dark red blood, which were connected to a strange machine between their beds—it reminded me of a dialysis machine, the blood being filtered through. *Blood-swapping* appeared to be exactly what it sounded like. Clean blood for diseased blood. They didn't value our lives—we were just *bodies*—but they valued our labor and our blood, the things our bodies could offer them. I closed my eyes and inhaled deeply, trying to breathe away the feelings of nausea and weakness.

There wasn't anyone else in the room that we could see. Hollister tried the door handle; it was locked. He input the codes he knew; they didn't work. "They must have different security clearances," Hollister whispered, so frustrated that he nearly punched the door with his fist. But I grabbed his wrist and shook my head at him. We stared at each other for a long moment before his eyes fell on the intercom on the wall beside the door. He glanced back at me with a question in his eyes—*should we?* Why not? There were cameras everywhere, as Leela had pointed out. They knew we were here, or they would know when they watched the security feed. We'd come this far. This was our fight.

I nodded at him and then held my breath as he put his mouth near the intercom and pressed the button. "Rick, can you hear me?" he asked. Rick instantly became alert, turning his head as he searched for the source of the voice, the voice of his friend. We stood outside the window, waving foolishly, but it didn't seem like he could see us. Hollister spoke again, "We're at the window. Can you see us?" Rick shook his head, mouthing something to us. He repeated it several times before we could read his lips—*one-way mirror.* Corey had taught me about this, how one-way mirrors worked. *If the light is the same on both sides,* he had said, *it just becomes a window.*

"We need to turn on these lights," I said, frantically looking for a switch, feeling the walls with my hands. I found it and flipped it without hesitation. It took a moment for the fluorescent lights to flicker on, but when they did, Rick's eyes went wide with recognition. He could see us. But so could the other young man, the one receiving Rick's blood. His eyes went wide also—but with fear.

"We're gonna get you out of here," Hollister said into the intercom. He backed up against the opposite wall and then charged at the door, hoping it would fly open. It didn't. He tried kicking it. That didn't work either. The door was metal, thick, heavy, and secure. During these attempts, the young man in the other bed was screaming for help. I couldn't hear him—the room must have been soundproof—but I knew that's what he was saying. Rick was hollering at him, probably telling him to be quiet, but he wouldn't stop. A door in the back of the room suddenly flew open. Someone—a woman—in a biohazard suit entered to assess the situation. When she saw us, she immediately pressed a red button on the wall. A loud, piercing alarm began to sound, and red lights flashed in the hallway. We stood frozen, torn, both of us looking at each other and then at Rick.

Rick was yelling at us, his blue eyes intense, his face red, his neck strained. He was telling us to go. Over and over, he said it. Images of his wife and his baby ran through my mind. How could I tell Angie that we'd left him behind? *We'll come back for him.* Rick looked at me, his eyes pleading with me to get us out of there, knowing his friend wouldn't be able to leave on his own. "We have to go now," I demanded, pulling on Hollister's arm, unable to make him budge. He and Rick were locked in an intense stare, Rick simply nodding and slowly, firmly saying *go*. I tugged on his arm again. "We can't help anyone if we're captured or dead," I repeated his own words to him.

Finally, he allowed his feet to move. He forced himself to look away from the window, away from Rick. We'd have to leave his friend behind. Our mission had failed. We ran toward the double doors, heading back the way we'd come. We'd have to get past the other doctor, the one who'd been recording his notes. But as Hollister and I pushed against the heavy metal doors, they wouldn't open. Hollister attempted to enter the only codes he knew into the keypad, pressing the yellow buttons with shaking fingers, the alarm still blaring in our ears. The word *LOCKDOWN* flashed on the small screen. Was the entire building on lockdown, or just this wing? Was Leela trapped somewhere too?

Hollister ran to the other end to see if the other double doors would open. *No*. They wouldn't. I looked through the large glass window again, glaring at the woman in the biohazard suit; she stared me down as well, no ounce of kindness in her dark eyes. There was a panel of switches on the wall beside the big red button she'd already pressed. I didn't know what they were for, but she slowly raised her arm, reaching for them, almost taunting me. "Hollister . . . ," I said, drawing his attention to the woman. He'd been looking at Rick, the two of them feeling helpless. The woman flipped a switch, which turned the lights off in the hallway; now they couldn't see us anymore, the one-way mirror back in effect. But we could still see her as she flipped another switch. The hall rapidly began to fill with smoke, pouring out of vents in the floor and ceiling. Hollister hit the glass window with the palm of his hand, shouting at her to turn it off. She couldn't hear us, and she didn't want to see us.

Coughing, I cried, "What is it?"

"Sleeping gas!" he yelled over the siren. "They used it on me before."

We were caged, and we'd soon be unconscious.

CHAPTER 20

[L E E L A]

We were back in the lobby. The alarm sound faded away once the double doors shut behind us, but the lights were still flashing red. Curwen sat on the marble bench beside the fountain; even though he'd said he felt okay, it was clear he was weak. Where were Laney and Hollister? They should have been back by now. We'd said ten minutes. It'd been longer than ten minutes. The longer we waited, the more tempted I was to go back to the children, to figure out a way to free them. Curwen protested, but I still attempted to open the door that led back to them. It was locked now, though. I tried all four sets of doors; all of them were locked. Were Laney and Hollister stuck somewhere? Could they get out, but we couldn't get in? I didn't even know which doors they'd gone through. It must have been one of the sets on the opposite of the lobby; both of them were labeled *LABORATORY*.

Curwen sighed; the medical face mask he was wearing almost made it inaudible. He was becoming more frustrated with waiting, and my pacing didn't help. I must have looked like a soldier marching back and forth, with the rifle tucked under my arm. He glanced at it with curiosity. It wasn't the first time he'd seen a gun, but there was a new, different, interest in his eye.

"What should we do?" I asked him, my voice calm but urgent, trying to conceal my growing panic.

“I don’t know.” He didn’t look up. “We can’t stay here much longer.”

“We’re not leaving them!” He’d already forced me to leave the children. I wouldn’t leave my sister.

“I wasn’t suggesting that.” He kept his head down, staring at the intricate tile floor, his elbows resting on his knees, his shoulders hunched, defeated.

“Well, there’s nowhere else for us to go,” I pointed out the obvious. All the doors that led to other parts of the building were locked.

“Maybe we go outside and look for another entrance,” he suggested.

His words were muffled from the mask. I was tired of straining to understand what he was saying, so I stopped in front of him and pulled the mask down below his chin. He looked at me with a worried expression. “You don’t need it right now,” I explained. “Just wear it when we join the rest of the group.” If *we join the rest of the group.*

Where was my sister? Was there another entrance, like Curwen suggested? Just then, I remembered the radio in my pocket. Before leaving us, Sheldon had programmed it to the same private channel as his. I pulled it out and flipped on the switch. What would I tell them? Would they help find my sister, or was I the only one they cared about saving, protecting? But before I could decide what to say, Sheldon’s voice came through, “Leela, are you there?” Curwen’s eyes lit up at the sound of his brother’s voice. “Leela?” he said again when I didn’t respond. Curwen nodded at me to answer, even though he also seemed hesitant about it, for different reasons. I was afraid they would make us leave my sister behind; he was afraid to see his brother, afraid to infect him with the disease.

Pushing the button, I put my mouth up to the speaker. “We’re here. I’ve got Curwen. But we got split up from Laney and Hollister.”

Sheldon replied, strong and steady, “We can hear the alarms going off from out here. Greer’s radio has reported that another group of guards are coming now. We can’t stay much longer.”

Durham took over. “What he means is, get out of there now.”

"No—I'm not leaving Lane—" I began to protest, but there was a gunshot, the sound of it reverberating through the enclosed lobby. I screamed, startled, and dropped the radio. When it hit the hard floor, the batteries popped out, scattering across the room. Curwen quickly rose to his feet, standing in front of me, shielding me, as our eyes rested on the shooter. A man, a guard, had come in silently through the front entrance. I squinted to make out the features of his face in the dark with the red lights flashing. His arm was raised high; he'd shot into the air—his intention was not to shoot us, but to scare us, to get our attention. I didn't recognize him. He wasn't one of the guards from outside the facility, the ones who'd chased the firecrackers. This was someone new, but at the same time, he felt familiar. He reminded me of someone. His demeanor. The madness in his eyes. *Whirl.* This man, whoever he was, was power-drunk like Whirl. I was frozen, motionless. It felt like I was face-to-face with Whirl, like in my nightmare, like in the grand hall as he stared us down. After what seemed like forever, I whispered to Curwen, "Do you know him?"

His voice was like steel, cold with rage, when he said, "It's Anderson."

Anderson. Laney had told me he was the one who'd held her at gunpoint. The one who'd arrested Curwen. The one who'd executed Muriel. My fear swung into action, and I swiftly raised the rifle into position, switching off the safety. I had no intention of shooting it, of shooting anyone, but he didn't have to know that. He needed to believe I was just as capable of taking a life as he was. Even though I wasn't. And could never be. When he saw the rifle pointed in his direction, he simply smiled. He savored a challenge. He taunted us, "I'm here."

"Why aren't you at the rally?" I demanded. "Did Whirl forget to invite you?"

What happened to my invitation? Whirl had yelled when he'd arrived at the wedding.

Anderson took a step toward us. "He had more important work for me to do."

Curwen laughed. "Keep telling yourself that." We wanted to make him angry so he would lose control. But would his loss of control result in our deaths? It was a dangerous game we were playing. Anderson took another step toward us. And then another. Going to his right, our left, as he went around the fountain. "You don't want to get too close," Curwen warned. "I'm already a dead man, and I'd love to share this sickness with you."

Those words caused Anderson to pause, to stand still and look confused. "What do you mean? You're infected?"

He didn't know. "My punishment," Curwen confirmed. He tried to mask his bitterness, but I heard it.

Anderson laughed. "That's genius." He was admiring Whirl's work. "But you won't put me at risk." He lifted the revolver, pointing at Curwen's head.

"Stop," I ordered him, raising the rifle higher to threaten him.

But he simply smiled. "You won't shoot me, girl." I had to make him believe I would. Taking aim at a spot on the wall just above his head, I fired. He ducked down. His reflexes were quick. Immediately, I ejected the cartridge, prepared to shoot again, if necessary. He wasn't scared. Instead, his fury had been further kindled; my fire had stoked his. Without hesitation, he shot at us. But Curwen's reflexes were quick too. He pushed me out of the way, both of us falling to the ground, Curwen coming down on top of me. As I braced for impact, the rifle flew out of my hands, sliding across the tile floor, hitting the opposite wall. Walking toward us, he shot again, but his aim was poor. He was inexperienced. *Not like Whirl.*

He attempted to shoot a third time, but the gun only clicked. He was out of bullets. Curwen realized it; he jumped up and charged at Anderson, staying low. But our enemy had already dropped the pistol and grabbed his stun gun. When Curwen made contact to tackle him, Anderson had the stun gun in Curwen's left flank. Curwen tried to fight through it, but I could hear the high voltage, and he began to slip to the floor. As he did, Anderson grabbed his face and slammed his head into the marble bench. Anderson immediately backed away from him, afraid of being contaminated with the virus. Curwen lay motionless, the side of his head bleeding.

Again, I felt frozen, unable to move. But Anderson glared at me and took steps toward me. Fear propelled me to move, crawling toward the rifle. But Anderson got to me first, grabbing my ankle and dragging me across the tile, farther away from the gun. Then the stun gun was in my side. I cried out in pain from the shock, struggling to get away, but he'd pinned me down, wrestling my arms behind my back as he handcuffed my wrists. *You're powerless. You've got nothing left.* He grabbed my hair tightly in his fist, pulling my head backward, forcing me to stand, steering me toward the fountain. "Wait, wait, wait," I begged. I *did* have one thing left. "What if you're infected with the disease?" I asked him. "You'll need me to break the curse." He had me on my knees again, beside the fountain; he held my face inches from the water. "But you need me," I said, my voice cracking, tears beginning to fall into the water.

This is how I die. This is how the Antonian people die with me. The curse is real. I realized then, in that moment, that I believed it. It was real.

Anderson put his mouth to my ear and whispered, "They don't need *you*." Then he pushed my face down into the water. I struggled against him, but he was too strong, his long fingers gripping my head, pressing firmly. I held my breath even though I wanted to scream and cry. I focused on the mosaic tile at the bottom of the fountain, shades of blue and white. My eyes stung. My lungs burned. If I stopped moving, would he think I was dead? Would he let go? Would I have a chance?

Just then, there was a loud sound, a gunshot. The pressure on my head ceased, but the weight of Anderson's body became heavier on top of me. And then, his head was beside mine in the fountain, blood mixing with water. This time, I screamed, my mouth and lungs filling with water, the bubbles surfacing as I exhaled. He was the second dead man whose weight had fallen on me, whose blood had surrounded me. Strong hands gripped my arms, lifting me up and out of the water, away from the fountain. Spitting out water—and blood—and gasping for breath, I tried to make sense of what was happening. Greer's hands held me, not letting go, supporting me. Curwen's hands held the rifle as he leaned against the wall for support, his head and face bloody. Durham was trying to help him, but he pushed his father away while repositioning the face mask over his nose and mouth. They'd come inside, without protection, risking infection.

Durham took the rifle from his son's grip, flipping the safety back on; he must have watched me earlier, at the bridge. Greer snatched the keys from Anderson's belt and removed my handcuffs. In the dark, the red lights were still flashing, and now the piercing alarm was sounding throughout the lobby as well. I couldn't hear anything else. They must have set off another alarm when they entered the building. How had they gotten inside?

"Let's go!" Durham yelled above the sirens. Greer still held my arm, my feet began to obey, and Curwen followed us. The doors Durham led us through were unlocked; I hadn't tried them before because they led to an exit. I didn't want to leave the building, to leave Laney behind.

"We can't leave Laney and Hollister," I protested without much fight. My fight had left me. It'd been washed away in the fountain. Through coughs, I weakly asked, "Will we come back for them?"

Durham stopped and turned around to look at me. "You want to come back here?"

"Yes." Laney had come back for *me*. I'd have to come back for her. And Hollister. And the children. *If they're still alive. If they aren't already dead.*

He nodded at me. "Good. We're coming back. But for now, we have to go."

I didn't object. I knew I should have. I should have kept fighting. My whole body, mind, and spirit were defeated. My fight had drowned to death in bloody water. It'd exited my body through that underwater scream.

Durham kept leading us out until we faced a wall of glass in a long hall that ran the length of the building. Benches and tables lined the rear, stone wall; it must have been a place for people—the scientists—to rest and enjoy their meals. The fountain had probably also been a place of rest and peace; now it was a place where Anderson rested in peace, where *I* had almost rested in peace. The four of us stopped in our tracks, soaking in the landscape before us. The rich green trees hugged the bottom of the mountains, like a child wrapping his arms around the legs of a parent, and the purple-hued mountaintops kissed the rainbow sherbet sunrise like something glorious, like a bride meeting her groom at the altar. Even with the alarm going off behind us, I still heard a holy song at the dawning of creation. It brought tears to my eyes. My mind couldn't reconcile the darkness behind me with the light in front of me.

A radio crackled. It was clipped to Greer's shoulder. "We can see you," came Sheldon's voice. "Look for the flashing light." There it was, among the tree line a hundred yards away, blinking like a firefly in the dark underbrush. We had to get there. The flashing light was home base. I was headed there without Laney. She'd lost the game; she'd been struck out. *I'd* almost been struck out. The fight for third base had been brutal. My fight had been left there.

The glass door was broken. That's how they'd entered the building to rescue us. Down the steps, running across the field, Greer supported most of my weight. Curwen was the one who needed to be supported, but none of them could go near him—Durham might have risked it because he loved him, but Greer wouldn't. The flashlight was still blinking for us. About halfway there, two of the guards from the front entrance came around the side of the building, running toward us, shouting for us to stop. Durham didn't hesitate, the gun still in his grasp, to shoot into the air in their direction; they immediately turned around and disappeared behind the wall again. We'd reached the trees, gasping for breath.

It might have been a sweet reunion between Curwen, Sheldon, and Mara, but he immediately told them to stay away from him, making sure the mask was secure on his face.

"Why?" Mara asked, her face falling. "What's wrong?"

"There's no time to talk. Come on," Durham ordered us.

Greer paused, still holding my arm. "Where are we going now?" he asked.

Durham's eyes lit up. "To the mountains. It's the one place they won't follow us. Leela will be safe there."

Safety is an illusion.

ABOUT THE AUTHOR

Rachel Langley is a Georgia native who graduated with a degree in communications and professional writing. She's always had a love of words and languages. When she was a young child, she would create characters and conversations in her head; when she learned how to write, she let them come to life on the page. She now makes her home in Charleston, South Carolina.

The Mark and the Match is the sequel to *Struck* and her second published novel.

Visit rachellangley.com for more information.

If you've finished reading this book,

would you please review it on Amazon?

Honest, thoughtful reviews are one of the best ways for independent authors and small publishers to gain exposure for their books. Your feedback in invaluable.

Thank you!

www.ingramcontent.com/pod-product-compliance
Lightning Source LLC
Chambersburg PA
CBHW060625310726
48982CB00003B/675

* 9 7 8 0 5 7 8 4 3 7 6 3 7 *